The Whitechapel Plot

The Displacers Series

Book 3

Simon Brading

For Gis, who still believes.

PROLOGUE

Paris, 1974.

The streets of Paris, which were usually so full of life and love, were deserted at three-thirty in the morning. Gone were the crowds of tourists that thronged the streets during the day; instead, the city slept, dark under a moonless sky.

The silence was broken only by the mewling of a cat that was roaming the nearby streets, searching for food, and the echoing footsteps of the lone security guard as he made his rounds of the streets around the Louvre Palace.

The guard wandered around the north side of the huge building and past the wing that was still occupied by the closed and deserted offices of the Finance Ministry. He checked each entrance and window in turn for possible break-ins and shone his torch into the deep shadows around the building, keeping an eye out for vandals and vagabonds.

There was nothing and no one.

The Louvre buildings were so well loved and respected, even with a government ministry inside, that they were barely ever targeted for graffiti and this late in winter there weren't any drunken party-goers on their way home attempting to relieve themselves, or young lovers stealing kisses in the bushes - the streets were dead and the guard was content in the knowledge that all was as it should be.

He had no way of knowing that his every movement was being noted by two youths, no more than 18 or 19, although it was impossible to tell because both were masked wearing tightly fitting dark grey clothing. They were crouching between the columns of the building on the other side of the street, motionless, blending in so perfectly with the shadows that even the scavenging cat wasn't quite aware of what they were and paused to sniff them and rub its scent onto the unfamiliar objects.

The larger of the two figures, a man by his shape and his voice, hissed and waved his hand at the cat to scare it off. 'Psst! Shoo!'

The cat jumped, startled, and fled, yowling.

Thankfully, the guard paid it no attention and just continued with his inspection.

As soon as he had moved far enough away down the street that the light from his torch no longer reached them, the two thieves jumped to their feet and ran swiftly and silently across the concrete, leaping up and vaulting over the fence, almost as if it wasn't there, and into the *Jardin de l'Oratoire*, a small garden nestled in a corner of the building. The smaller of the two actually somersaulted off the top of the fence and rolled on the gravel beyond.

The man tutted, shook his head and breathed a single word, 'showoff' as they jogged to the wall of the museum.

'Last one up smells of onions!' The voice was that of a young woman and her blue eyes twinkled from behind her mask as she started to climb the museum from the dark corner on the *Rue de Rivoli*.

They made their way up the wall, climbing with the almost supernaturally strong grip that they had developed during years of training, using almost non-existent handholds. They leapt from hold to hold, occasionally helping each other over the most difficult parts, but more often going alone, using flashy moves and showing off, almost playing as they all but ran up the wall.

The pair always did jobs as a team. They didn't have to; either one of them could have accomplished the theft easily enough on their own, but they enjoyed working together and had developed a bond over the years, which meant that they often knew exactly what the other was intending before they did it and that had gotten them out of more than a few sticky situations.

In short order they had reached the grey roof of the Richelieu wing of the museum and they padded catlike along the edge, to where the Richelieu wing met the Sully wing. There they paused to survey the Napoleon Courtyard and the U-shape of that part of the Louvre in its entirety. Their objective was opposite them, in the Denon wing, directly across the courtyard where the glass pyramid wouldn't stand for another fifteen years.

Their gaze was naturally drawn up from their target to the spectacular views of the *Arc de Triomphe* at the end of the *Champs-Élysées* and the *tour Eiffel* looming over the city and as one they turned and wrapped their arms around each other, pulling close in a hug.

'We've got to come back some day and do some proper sightseeing.' The woman said, nestling her head into the man's shoulder with a sigh.

'Not for a while though... Maybe in forty years, give or take.' His smile was obvious in his voice, even though it couldn't be seen.

The woman chuckled softly and lifted her head, reaching up to stroke the man's masked face with a gloved hand. 'It's a date. Now come on, we have a job to do.'

He laughed gently and they separated, pulling apart until they were holding hands, facing each other. They stayed like that for a second, then, at an unspoken signal, they were off and running. They went around the entire circumference of the building, sprinting from shadow to shadow behind the statues and balustrades, using them wherever possible to hide from the dim light of the yellow sodium lamps scattered everywhere.

They raced over the roof of the Sully wing, going over the top of the *Pavillon de l'Horloge* past the clock and then turned onto the roof of the Denon wing.

Only a couple of minutes after they had started their attack on the building, they reached their entry point - a tiny window on the top floor of the building with a laughably simple lock. They had it open in seconds and squeezed through into the dusty and unused space directly underneath the roof that lay beyond.

Perfectly balanced, like circus performers, they ran across the narrow beams of the room to the hatch in the floor that extensive study of the blueprints of the building had revealed was there, then made their way down through the building. They passed through empty storerooms and descended hidden back staircases, which looked like they hadn't been used for a hundred years, easily keeping away from public areas and the beats of the night guards, which they had mapped out in weeks of painstaking observation and preparation.

These forgotten passageways took them all the way down to the first floor, where they entered one of the dimly lit galleries, finally finding themselves among the works of art that brought multitudes of visitors from all around the world. They made their way past countless works of art worth countless millions until they found themselves in the *Salle des États*, standing in front of what they had come for, what they had come to *steal* - the most famous work of art in the world and the motive behind most people's visits to the huge museum: *La Gioconda*, better known to the English speaking world as the *Mona Lisa*.

The smaller figure pulled off her mask, revealing a good-looking young woman with long blond hair, which she shook out before leaning forward to get a better look at the painting. She put her face right up against the glass that was protecting it and frowned. 'It's a lot smaller than I thought it would be…'

'Rachel! What are you doing? Put your mask back on!'

She turned and smirked at the man. 'Come on, Sam, it's 1974! There aren't any cameras, and besides, even if there were, the images would just disappear when we went home, wouldn't they?'

He hissed and pulled his mask off, freeing an unruly mop of brown hair. The expression on his beardless, handsome face revealed that he was annoyed with himself. 'I still can't get used to all these silly rules.'

'Don't worry, you will eventually… Maybe.' She grinned at him before they turned to peer at their objective.

Sam shrugged. 'I really don't get what's special about this thing.'

'Philistine!'

'No, I mean, just look at it! The girl's not even especially good looking; her smile is a bit weird and she looks a bit, well, mannish… I really don't see the attraction.'

Rachel stood and looked at it for a second. She tilted her head to one side and squinted at the painting. 'To be honest… me neither, but who cares? Come on, let's do what we came for and get out.'

However, before they could even move, the sound of a voice rang out from not far away. 'Say "*fromage*", if you please!'

They spun in place to face the voice and were therefore looking directly at the flash of intense white light, which was made painful because their eyes were dilated and fully adjusted to the faint lighting of the night-time gallery.

They cried out in sudden shock and covered their suddenly watering eyes with their hands, blinking rapidly and trying to regain some vision, while the voice continued to speak in its thick French accent.

'Congratulations on passing the first part of your graduation test!'

When they were finally able to see again, they found that the voice had come from the man who was leaning casually against the wall less than five metres away. He was similarly dressed to them, although his clothes weren't quite so form fitting and had slicked back black hair, a pencil-thin moustache and a mischievous glint in his eye. There was a

Polaroid camera swinging from its strap around his neck and he was waving a developing photo in his left hand.

'It was a bit of a cinch, actually, I don't think much of your test.' Sam was slightly annoyed at the man's destruction of his night vision, but wasn't at all worried at his sudden appearance.

'Yes, well, congratulations, but don't be so, how you say? *Cocky*. You haven't passed the whole test yet.' He pointed a long thin finger at the *Mona Lisa* hanging behind them. 'When you tried to pull that painting away from the wall an alarm would have gone off.'

They watched, hypnotised, as the finger moved gracefully through the air until it was pointing at a painting on the wall right next to him, while all the time his other hand was waving the picture to dry it. 'The same alarm that goes off when this one is pulled away from the wall too.'

He glanced down at the Polaroid in his hand. 'Magnifique! C'est une très belle photo!' He turned back to the would-be thieves with a huge smile on his face. 'And now for the second part of the test.' The finger hooked into the base of the painting and he smiled cheekily. 'See if you can get away.' He pulled the painting a couple of inches away from the wall.

Suddenly, alarms blared and wailed.

Nonchalantly, the French man waved. 'Au revoir mes petits!'

Sam and Rachel looked around in shock, panicked for a second and unsure of what to do. When they looked back the man had disappeared.

They glanced at each other and took a deep, apprehensive breath, as angry shouting started up at both ends of the long gallery. They pulled their masks back on and bolted.

It took them an hour to escape the museum, being chased around the hidden stairwells, playing a deadly game of hide and seek with about a dozen armed and increasingly annoyed security guards. Despite the danger, they were nevertheless having the time of their lives, leading the guards on a merry dance, and when they thought back to it later, they inevitably compared it to a scene from *Scooby Doo*. Their progress through the museum took them in and out of the galleries and they occasionally stopped to appreciate the art when they had a big enough lead over their pursuers, taking advantage of having the place to themselves, well, almost to themselves.

Eventually, though, the sound of sirens coming from outside the building meant that play time was over and they swiftly lost the guards, with almost insulting ease, and made their way from the building. They went back over the roof and down the east side of the complex this time, before crossing the river towards *Notre-Dame*. There, they removed the masks and became just another couple of Parisians making their way through streets that were starting to come back to life.

The Frenchman was waiting for them in an alley a mile away.

'That was not very funny, Jacques!' Rachel went straight up to him and punched him on the arm.

'Au contraire, ma chère! I had a wonderful time watching you lead my men around like headless chickens on a wild-goose chase.'

'I think you're mixing your metaphors a bit there.'

He reached behind himself and grabbed a couple of small paper bags that were on a wooden crate, opening them to produce fresh croissants. 'Please accept my apologies?'

Sam and Rachel's eyes lit up when they realised they were sitting in the alley behind a bakery and the pastries had just come out of the oven. They were even more pleased when Jacques produced a flask of coffee and a small bottle of brandy "for the cold".

'Apology accepted!' Rachel grabbed them from him eagerly and they sat down on the crates to have breakfast and dissect the night's work that three years of training with the man had led up to.

Jacques was an ex-cat burglar who now worked as a consultant for a security company. He was another one of Rachel's "contacts", one of the people who she had met during her previous journeys through time or had researched as having skills that she would like to learn.

Sam Vives and Rachel Evans were "Displacers", members of a small group of people with a special talent: the ability to travel through time, or "Displace", as they called it. Rachel had been Displacing for several years longer than Sam and she liked to collect abilities, mostly martial arts, but occasionally something else equally physical. In this case she had decided that the ability to climb all over buildings and break into them at will might be useful at some point in the future. Sam, while not actually agreeing about the breaking into buildings part, had thought that it would be fun and had readily agreed to come with her. He would never admit it, but the attraction of the journey had not so much been the opportunity of spending a few years learning from Jacques, but rather the chance to spend those years with Rachel, who he had more than come to care for over the few months and more than six years that he had known her.

They had originally met up with Jacques in his home town in the Alps. He had "retired" from his life of gentlemanly crime and was tinkering around with a few things in his workshop. He had actually been quite pleased to see them; he had been getting very restless, bored with staying "clean", as he put it. They spent the following two years training with him; climbing various mountains to strengthen their grip and hone their skills, learning everything that Jacques knew about alarm systems and safe-cracking, which turned out to be quite a lot, and the time just sped past.

Rachel had done her research well and timed things just right; with a foresight, or a hindsight, that was impressive as well as highly convenient, just as they were running out of things they could possibly do in the French Alps and still call it training, Jacques received a phone call. He was contacted by an old friend who had just been elected to the board of Governors of the Louvre Museum. He knew of Jacques' shady past and wanted him to consult with them and completely overhaul the security systems. Jacques leapt at the chance and so they had left the Alps behind.

The year they had spent in Paris had been memorable, exciting and more than a little bit romantic.

'Well it looks like I still haven't quite got the security at that place up to scratch, but it's close,' Jacques mumbled around a mouthful of croissant. 'Thank you for helping me test it out.'

Sam grinned. 'No problem; it was fun! But maybe, instead of more alarms you should just get some decent guards?

Jacques shrugged. 'There have been budget cuts. The museum preferred to spend their money on the new Monet instead of hiring a professional security firm, I'm sure you can understand. The guys we have are all ex-army, though and some of them have even been to war... the Second World War, unfortunately. I'm actually pleasantly surprised none of them had heart attacks chasing you around tonight.' He shook his head, and smiled wryly. 'I think the people who run the museum are counting on the police getting involved if anything is stolen and the police won't cost them anything. But still, the alarm worked, which is nice.'

Rachel looked at him, scathingly. 'Yes, the alarm worked...'

Jacques gave her a winning smile in the way that only a Frenchman can. 'Anyway, I have something for you, a souvenir.'

'Is it the *Mona Lisa?*' Sam asked with a raised eyebrow and a cheeky grin.

'No, I'm afraid not!' Jacques laughed as he fished in his pocket. 'Here.'

He handed over the Polaroid photo.

Sam and Rachel held it between them and looked at it together. Their faces had been caught in identical expressions and postures of surprise while the *Mona Lisa* smiling down at them.

'Well, it's quite original as souvenirs go, thank you, Jacques!' Rachel leaned forward and kissed him on the cheek.

Jacques smiled and stood. 'Well, I must be off; the board of Governors will be waking up from their beauty sleep soon and I must give them my report. Are you sure that I cannot entice you to stay a little bit longer? I'm going to be going to the Smithsonian in a couple of weeks to test their new exhibition wing…'

The two Displacers shared a look and silently decided to stick with the decision they had made.

Jacques saw it in their eyes and shrugged, a lopsided smile on his face. 'Well, maybe some other time then.' He walked to the end of the alley and stopped to look back at his friends. They were sitting close together on the stacked up wooden crates, leaning in to each other. He sighed and put his hands over his heart. 'Ah, to be young and in love again, in belle Paris!' He turned and walked away, waving once over his shoulder. 'Au revoir mes amis! Until we meet again!'

Sam and Rachel watched him go, then shared a look and a nod. They closed their eyes…

… and opened them back in present day Barcelona.

Gone were the young man and woman and in their place were two teenagers. This was one of the drawbacks and advantages of being a young Displacer, an incongruity that had seen Sam grow into a young man twice already. Although his physique had changed and developed considerably since the Displacement to Okinawa with Rachel where she introduced him to her unique hobby, in the present day he still had the face and height of the 15 year old boy that he was and, even though they had gotten into the habit of training every day over the summer, he still hadn't lost his boyish look.

They smiled at each other, still holding hands, but the mood was broken when Sam's eyes wandered to the open door and the suitcase that was standing ready in the hallway.

His smile faded somewhat. 'Thank you for letting me have these last three years with you before you leave.'

'As always it has been a pleasure.'

'Are you sure you have to go?'

She raised an eyebrow. 'Aren't you sick of me, yet?'

'A little bit maybe... but I reckon I could still put up with you for a few more months.'

'I'm sorry, darling, but my mother is expecting me back.'

'Right...' Sam's head dropped and he sighed.

'Hey! Don't look so down!' She lifted his chin with a finger. 'We've had a great time over the last couple of weeks that Andrew hasn't been here, so there's nothing to regret, and besides, you have school next week - you're not going to have time to miss me.'

She leaned forward and they kissed, tenderly but chastely. Their passions for each other had developed quite naturally during the years they had spent together in the past, but they had an agreement to keep the more physical side of their relationship to a minimum in the present day where they were both still too young, at least in the eyes of their parents and the rest of the world. It was all very confusing sometimes, but it was an essential part of keeping their secret.

They shared a moment, looking into each other's eyes, before Sam smiled. 'So, who keeps the photo?' They looked down; the Polaroid photo was still clutched in their hands.

'Why don't you keep it?' said Rachel. 'It can go in your files, help to pad them out a bit, make them more interesting; your Displacements till now have been a bit on the boring side.'

She grinned, knowing full well that it wasn't true.

Aside from their three year trip to Okinawa, Sam had had two very notable, very important Displacements to Egypt and the Caribbean, both times foiling the plotting of Quentin Price, a member of a rival time-travelling group who were interested only in their own profit, marauding through time with careless regard for the welfare of the time-line, a time-line that the Displacers worked hard to protect, often losing their lives in the attempt.

'OK, but at least take a photo of it with your phone, that way we both get a copy.'

'Good idea. But then we have to get a move on, we don't want to be late for dinner.'

'Do you think you can face my mum's cooking after all those restaurants Jacques took us to?'

Rachel chuckled as she shook her head. 'If I never see another snail or frog's leg again it'll be too soon!'

'You know, they eat a lot of snails here too. My mum hates them, but my dad loves them and he's always trying to get me and Violeta to try them. I can always ask him to get some for you…'

'Don't you dare!'

Sam laughed and held the photo in place while Rachel snapped it with her phone. That done she kissed him again, then went to the door.

The smile faded slightly from Sam's face as she led the way out; he didn't know how he was going to get through the next few months without her.

Rachel had been a firm fixture at Vives family dinners ever since Andrew, the head of the Displacers and both Sam and Rachel's uncle, had gone back to London a couple of weeks before, leaving her on her own in his flat. She had gotten to know Sam's family quite well; they had quite naturally wanted to meet the girl that Sam had been spending so much time with.

Sam had expected the first time Rachel met his parents to be rather awkward; there were so many things that she couldn't talk about, so many things that she couldn't even hint to knowing or having done. In the end, though, she had coped very easily because she was far more used to covering up for herself and it had been Sam who had had the most trouble - there had been quite a few times when he had started to tell his family something, but had realised as soon as he had opened his mouth that he couldn't and had to stop, leaving everyone staring at him as if he was an idiot while he mumbled and tried to cover.

Luckily his parents put it down to his being shy around his "girlfriend" and to his shame shared many a knowing look, seemingly glad that there was now somebody in the life of a boy who had been a bit of a loner up until then - Rachel was a more than welcome addition to the family in their eyes.

Violeta had been immediately won over by her as well; Sam's sister was a bit of a chocoholic and he had advised Rachel to bring a box or something. She brought a *Caja Roja* with her and immediately made a friend for life.

Rachel had also been there when they had celebrated Violeta's eighth birthday in August. She had dressed up as a princess and played with Violeta and all of the girls who had come as guests. Sam had taken a lot of photos and, despite the fact that she was dressed silly and pulling faces most of the time, he had to admit that they were some of the best pictures he had of her. One of them in particular, where he had caught her laughing with Violeta, was the background to his desktop on his computer.

That night's dinner was another special occasion; it was a farewell for Rachel. The next day they were giving her a lift to the airport and she was catching a flight back to London. There was a note of sadness about it for both her and Sam, but they tried to enjoy it as best as they could, which wasn't too hard because, despite Sam's jokes, his mother's cooking was superb and there wasn't a snail in sight. They ate, laughed, played games with Violeta and did the best they could to forget the shadow hanging over them.

Sam said goodnight to her at the door afterwards and kissed her on the cheek because they were being watched - subtly by his parents, who were pretending to have a conversation down the hallway, and not so subtly by Violeta who was standing a few feet away and staring up at Rachel with wide eyes.

'I'll see you tomorrow. Get some sleep, we both need it.' Rachel gave his hands a last squeeze and then left.

He watched her until she was out of sight around the corner of the stairwell and then closed the door. Turning around, he came face to face with his grinning parents and shrugged. 'What?'

As always, Displacing had taken a lot out of Sam and he went to bed soon after Rachel left, even though it was still quite early. He slept until late the next day, not as late as he had done when he'd previously returned from Displacements, but still long enough to go straight to lunch instead of having breakfast.

They took Rachel to Barcelona airport in the afternoon and Sam said goodbye to her before she went through customs. They had to force themselves to keep the emotion to a minimum; Sam's mother had accompanied them and they didn't think she would understand a tearful goodbye if, as far as she was concerned, they had known each other for less than three months. The reality was that this was the first time, the first *day* for more than six years that they were going to be apart.

They promised to speak to each other every day, hugged, then she turned away and disappeared into the crowds.

Sam walked slowly back to the car with his mother, heading out into a sunny day in September that suddenly seemed very grey.

CHAPTER 1
SCHOOL

The coming school year was an important one for Sam; it was the final year of his *ESO*, his compulsory education, and at the end of the year he would be able to decide whether he would continue at school or not. There were exams to be studied for, important life decisions to be made and he still had no idea what he was going to do.

Despite all this, and the fact that he was going to be without Rachel for a few months, Sam was actually quite looking forwards to going back to school. Usually he dreaded it; not as much for the work, but more for the company, and there was one boy in particular who made things very uncomfortable for Sam - a bully named Rafa Sánchez.

Sam had always been one of the smallest boys in the class, making him a natural target for the large and brutish Rafa, but there had also been an incident on Sam's very first day of school, when they were seven, that had turned Rafa against him forever - an insignificant matter of a gold star won by Sam that Rafa thought he should have got instead.

This year, though, he didn't have to worry about Rafa; his first ever Displacement to Port Royal had given him the confidence to stand up for himself, something that will always give a bully pause for thought since they are usually cowards, and then his journey to Okinawa with Rachel had given him the martial arts skills to back up that confidence if he needed them. Sam could have used those skills at any time to give the big boy a taste of his own medicine, but he just wasn't that kind of person, so he had made do with showing Rafa up in front of his friends, almost the worst fate that could befall a bully - Rachel and he had put on a bit of an exhibition for all of the neighbourhood thugs over the summer, training in the local park in front of them. Seeing Sam's level of skill had permanently put them off pursuing Rafa's personal quest for vengeance.

The only time that Sam was expecting Rafa to try to make trouble that year was during fencing practice, where the bully would have the perfect excuse to use violence. Rafa was on the team with Sam, but didn't quite get the gentlemanly aspect of fencing. He very often used much more force in his bouts than was necessary, as an intimidation tactic, and more often than not the other members of the team, and especially Sam, ended training sessions with large bruises. Even so, Sam loved fencing and he was good at it; something that had stood him well in Port Royal, saving his life and earning him praise from many a hardened pirate.

The first practice of the fencing club was Thursday of the first week of term. The club was run by a couple of teachers, but there was also a professional coach brought in by the school to take the private lessons and help with the team. As usual, they split the thirty or so students into two groups. While the teachers took the new members of the club and the non-team members to one side of the sports hall to work on some basics, Sam went with the coach and what was left of the team to the other side of the room and, because they were doing try-outs for the team, a few of the other boys and girls joined them - new students who had fenced before, as well as a few of the older club members who had never quite been good enough, but had worked hard and wanted to try their luck.

Before they started, the coach gathered them round to speak to them. 'Alright, everybody, three people left last year so we've got three positions to fill. However, that doesn't mean that those of you who were on the team last year have a guaranteed place; don't think that I won't kick you off if you haven't been practising and somebody else is better than you.'

As he continued he looked pointedly at Sam and Rafa in turn. 'We also need a new captain and I'm hoping that *someone* will show me something good. OK, grab some foils, pair up and let's see what you've got.'

Sam was partnered with one of the new members of the club, a young boy of twelve called Marc, who was looking very nervous. They put their helmets on, saluted and started to fence, not really competing in earnest or counting points, but just fencing and getting into the swing of things. The boy wasn't bad once he got over his nerves; his technique was quite clean and disciplined, and Sam thought that with a bit of work he might well become a useful member of the team.

Sam found that he was having no trouble at all remembering all the techniques that he had learnt over the last few years and was very quickly able to let go and have fun. However, his enjoyment was completely ruined when there was a scream from nearby and he looked up to see a small boy, one of the youngest of the new members, probably a first year, and smaller even than Sam had been at his age, lying curled up on the ground, crying and clutching his arm. Standing over him was Rafa, shrugging and pleading innocence, his fencing mask with its painted skull pulled back onto the top of his head. He saw Sam watching him and grinned, giving him a thumbs-up.

Sam shook his head in disgust; trust the bully to pick the smallest boy available to pair up with - it looked like he had started to look for new targets now that Sam had escaped him.

The coach hurried over and helped the boy to his feet and over to sit on a bench by the side of the room. Everybody else just stood watched, their bouts forgotten, and Sam saw that many of the newbies, including his own opponent and not a few of the team members, were looking a bit white and he decided to do something about it.

He nudged his opponent. 'Hey!' The boy, Marc looked up at him, wide-eyed. 'Don't worry about it; Rafa's strong, but his fencing isn't very good. Once you've learnt how to deal with him he won't be able to hurt you. I'll show you sometime, if you'd like.'

'Please.' Marc nodded, somewhat comforted, and Sam smiled at him.

They looked up as the coach came back over and addressed the group. 'Alright, I'm going to start assessing you all one by one. We'll start with you, Rafa, seeing as you don't have a partner right now.'

Rafa flashed Sam a last grin and then followed the coach to a clear space in the corner of the room.

Sam turned back to his own partner and tried to forget about the big boy, but he was too distracted and could only half concentrate on his bout.

It wasn't long, though, before they were interrupted again, this time when the coach ripped off his mask in obvious annoyance and almost shouted at the bully, his voice easily carrying to everybody in the hall. 'You're going to have to do a *lot* better than that, Rafa, if you want to keep your place in the team! Sam! Get over here!'

Sam shook hands with Marc and headed over to the coach. He smirked at Rafa as he passed him, but then went cold as he realised that

Marc was the only fencer available and the bully was going to partner up with him - Rafa would certainly try to take out his frustrations on him. He ran back to the boy, who was already looking at Rafa with fear, and leaned in to whisper. 'No need to worry; you're good enough to out-fence him. Don't get scared by his tactics, just keep moving back out of his reach and when he overcommits get the touch.'

That was all he could say before Rafa got there.

'Bugger off, Vives. Oh, and watch yourself; Coach is in a bad mood - I *so* hope he doesn't kick you off the team.'

'Not likely; you're the first on the drop list by all appearances.'

Rafa just snarled in reply, then turned to his new partner. He grinned evilly. 'Alright, short-arse, it's your turn for some pain!'

Marc looked up at Sam, almost pathetically pleading with him, but Sam just gave him a reassuring look and a nod. 'Just remember what I said.'

'Sam!' The coach called him again and Sam had to hurry away.

The coach was tapping his foot impatiently. 'Come on, Sam, we've got a lot to do this evening. I haven't got much time and I've already wasted enough of it on Rafa. Oh, god, just look at him…' He groaned and shook his head.

They watched as Rafa charged at Marc, his normal and only tactic. Sam was relieved to see that his advice was being followed and the boy was steadily backing away, avoiding Rafa's wild stabs and waiting for his chance to score. Unfortunately, that meant that the bully was quite obviously becoming frustrated, which was never a good thing.

They watched three points, each of which ended quickly and the same way, with a point for the boy and the bully raging, before the coach sighed and turned back to Sam. 'Right, let's fence, and *please* don't disappoint me. First to five points, OK?'

They saluted, put their masks on, and began.

The coach was a professional, a former member of the Spanish national team, and his technique was far beyond anything that the students could lay claim to, which meant that serious bouts with him would have been very one-sided affairs. Private sessions with him usually weren't competitive, therefore, but rather he used them to do things like teach combinations of parries and ripostes, getting the students to repeat them over and over until they came automatically. However, occasionally, when the coach wanted to see what the students were capable of, for example during try-outs like that day, he would fight a match with them, adjusting his technique to suit their levels.

They started off easily, with the coach using only relatively basic techniques, as he had done in the past.

Sam won the first couple of points fairly easily, but he knew that the coach was just testing the water, feeling out his enemy, just like Master Hamato had taught Sam.

The third point took Sam longer to win, but he still did and gained a nod of approval.

He won the fourth as well, barely, but that was the last one because from then on the coach no longer held back.

Strangely, it was when Sam stopped winning that he really started to have fun; there was something about a challenge, especially a physical one that had always appealed to him and he was almost enjoying himself as much as he did in his sparring sessions with Rachel. It was also when he finally figured out that he could use a lot of what he had learnt in Okinawa, especially the footwork, to improve the techniques that the coach himself had drummed into him over his years in the club.

The more they fought, the better Sam got, but he still couldn't beat his opponent; the man had been fencing for too many years and was too rehearsed in the very specific techniques used in fencing that not even Sam's three years of intense martial arts training could compete.

The coach took four points in a row, lightning-fast exchanges that had Sam's heart racing in excitement, before calling a halt in the middle of the piste.

'Four to four, Sam, but who's counting?' The coach laughed and shook his head in admiration. 'You're doing really *really* well, but I think you can do better. One more point - give it all you've got!'

He put his mask on and saluted as he backed away to his starting position.

Sam returned the salute, grinning behind his mask.

The coach was right; even though he was fencing far above the level that he had had at the end of the last school year, he knew that he wasn't fighting nearly as well as he had in Port Royal. That was understandable, though; in Port Royal he had temporarily taken on the persona of a pirate captain, with skills picked up over a lifetime of handling a sword in life or death fights. He had, of course, lost those skills when he had returned home, but he could still remember how it had *felt*, especially during his duel with Bonnie, and he knew that he would have to recapture some of that brilliance and combine it with the martial instincts that Master Hamato had nurtured in him if he had any hope of winning. The only trouble was that the rules of fencing meant that he had to stay within the bounds of the thin piste and couldn't do things like leap off barrels, swing from ropes, climb masts, or balance on the rail of a pitching ship and couldn't use some of the more flamboyant moves he remembered from that fight to surprise his opponent. Instead, he was going to have to do something a bit more conventional.

They engaged in the centre of the piste and, right from the start, Sam tried to take the initiative and attack from different angles. Predictably, though, the coach adapted expertly to his change in tactics and Sam's every attack was met and riposted, forcing him to use all of his skill and agility to keep his opponent's sword from making contact with his body.

Sam's mind worked frantically on the problem, just as it did in every fight he had with Rachel. He analysed the coach's responses to his attacks, trying to find a pattern to them or a weakness to exploit - he desperately needed something that would allow him to get a touch and beat a man who was clearly better than him.

He spotted something - every time the coach executed a particularly low circular parry, there was a split second when he was open to a blow on the opposite side of his body, just under his collar bone. Sam would have to be inch perfect and time his strike just right, but it was the only opening he had found and his only chance, so he committed to it.

He went through a series of attacks, setting up the exact circumstances for him to be able to take advantage of the weakness and then, when he was ready, he feinted the strike that would make the man do the circular parry, then changed direction at the last moment and lunged.

He had carried his plan out perfectly and the point of his foil flew unerringly towards exactly where he had wanted it to go, but suddenly, somehow, the coach wasn't there in front of him anymore and, not only that, but there was a sharp pressure on his back as the tip of the man's sword touched him, taking the point.

He had lost.

Sam tore off his mask and blinked at the man incredulously. 'What did you do? What was that?'

Panting gently, the coach pulled off his own mask to reveal a huge grin. 'That, Sam, was a flick technique.' He laughed at Sam's blank expression. 'Oh, haven't I taught you them yet? Very flexible swords, foils, you can do a lot with them that isn't just stabbing...'

Sam shook his head and smiled wryly. 'No, you haven't taught flicks to me yet. Perhaps you should...'

'Don't worry, I will; you weren't ready for them before, but boy are you now; that was *superb*! And, by the way, what the *hell* have you been doing over the summer?'

'If only you knew…' thought Sam to himself, but instead he just shrugged. 'I've been keeping fit and doing some martial arts. Nothing special,' he said.

'Well, whatever you did, it worked!' He reached out and shook hands with Sam. 'And we *have* to talk about the national championships sometime.'

'OK.' Sam nodded and turned to leave, but immediately halted in his steps when he saw that everybody was staring, open-mouthed, at him. He looked around the faces, noting Rafa's angry scowl, but mostly seeing astonishment and even a little bit of hero worship from many of the new members. He was suddenly very self-conscious and there was an awkward moment of silence as he reddened in the face and tried not to meet anybody's eye.

The coach slapped him on the back, breaking the spell as he called out. 'Right! You've all seen what you've got to beat if you want to be captain! Switch partners and keep practising!' He pushed Sam gently away and motioned for another fencer to come over.

Sam took the boy's place, facing off against a girl this time.

For the next half an hour Sam fenced with several different boys and girls, members of the team as well as new aspirants. They were all good; they had to be, to be considered for the team, but none of them came even close to having his level of skill and, exactly like the coach did, he had to modify his level of technique so as not to humiliate them.

He should have been pleased to be the best at something for once, but instead he grew more and more upset as the evening went on and at first he had no idea why.

Finally, though, he figured out what was wrong - the only reason he had an advantage over the other students in the sports hall was because he had spent three years learning martial arts from a master, three years dedicated *solely* to learning martial arts, which was something that none of them could ever even *dream* of doing. That meant that his superiority wasn't *fair*; he had *cheated* to obtain it.

He thought back to what Rachel had said about Displacing, about growing up too fast and having to leave behind everything you had known previously, like family and friends. So far he had been able to avoid feeling that way about his family, but this was only his first week back at school since becoming a Displacer and he was already feeling the effects of his actual age and experience compared to his fellow students and, while he had to admit that fencing was fairly trivial in the larger scheme of things, he couldn't help but feel a bit depressed; Rachel was gone and now so was the pleasure he had previously felt practising his favourite after-school activity.

That feeling of unhappiness got worse and worse as the time passed and he was starting to think that he would have to give up fencing all together, but then, the next time that the coach called for them to switch partners, instead of losing himself in his thoughts and waiting for someone to come to him, he looked around and noticed what had been happening - rather than go to someone who they knew they had a chance to beat, the other students were actually queueing up to spar with him.

In that moment, Sam had an epiphany - an advantage like his wasn't something to be ashamed of, neither was it something to be used to demoralise or humiliate his opposition, which he instinctively knew was what somebody like Rafa would do, instead it could be used to inspire and even to teach his fellow teammates. Being the captain of fencing wouldn't be so different from being the captain of a pirate ship; he could be a leader and an example, if he got the job. Finally, he would be able to use some of the skills that he learnt on Displacements to help people in the present and not just defend himself from Rafa's bullying.

His chin immediately came up and he smiled at his new opponent, another one of the newbies, 'OK, show me what you can do!' He saluted and the boy tentatively smiled back at him before they put their masks on.

He used the rest of the session to teach as much as he could, giving his opponents as much positive feedback as he could and when it came time to spar with Rafa he took it in his stride, with a smile, and instead of simply humiliating him, which was very tempting, and which he could have done easily enough, he tried to get the big boy to change his tactics and do something else apart from brute force his way to victories. It didn't work, but he resolved to keep trying; Sam was not a vindictive boy and now that he himself was safe from Rafa he was going to try to get him to stop being a bully. And if that didn't work he could always take Rafa's next victim under his wing, at least while they were at school or in the fencing club.

Sam was made captain, much to Rafa's disgust, but the delight and approval of the other members of the team and was congratulated on all sides; this was the most popular he had ever been at school. He was pleased to see that his first opponent, Marc, had also made the team;

the boy had showed promise and he had had the courage not to be frightened off by Rafa. The bully hadn't managed to hurt anyone else either, beyond his first partner; Marc had passed on Sam's advice to Rafa's next opponent and he in turn had done the same to the next and so on, and every single one of them had been able to avoid getting hurt too much.

His parents decided to celebrate his appointment with pizza, Sam's favourite food. Sam's father had an unfortunate tendency to burn pizzas, even though they were simple enough to put in the oven, so thankfully they went out. They ended up in a place just down the road, which they had been to several times before, where they were always welcomed with a smile by the Italian owner and with free breadsticks for Violeta.

They had a very good evening and Sam stuffed himself with the spicy *Diavola* pizza that he loved, all the while laughing with Violeta as she struggled messily with her spaghetti.

For the first time in days he didn't miss Rachel so very much.

CHAPTER 2
87

Two weeks after Rachel had left, on Saturday morning, Sam woke up knowing that he was able to Displace again. It was a unique feeling, being ready to Displace, and there was no mistaking it for anything else - like an exciting tugging sensation in the stomach that pulled him towards the past and adventure.

He grabbed his phone from the nightstand, then rolled onto his back and stared up at the ceiling while it started up.

A couple of days before, Andrew had sent him a message, telling him to get in contact as soon as he could Displace again, that there was work for him to do - an official Society mission. He had been excited, wondering what his uncle had in store for him, but at the same time he had been a bit disappointed that once more he wouldn't be able to choose where he went; he had a long list of places that he wanted to go to and things he wanted to do, but he never seemed to be able to get around to doing any of them - although he had to admit that more than a few of the items on that list now seemed quite childish to him and besides, if he was going to have an adventure, he wanted Rachel to have it with him.

His phone connected and he wrote two WhatsApp messages, the first, as always, to Rachel, bidding her good morning, and the second to Andrew reporting his readiness. He received an immediate reply from both - Rachel returning his message with an emoji, and his uncle telling him to go to his flat and connect to Skype as soon as he could.

Andrew had given Sam a key to his flat when he had gone back to London so that Sam could use the computer for Skype meetings with the group and he hurried there as soon as he'd had breakfast, telling his parents that he was going on a run.

He went straight to the study and turned on the computer, then wandered around the flat while he waited for it to start up.

The flat seemed so empty, with nobody living in it. Most of Andrew's souvenirs and books were still on every shelf, of course, but there were none of the little signs of life that he had taken for granted when his fellow Displacers had been there, no toothbrushes, no empty mugs, no open biscuit packets on the coffee table. It also smelled slightly of damp, because it had been completely shut up since Rachel had left and as he went he opened a few window to let the warm, late-summer air in.

He walked along the hallway, past the door to the mysterious room that Andrew had never let either him or Rachel go in and idly tried the handle, wondering if his uncle had left it unlocked, but he hadn't - it looked like what was in there was going to stay a secret for at least a little longer.

He paused at the kitchen and briefly considered making himself a cup of tea, more out of habit than anything else; he had always had one shoved into his hand by Rachel or Andrew as soon as he'd gotten there every morning, but swiftly rejected the idea and went back to the study. The computer was on and waiting, so he logged in to his Skype account and sure enough he found Andrew online waiting for him.

When Andrew appeared, Rachel was sitting next to him.

'Hi, Sam!'

For a moment Sam was so surprised to see her that he just gaped at her with his mouth open.

She raised an eyebrow. 'Have you forgotten me already?' She grinned at him.

'Sorry! Rachel! Sorry! It's just I, well, I wasn't expecting to see you!' He returned her smile warmly.

'Well, I'm helping Andrew with the Displacers now, aren't I? And you're a Displacer. So…'

'Right!'

'Yeah, hi to you too, Sam.' Andrew chuckled, not too put out by the fact that Sam had ignored him completely.

'Oh. Hi, Andrew. Sorry, didn't see you there!'

Andrew chuckled and shook his head. Andrew was leader of the Displacers, which made him Sam's boss, but he was also family, which gave Sam a lot of leeway for cheekiness. 'Yes, right, well. If you don't mind, can we get to the job at hand? As I told you a couple of days ago, I have a mission for you. Once it's done I'll leave you two to chat while I go off and do something that's actually worthwhile, OK?'

Sam and Rachel just grinned at each other.

'I have a nice, easy job for your first official mission and you can put to good use those thieving skills Rachel has been telling me she helped you pick up and that I heartily disapprove of...'

Pennsylvania. November 19, 1863

Sam stood on a slight rise and looked down at the crowd of people milling around under a bright blue sky in the lush green field, talking solemnly and patiently awaiting the appearance of the dignitaries who would dedicate the cemetery that afternoon. The mood was solemn, but Sam could feel a hint of jubilation, a hint of hope; the battle that had been waged on this field had been a great victory for the side of the Union and had marked something of a turning point in the fortunes of the northern armies.

Most of the occupants of the field were wearing black suits and dark clothing, befitting the sombre nature of the occasion, but there were a few blue uniforms scattered here and there among them. A quick glance down at his own clothing revealed that Sam was dressed in one of the blue uniforms, with the golden bars of a captain in the Union Army on his shoulders, a heavy pistol strapped to his side and a hat on his head.

He gazed around, taking the time to acclimatise before he took care of the mission. It was hard to tell that this was the site of the bloodiest battle in the American Civil War, the setting was actually rather peaceful, but he supposed that the weapons involved were not quite the same as the ones he had encountered on his brief but memorable visit to the battlefields of World War One; they didn't leave such a lasting mark on the landscape.

Sam made his way through the people, heading towards a large tent set up near to a rickety looking wooden stage; this close to the beginnings of proceedings he was fairly sure that was where he would find his target.

He returned the salute of the guards outside the tent and went in.

President Abraham Lincoln was alone on the far side of the tent with his back to the entrance.

Sam stood just inside the entrance and studied the great man. He was tall, over six feet, and he had a beard framing his chin but no moustache. Unsurprisingly, he looked exactly as he did in the pictures that Sam had seen on the Internet. He was a formidable presence in the largish tent, seeming to fill the space.

Sam saw a hat on a table just a few feet away, along with a pair of gloves and a scarf. It was a round hat, like a flattish bowler.

According to Andrew, Lincoln had somehow got it into his head to try a new style of hat. He was going to wear it today and ruin the image that history had of him. To Sam it all appeared rather trivial, but Andrew seemed to believe that it was important, that it would have disastrous consequences, so, bizarrely, he had ordered Sam to come and steal it.

Lincoln was reciting his speech, referring to a piece of paper that he was waving in his hand every so often.

'Eighty-seven years… Three years short of nine decades… No, that's not right either…'

Sam was just starting to reach out for the hat when Lincoln turned and spotted him. He raised an eyebrow. 'Yes?'

Sam almost panicked, but caught himself in time and drew himself to attention, remembering that he was dressed as a soldier and that the best way to blend in was to look like you belonged.

'Er, Mr President?'

'Yes, son?'

'They're almost ready for you, sir.'

'Thank you.'

Lincoln turned away again, waving his paper in the air. 'Seven dozen and… aargh!' He growled, reaching up to tug at his hair in frustration.

Sam used the opportunity provided by the man's distraction to step forward and grab the hat from the table. He was about to leave when something occurred to him and he hurriedly stuffed the hat up into his uniform coat to hide it. Not quite believing that he was doing it, he called out. 'Four score, Mr President.'

'I'm sorry, captain?' The tall man turned to frown at him.

'Four score and seven, sir. It has a nice ring to it, don't you think?'

'Four sc… why yes, I believe it does!'

Lincoln faced the wall of the tent again and declaimed in a deep voice, holding his arm to the side for effect. 'Four score and seven years ago, our forefathers…'

Sam took advantage of Lincoln's distraction to beat a hasty retreat. He headed around the side of the tent and out of the way just in time to avoid the group of dignitaries who were coming to get Lincoln for the speeches. He grinned as he heard Lincoln's shout. 'Where the hell is my new hat?'

Sam had never really liked history lessons at school before becoming a Displacer, but since he'd started putting together his list of possible destinations to go to he'd developed a bit of an interest and it was too good an opportunity to miss, so he stuck around to watch. He stood through Edward Everett's two hour speech on what had happened at Gettysburg, just so that he could hear Abraham Lincoln's two minute address, one of the most famous, yet shortest, speeches in history. He joined in the thunderous applause, still not quite believing that he could have witnessed such a momentous occasion and stayed to see the dedication of the cemetery.

When the people started to break up and go their separate ways, he clutched the stolen hat tightly in his hands and closed his eyes…

…then opened them again and smiled at Rachel and Andrew. He put the hat on his head and it slipped right down to cover his eyes; Abraham Lincoln had a big head apparently. 'How does it look?'

'Very sexy…' came the dry reply from Rachel.

Sam pulled the hat off and grinned at her.

Andrew frowned and squinted as he leaned forward in his seat. 'Was there something inside the hat?'

Sam looked down at it, turning it over in his hands. 'No, it looks new. Why?'

'Then what's that on your head?'

Sam reached up and ran his hand through his hair, but he couldn't find anything so he expanded his own image onto one of the empty screens and leaned forward, looking closer - there was something white in his hair. 'I'm sure it's just from some bird, there were plenty of them around.' He laughed and put his hand up to tug at the white mark, but stopped; it wasn't that he had something white *in* his hair, his hair *was* white - a lock of his hair above his left eye had turned bone white. 'Whoa, what the hell is this, Andrew?'

'I have no idea!'

Suddenly, Sam felt very weak. His eyes unfocused and the world receded from him as if he was tumbling dizzily down a dark hole. He fell back into his chair, blinking rapidly, trying to force away the blackness that was overcoming him.

'Sam! Sam!' Rachel's voice seemed to be coming from far away and he struggled to focus on it, drawing himself back from the brink of unconsciousness.

His vision cleared slowly and he looked up into the concerned faces of his uncle and his girlfriend on the monitor. 'OK, that was weird. How long was I out of it for?'

'Only a couple of seconds. How are you feeling?'

'I'm OK, Rachel, just a bit dizzy. What was that?'

Andrew sighed. 'I was afraid something like this might happen. You've been going on twice as many Displacements as everyone else and you don't seem to be taking it as well as we thought you were.'

'What does that mean?'

'It means I think you should stop Displacing for a while.'

Sam stared at him in shock. 'No! That's not fair!'

'It's just for a little while, Sam, to give yourself time to recover. We'll see how you are in a few weeks and if you're OK, then you can start again, but only once a month, alright? We don't want you burning yourself out; you're too young and dumb to be an Elder.' Andrew grinned, making an effort to take the edge off of what was a very worrying situation.

'Andrew, look!' Rachel called out in surprise. 'His hair is turning brown!'

Sam leaned forwards again to get closer to the webcam and they all watched astounded as the white hairs on his head started to go back to their normal colour. Eventually, the white disappeared entirely, leaving Sam looking exactly the same as he had before the Displacement.

Andrew was somewhat relieved, but he was still deadly serious when he spoke next. 'Sam, I mean it, you have to take a break. Just because your hair went back to normal *this* time doesn't mean that if you push yourself too hard you won't do permanent damage *next* time.'

'And I don't want to go out with an old man! No offence to old men, of course.' Rachel patted Andrew on the shoulder, trying to lighten the mood, but her face was still creased with concern.

Sam sighed. 'Alright, I'll rest for a while. What are we talking about, here, Andrew? A month? Six weeks?'

'Actually, I think it would be best if you didn't Displace again until Christmas. That way you'll be here, one of us can go with you, and we'll be able to take care of you if something happens when you come back.'

'And we can poke and prod you and do experiments if you go white again!' said Rachel with a grin.

Andrew laughed, but Sam wasn't in the mood for jokes. 'Christmas! You want me to wait until Christmas! That's more than three months! Come on, Andrew, that's not f...'

Andrew cut him off sharply. 'Sam! No arguments! We need you healthy!' He took a breath and calmed down, continuing in a more controlled voice. 'I've told you before, we don't know exactly what you're capable of yet. I've been letting you Displace whenever and wherever you want, but that has to stop. Now. Some precautions need to be taken it seems and while you are a member of the Displacers you are *my* responsibility and are under *my* orders. And I'm ordering you,' he sighed. 'No, I'm *asking* you, Sam. Please take my advice this time and stop.'

Sam didn't like it, but he saw some sense in Andrew's concern, especially seeing as his head was still swimming. 'OK, then.'

'Good. Now, I'm going to leave you to have a chat with Rachel, but please don't be long; you have to get home and get to bed. And make sure you eat and drink something - there should be some Jammy Dodgers and some tea left in the kitchen.'

'Yes, Andrew...'

'OK, OK, I'm going! Just take care of yourself, alright? And if anything else happens let me know as soon as you can.' With that he stood up and left.

Rachel watched Andrew go and as soon as the door had closed behind him she frowned at Sam, still worried. 'Are you sure you're alright?'

'Yeah, I'm fine. I felt worse after the run the day we arrived in Okinawa.'

Rachel smiled for the first time in a good few minutes; Master Hamato had made Sam run until the point of exhaustion, more as a test of his determination than his stamina, and he had waited for her to be out of sight, but unfortunately not out of earshot, before getting rid of his breakfast. 'I'm glad the white hair isn't permanent.'

Sam nodded. 'That was strange.'

She shrugged. 'The whole Displacing thing is pretty strange, I don't think anyone knows what is normal and what isn't. I'm pretty sure the Elders are going to want to investigate, though, look in the archives to see if something like this has ever happened to anybody else, that kind of thing.'

'Just as long as they don't want to take any blood or anything; I'm not a big fan of needles.'

'Wuss!'

They laughed, the fright of a few minutes before almost forgotten.

'I miss you.'

'I miss you, too... Christmas isn't too far away, be patient please, Sam.'

He smiled. 'I'll try. But you know me; one day I might just wake up in China by mistake.'

Rachel laughed. 'I really wouldn't put it past you.'

'Can you stay online for a while?'

'Of course!'

'Great! I'm going to go and get a drink and some of Andrew's biscuits. I think there's a coke left in the fridge. Don't tell Andrew, but I got pretty fed up of having tea all the time.'

'Sacrilege! I think it's in the Society handbook somewhere that tea is compulsory whenever Displacing is discussed.'

'That's it! I'm leaving and going over to the dark side.' Sam stood up and started to leave with a big grin on his face. He paused in the doorway and looked back at her. 'Don't go anywhere, I'll be right back.'

'I'll be here, don't worry, Sam.'

CHAPTER 3
RESTRICTED

After his Displacement, Sam became obsessed with his hair and he couldn't go past a mirror without checking to see if there was any white in it. It wasn't just that he was afraid of the ill effects of Displacing, he was also worried about what his parents might think - when he had got injured during his disastrous trip to World War One, Andrew had been able to explain away his broken arm and bruises as a hit and run accident, but it would be difficult to find an excuse for why his hair had lost its colour, beyond an accident involving bleach or perhaps a radioactive insect. He had nightmarish visions of his parents taking him to hospitals, having tests done and looking for all kinds of strange diseases. In one of his more lucid daydreams he actually pictured himself taking part in an episode of *House*, with Hugh Laurie accusing him of lying over and over and forcing him to admit to his ability to time travel, while his parents looked on with disappointment and repugnance. His obsession continued for a couple of weeks, well beyond the time when he knew that he was capable of Displacing again, and it wasn't until Violeta found him in the bathroom, staring at his hair in the mirror, running it between his fingers, inspecting it for the minutest of changes and asked him 'are you going to be a hairdresser when you grow up, Sammy?' that he realised how ridiculous he was being. After then, he checked a couple of times a day, only because Andrew had asked him to just in case, but there was never any noticeable change.

With Displacing completely off the table, Sam's life more or less went back to how it had been before he had gotten his powers.

He threw himself into his schoolwork, using the time he usually spent on researching possible destinations to do the homework he normally neglected. He would much rather have been doing something related to Displacing, but his grades improved steadily as a result, which made his parents very happy and he figured that, if he was going to have the best chance of persuading them to let him leave school at the end of the year and work for Andrew, then he had to at least make sure to pass all his exams.

Fencing became his other main focus. He got to know and became friends with all of the new members of the team, but made sure not to ignore all of the other people who hadn't made the cut; it was after all a club and not just a team. He did his best to help anyone who asked for it, while trying not to flaunt his superiority or rub it in anybody's face. He also continued to do his best to "rehabilitate" Rafa, but he didn't get very far and feared that the bully might be a lost cause.

He also made time to keep up with his training, but it wasn't the same; running up and down Collserola alone wasn't nearly as much fun as it was with Rachel and going through techniques on his own wasn't ideal. He kept up with it, though, going out most evenings after school for an hour or so when he didn't have fencing, both because he knew Rachel would make fun of him if he lapsed and lost his, all-important, six pack, but also because he owed it to Master Hamato to maintain his discipline.

The highlight of his days, though, and the only real contact he had with the Society, was the time he spent talking to Rachel on Skype. During the week he didn't have a good excuse to leave home in the evenings, so he had to use his own laptop in his room for their calls. That meant that they had to limit themselves to very day to day topics of conversation, like schoolwork or how much they missed each other, in case they were overheard. However, at the weekend he was free to go to Andrew's flat and use his computer to speak more privately and it was then that she could keep him up to date with what was happening with the Society.

The first thing he asked her every time he saw her was whether there had been any progress with the investigation into what had happened to his hair. She told him the same thing every time, though; that the Elders were looking into it, but the only explanation they had been able to come up with so far was what Andrew had already supposed, that he was overly stressing himself by Displacing too often.

Everybody knew the cost that it had on the body, indeed that was the reason why Displacers went through the Transition and became Elders - the strain became too much and their bodies just refused to do it anymore. Without finding anything in the archives that specifically referred to what had happened to Sam, the Elders were unwilling to say what should be done, so they were of the same opinion as Andrew; that the best thing for him to do was to rest and wait for Christmas and have a supervised Displacement then.

While it was disappointing to hear that the Elders weren't able to come up with something that would allow him to Displace safely, Sam was still glad to hear all of the other news from the Society and it made him feel at least a part of things when she read him the reports of the other active members, telling him about the missions that they and she had been on.

However, there was one thing that was bothering Sam. He had spent enough time with Rachel to know when she was hiding something from him and every time he spoke to her he got the feeling she wasn't telling him all of the news. Eventually, on a Sunday afternoon a few weeks after his Displacement to Gettysburg, he pressed her about it.

'Well, there have been some doubts and not a bit of disappointment...' She grimaced, reluctant to continue. 'There are some people saying that this means the prophecy isn't about you after all and, of course, Ralph is using this to attack Andrew again, telling everybody that he knew that and has been deliberately giving everybody false hope.'

'I really don't like that guy. I don't trust him either.'

'I know what you mean, but leaving his son and his bitterness to one side, Ralph has actually done a lot for the Displacers. He's one of the good guys.'

Sam didn't quite believe her, but he accepted her words for the time being and changed the subject - now that he knew what she had been hiding from him he didn't particularly want to talk about it, especially seeing as there was nothing he could do about the situation until he could Displace again. 'Oh, I keep forgetting to ask - what's happening with that vase I brought back from Egypt?'

'Philip still isn't ready to open it yet. He's been studying it this whole time with x-rays and stuff... Actually, I'm not entirely sure what he's been doing, I just know that he doesn't want to rush things.'

'Not rush things? He's had it for months!'

'Yeah, well, if you thought us active Displacers were patient wait until you have to deal with the Elders… And on top of that Philip is a scientist - he's not going to hurry into anything.'

'I kind of understand that in this case. I wouldn't want him to open it and have what's inside fall apart; I went through too much to get it. Let me know if anything happens in the next few years please…'

Rachel laughed. 'OK! In the meantime Andrew is going to go to Egypt with Lisa and John to have a look around that temple of yours. He wants to see if there is anything there that can help us with the vase or the prophecy.'

'Ask them to look out for Bertram please, I'm a bit worried about what happened to him after I left.'

'I will. Anyway, enough work stuff, tell me what's been going on with you? How's school going?'

Sam smiled and settled back into Andrew's comfortable office chair as they moved from Displacer business to more personal topics - even though they seemed to talk about the same things every time they connected, he didn't mind; if they had to be apart he would take what he could get.

Time passed quicker than he had feared it would and soon it was the first of November and Sam celebrated his 16th birthday for the third time, but the first time as far as his family were concerned.

His parents proudly presented him with some new fencing gear - one of each type of sword as well as a glove and a helmet saying that, now he was captain, he had to look the part.

Rachel sent him a box set of *Back to the Future* blu-rays, which he loved, and a bottle of "Just for Men" hair dye, which he couldn't stop laughing at, but that left his parents completely mystified.

Andrew and James sent him books - around thirty historical novels were delivered to him in one big, very heavy box. They were all in English and covered a wide range of time periods and events from the Wars of the Roses to the Hundred Years War, as well as some set in Medieval Arabia, Spain and France. He had no idea how he was going to find the time to read so many of them, but they all looked so interesting that he resolved to try.

The days went by and each and every morning Sam woke up knowing that he could Displace if he just closed his eyes and concentrated hard enough, but he wasn't allowed to. It was very frustrating; his Displacements, especially the ones with Rachel, had been the highlight of his life, something to look forward to every couple of weeks.

He was sorely tempted to Displace anyway, but in the end common sense won out and he resisted the temptation; he didn't want to do anything to jeopardise his future. So he contented himself with reading about the past and dreaming his usual dreams of being a knight in shining armour. Just now the damsel always had Rachel's face.

CHAPTER 4
JUST CHECKING

Egypt, 1907.

Night in the desert was quiet, usually, but as the three cloaked figures stood looking down a gentle slope between the rock walls of a canyon at the encampment below them they were assailed by the sounds of drunken revelry.

'Are we really going to go down there into that, Andrew?'

The tallest figure shook his head and sighed. 'Yes, John, that's why we're here - we need to get Lisa into that complex. We need to get her to the temple that Sam discovered and see if there's anything we don't want Quentin getting his grubby mitts on.'

'But it's crawling with bad guys!'

'"Bad guys", John? Really? Just because they are wearing black?'

'No… not *just*… I mean, well, look at them…' John waved in the direction of the camp vaguely as he searched for words. He didn't find them. 'OK, yes, because they're wearing black, but you've got to admit they do all look like bad guys.'

'I think they look like Bedouins…'

'Children, please!' Lisa hissed in exasperation. 'Look!'

She pointed down the slope to where there was a small door at the end of the canyon set in the rock face. It was illuminated brightly by a constellation of burning torches. Two huge figures accompanied by several black-clad Bedouins had come out of the door and into the firelight.

'That must be Tristan and Tessa, the so-called "Twins",' said John. 'I've never seen them before, but there can't be two other people who look like that.'

'Damn it, I should have known they would have come back.' Andrew said, gritting his teeth in frustration. 'We should have come here as soon as Sam got home; who knows how much they've been able to take already.'

'Well, if they're here, then we can't do anything; they'll have set the time-line.' John said. 'We might as well just go home.'

They watched as the group stood around just outside the door having a brief conversation before they split up. The two giants each hefted a couple of large bags onto their shoulders as if they were nothing, closed their eyes, then disappeared.

The Displacers looked at each other and grinned.

'That's a stroke of luck,' said Lisa, chuckling.

'Indeed! Now we just have to hope that we can get tonight's work done before they come back.' Andrew suddenly frowned and looked around the camp thoughtfully. 'I haven't seen Bertram Campbell or anyone who could be that Francis person Sam described anywhere, have either of you?'

'Maybe they've left them in the temple complex?' Lisa sounded hopeful, but they all knew that there wasn't much possibility of that.

Andrew sighed. 'We'll keep an eye out for them when we go in. I think we'll wait for a couple of hours; with the amount they've been drinking they'll probably all go to sleep soon and we'll be able to walk right past them.'

'That's so boring!' said John, whining like a child. 'Come on! We've got guns and most of them have only got big swords... We can fight our way through! Haven't you guys seen *Raiders*?'

Neither Andrew or Lisa deigned to answer him, they just walked away over to the wall of the canyon and sat down to wait, ignoring him as John softly called after them.

'Guys?'

In the end it took less than an hour for the camp to become quiet; whatever the men were drinking was obviously quite strong and had sent them to sleep very quickly.

They waited another hour, just in case, then Andrew waved them forwards. 'OK, let's go. And don't forget the symbol.'

The Displacers made their way swiftly and silently down the slope and through the camp, sticking to the shadows as much as possible.

Following the plan that Andrew and James had come up when they had prepared the mission, they paused every so often to roughly scrawl a symbol on the floor or a tent wall in charcoal, or with their fingers in the ashes of fires that had gone out; subtle marks that would attract the eye of the curious, but not be too obvious to the casual observer.

Despite their artistic efforts they still got to the door quickly and they grabbed torches off the wall and went straight in.

They made their way rapidly through the deserted tunnels and found that the traps that Sam had described in detail in his report had been made safe by the Bedouins. In the first chamber the correct door had been marked and the other entrances blocked off, the tiles on the floor in the second chamber had been painted white to indicate the ones that were safe to use, and the third chamber had received the same treatment as the second; the thin walkway was covered in white paint and they had even managed to splash the ceiling somehow, which considerably lessoned the dizzying effect that the white bands had.

John grinned when he saw the paint everywhere. 'Looks like Health and Safety got here before us.'

Andrew, though, was quite annoyed, although he understood the necessity. 'Bloody vandals. Come on, let's see what they've done to the temple.'

Surprisingly, the temple was almost completely untouched. The markings on the walls hadn't been defaced and the Pharaoh was still sitting on his throne, intact, aside from the missing mask. Lisa held her torch high and gazed around, a yearning look on her face, but was too disciplined to say anything and just followed the others as they made their way directly to the secret door at the back.

The room was almost half empty and there was a large semi-circular void around the door where items had already been taken away by the Twins and the Bedouin, but even so the amount of gold and jewels left in the room, glistening and gleaming in the light from their torches, was staggering.

John gave a low whistle. 'Oh my… The fun I could have with that amount of money.'

Andrew glanced at him, scathingly. 'I really don't want to know.' He turned to Lisa, about to tell her to get to work but there was no need; she had already begun to inspect the remaining treasure. Instead he turned back to John. 'You've got the bags, go with her.' He pointed a warning finger at him. 'Just take what she tells you to, not whatever catches your eye; we can't carry much with us.'

'Spoilsport.'

Andrew sighed. 'Alright, if there's room in the bags maybe I'll let you take a bauble or two, we'll see.'

'Yay!' John skipped over to Lisa and started picking up the objects that she pointed out and putting them carefully into several small sacks.

Andrew left them to work and went back into the temple. He walked up to the wall by the door and scanned the writing there. Finding what he wanted he took out a piece of charcoal and started making a few subtle lines on the wall, taking a few paces back every so often to inspect his work, moving around to look at it from different angles before going back to draw some more.

It took over an hour, but finally he was satisfied with his artwork. The lines he had made weren't anything in themselves and weren't individually obvious, but collectively they drew the eye towards a symbol at head height on the wall - the same symbol that they had been drawing around the camp: the symbol for "death" in Egyptian hieroglyphics.

He turned as Lisa and John came out of the treasure room carrying the now bulging sacks between them.

'There's still some incredible stuff in there but I've got the most important pieces, I think.'

'Good, well done, Lisa. Get home you two, I'll see you when the job is done.'

He watched as Lisa and John disappeared and then, with one last look at the symbol on the wall, he left the temple.

Two days later Andrew was starting to think that he would have to go back into the temple and make things a bit more obvious when there was a rumbling noise and the ground started to shake.

He stood up from his place of concealment, walked over to the lip of the canyon and gazed down at the chaos unfolding below.

The Bedouins were looking around in fear as the ground shook beneath them and sand and loose rock rained down around them. As the tremors worsened, the rock face at the end of the canyon started to crumble and crack, coming apart in a pattern that was far too regular to be natural, and blocks started to tumble from it. Suddenly, lava burst through the door and the gaps in the rock and started to pour into the canyon, oozing quickly up the slope.

The men broke instantly, sprinting in the footsteps of their camels, who apparently had more sense than their owners did and had galloped away the first time the ground had shook. In no time at all they had disappeared up the long slope and out of sight.

Andrew shook his head and chuckled; there was always one person who would reach out and touch something or push a button that they weren't supposed to.

Fascinated, Andrew remained where he was and watched the lava pour into the canyon, but when the ground beneath his feet started to crumble he realised that it was much too dangerous to stay.

With the walls falling, soon the canyon would be gone without a trace and any remaining secrets would be lost forever. It was a shame, but at least that would keep the rest of the treasure out of Quentin's hands.

Satisfied with how things had turned out, he closed his eyes and went to join his friends back in the present.

CHAPTER 5
A DISTURBANCE

The Christmas holidays couldn't come soon enough for Sam and his excitement at the prospect of Displacing again was rivalled only by his eagerness to be reunited with Rachel. He was fairly sure he loved her, but his feelings were very mixed up; he had twice spent three years with her in the past and he was pretty sure he had fallen in love with her each time, but then when he came back it was a return to the hormones and confusion of being a teenager going through the worst of puberty and things got very complicated again. The only thing he could really say for sure was that he missed her a lot and couldn't stand to be apart from her.

When December finally rolled around and the weather started to turn nasty he knew that there wasn't long to go. Schoolwork began to wind down and he led his team to victory in one last fencing match before the break, playing against a local school. The win was very much a team effort with most people winning their bouts. Marc, the new boy, had won his match easily; he was improving at a steady rate and was moving rapidly up the ranks of the team. Even Rafa did fairly well and seemed to have calmed down at first, using actual technique rather than charging straight in like a bull in a china shop from the get-go, but it didn't last long before he lapsed back into his usual tactics. Still, Sam saw it as an improvement and the coach didn't have as much reason to be ashamed of the bully as usual.

Aside from fencing, Sam's life was fairly boring, as many schoolchildren's lives are, but in his particular case, adding insult to injury was the fact that everyone else was Displacing without him - Andrew had gone to Egypt and brought back a fair amount of interesting treasures that unfortunately didn't look like they were going to help with the vase and even Rachel had carried out a couple of missions on her own. He was happy for her, but he wished he could have gone too.

There was one bit of excitement, though; midway through the month Sam received a WhatsApp from Andrew asking him to connect to Skype urgently.

Sam was half way through his evening run, a mile or so away up the hill in Park Güell, but he sprinted straight back and connected as quickly as he could. He was hoping that Rachel would be there as well, but was disappointed when only Andrew connected.

'Sam! Thank you for connecting so quickly.'

'No problem, what's up? Where's Rachel?'

'Rachel's with her mother today, I'm on my own.'

'Oh…'

Andrew grinned. 'Don't look so disappointed, please, I'm still your uncle and you should be satisfied with just me!'

'Yeah, right! Sorry, Uncle Andrew, but you're just not as good looking as she is.' Sam returned his grin.

'That's a matter of opinion. Anyway, I need to talk to you seriously and it'll help that you're not being distracted by the sight of your girlfriend pouting at you; we've got a bit of a situation brewing.'

Sam raised an eyebrow. 'Really? Let me guess... Quentin?'

Andrew nodded. 'Probably. You know how the Elders can sense changes in the time-line before they happen?'

'Yes.'

'Well, they're pretty sure that there's something coming, something big. There's a "disturbance in the force" as John puts it and we're pretty convinced it's Quentin and company because it's too big to be our usual bread and butter slip in the time-line. We think he has an operation in the works and the fact that the time-line is already shifting means it'll be a disaster for us if they carry out their plans. So we need to pull out all the stops to prevent them from succeeding.'

Sam frowned. 'But if the Elders can feel a change, doesn't that mean they are already in the past? And if they are, isn't there nothing we can do? Isn't it already fixed?'

'No, thankfully this is only a precursor - a sign that a change will occur soon. It doesn't mean that they are already in the past because then the time-line would have changed already.' Andrew sighed.

'Quentin and his people have been making quite a few changes to their own advantage for several years now and we're having a bad time of it, but thankfully we're learning to recognise the signs. Unfortunately, the last few times we only realised what was happening the same day, but this time it's a much bigger change and we're hoping that we'll have a few days, or maybe even a few weeks to react.'

'So what did you do last time? Did you manage to stop him?'

'Yes, last time he was stopped.'

'Fine, then you can just do that again.'

Andrew looked at him, absolutely seriously. '*We* can't do it, because it was *you*. You stopped Quentin in Port Royal and the Elders felt you doing it. We ourselves didn't get anywhere *near* figuring out what they were doing before they tried to do it.'

'So, what can I do then?'

Andrew chuckled wryly and shook his head. 'We really don't know. We were hoping something would occur to you.'

'Oh.' Sam sat back in his seat, unsure what to say.

'We know this is a big responsibility to put on your shoulders, but we've never had any success trying to stop them and you're our only hope to do something this time.' Andrew wanted to say more but he didn't. There was enough pressure on Sam already without telling him how close they were to losing everything.

Sam shrugged. 'Well, I don't know what I can do but I'll try.'

Andrew smiled weakly. 'For now, just let us know if you have any sudden urges to jump into the past or anything like that.'

'OK, will do.'

'And if anything else occurs to you, you know where to find me.'

Sam nodded. 'OK. Tell Rachel I said hi, please.'

'I will. See you soon!'

Andrew signed off, leaving Sam staring at an empty screen.

His smile instantly disappeared and his fists clenched on the arms of his chair angrily; once again things were being hidden from him. First, "for his own good", they had kept the prophecy a secret from him for months, and now Andrew had suddenly revealed that he had lied about Quentin's motives, that the man was actually changing the time-line to suit himself, whereas before he had insisted that he was only interested in monetary gain.

How much else wasn't he being told because his uncle thought it would put too much pressure on him or some other equally stupid reason?

There was nothing he could do to confirm his suspicions until Christmas and could talk to James or the other Displacers, so he put them out of his mind and closed the lid of his laptop, determined to concentrate on the newer, more urgent problem.

He stood and began pacing up and down.

At the time, everybody had assumed that his encounter with Quentin in the Caribbean had been an accident, that he had just happened to go walking in the rain at exactly the right time - the odds were against it ever happening, but it wasn't inconceivable. The problem was that he had done it again and had met up with Quentin in Egypt. Once could be explained, twice couldn't; it was far too improbable, which meant there had to be more to what had happened than just coincidence. Either he had some kind of link with Quentin or...

He frowned as something occurred to him - he remembered thinking something like "I hope I don't meet Quentin this time" just as he was Displacing. That must have cancelled his lock on Blackpool in the fifties and transferred it to Quentin, using *him* as a focal point instead of a place and time. Obviously that wasn't what had happened when he'd gone to Port Royal; he hadn't known who Quentin was then, but it had to have been what had taken him to Egypt.

He sat down on his bed and closed his eyes. He began to Prepare himself, feeling the familiar tingle flowing and swirling, spreading throughout his body. He didn't want any accidents so he cleared his mind, making sure not to think of anything that would cause him to go somewhere he didn't want to. Then, when he was ready, he allowed himself to think of Quentin, picturing the face of the man who had tried to kill him twice now, who had come to his hospital room and signed his cast while he'd been unconscious, who had sworn to destroy him. He concentrated, reaching out and...

...nothing. The tingling feeling washed away from him slowly, leaving him cold and empty and he opened his eyes again - either it wasn't possible to use a person as a focal point or Quentin wasn't in the past at that moment.

He sighed; it had been too much to hope for to get confirmation of his theory at the first attempt. He would have to talk to Andrew about it; the Elders would have some more research to do.

He slipped off the bed onto the floor and started to stretch - in his eagerness to connect he hadn't had time to do so after his run. He hadn't showered either and he could feel his clothes sticking to him, but he needed to take care of his muscles first; Master Hamato's lessons were too well ingrained in him.

He replayed the conversation in his mind as he spread his legs and bent down to touch his nose to the floor between them. While he was still seething over the way he was being treated by his uncle, he couldn't help but be concerned; Andrew was very worried and even though he was trying to make less of the situation it was obvious that things were a lot worse than he was saying - the Society was desperate and hoping that Sam would come up with something, pull a rabbit out of the hat, like he'd done before.

CHAPTER 6
REUNION

On the 20th of December the Vives family flew from Barcelona El Prat to London Gatwick where they were met by Andrew in a brand new, bright red Mini with a Union Jack on the roof, which had Violeta in stitches. Once again Sam was disappointed not to see Rachel but, as Andrew rightly pointed out, there wouldn't have been room in the car if she'd come along and it was going to be a squeeze as it was.

The drive in to London was long, made longer and almost unbearable by the ever-present traffic and the journey took them the best part of two hours, even though they weren't going into the city itself, but rather to James' home, near Brixton in South London, where they usually stayed while in England. The house wasn't overly large, with three bedrooms and one bathroom, but it was enough for the five of them to be comfortable, even though Sam had to share a bedroom with Violeta.

It was after dark when they pulled up outside the white two-storey house on the corner of McKay Road and by that time Violeta was grumpy and sleepy and probably a few more of the dwarfs as well after the long journey, so Sam's parents greeted James, who had come out onto the doorstep to welcome them, and then rushed to get her inside and to bed.

Sam was very pleasantly surprised when Rachel followed his grandfather out of the house. He could have jumped into her arms and kissed her right there, but they shared a glance and came to an unspoken agreement that Sam's parents probably wouldn't be a hundred percent happy with such public displays of affection, so they smiled and said hello to each other, then carried in the suitcases, waiting for a bit more privacy before they said a proper hello, settling for a few inconspicuous nudges and caresses while they were unloading the car.

This was the first time that Sam had been in the house since becoming a Displacer and, as he brought the suitcases in, he looked around with different eyes, taking note of the items that were on display - there were souvenirs in every room, just as there had been in Andrew's flat in Barcelona, but James didn't have nearly as many of them and they weren't so haphazardly scattered about the place, instead he had them catalogued or at least grouped logically and Sam wondered if there was a mental change involved with going from being an active Displacer to an Elder, whether they became more focussed or organised or something. It was either that, or they had more time on their hands to sort through the bric-a-brac that they'd picked up over their lifetime, or lifetimes. Of most interest to Sam was a collection of Japanese swords that were hanging on the wall in James' study, thankfully out of reach of Violeta's hands. He knew something about them, both because he was interested in Japan and also because Master Hamato had had his own collection, and he could tell that they came from quite a wide range of periods. He didn't have time to look at them properly at that moment, though, because Andrew was saying goodbye and Rachel was going out the door with him.

He rushed out after them, catching up with them on the street. 'You're leaving?'

She turned back and grinned. 'Of course! You know, for a second there I thought you weren't going to say goodbye.'

'I've barely said hello.'

They glanced at the house - Sam father was disappearing upstairs with a suitcase and his mother was out of sight, occupied with Violeta - then they turned back to Andrew, who was smiling sarcastically at them.

'I think I'll just get in the car...' Andrew looked at them pointedly, then got in the car and closed the door loudly.

Sam's eyes met Rachel's. 'I've missed you.'

'Shut up and kiss me.' Rachel pulled him close and locked her lips to his.

Sam held her close and it was a good few seconds before they separated again, but when they did there was a knock on the car window.

'Sorry to break up the reunion, but it's time we should be going, Rachel. Sam, don't worry, you'll get plenty of time with her while you're here; James is going to tell your parents that he wants to spend some quality time with you and he'll be bringing you to Headquarters for the next few days, starting tomorrow.'

Rachel gave Sam one last peck on the cheek, 'I'll see you tomorrow. Bring something to train in and we'll go for a run in the park.' She climbed smoothly into the car and Andrew pulled away.

Sam watched them turn the corner at the end of the road and then went back inside.

His parents were still upstairs, so he was left alone with his grandfather.

'Fancy a cuppa?' asked James.

'No thanks. Uh, isn't it a bit late for a cup of tea?'

'It's never too late, especially when you get to my age and you already know you're going to be awake most of the night anyway. An extra trip to the toilet doesn't matter much in the grand scheme of things.'

It was a little too much information, but Sam didn't mind; he loved his grandfather and all his little foibles. He followed James into the kitchen and watched him put the kettle on and prepare a mug with a tea bag and sugar.

He had so many questions that he didn't know where to start, but it was obvious that James knew exactly what Sam was thinking and as soon as he had his tea in his hand he led the way to the sitting room, pausing briefly to peer up the stairs and make sure that nobody was going to disturb them for a while. He closed the door behind them, then went over to his favourite armchair and sat down. He sipped from his tea, looking over the rim of the mug and huffed in amusement as Sam flopped bonelessly on the sofa opposite him. 'Well, you look alright to me. Tell me about the hair.'

Sam fingered the strands of hair that had turned white after his last Displacement. 'It's nothing.'

James shook his head. 'One thing that I've learnt over my many years is that in our line of work it is *never* nothing. Andrew said that some of your hair went white and you got dizzy.'

'Yes.'

'I can see your hair is back to normal, but have you had any more dizziness?'

'No.'

'Have you tried preparing since then?'

'Yes.'

'And?'

'No problem. It was as easy as ever.'

James nodded in approval. 'Well, it seems that one thing you've gained since I saw you last is a bit of confidence and it's about time! Having a girlfriend definitely agrees with you... or are you going to try to tell me that she's not your girlfriend, like you did last time?'

Sam reddened, but shook his head. 'I don't think there's any point, is there?'

'Good man! I've been reading between the lines of your reports and it's plain to see that there's a fair amount that the two of you aren't telling us, but that's none of our business.' He grinned mischievously. 'However, I'm also your grandfather and I'm *supposed* to care for you, which *makes* it my business. And, as far as I can see, she is perfect for you.'

'Yeah, I quite like her.' Sam grinned back at him.

'I bloody well hope so!'

'Anyway... Can we change the subject please?

James laughed. 'Of course, my boy!'

'Thank you. So, does anyone have any idea why my hair went white and I got dizzy? Has it ever happened to anyone else?'

'Nope, never. It seems like you're special.' James chuckled wryly. 'We're still scouring the library, rereading diaries and reports, but so far we've found nothing and frankly I don't think that we're going to. We do have a theory though; some of the Elders have suggested that it's not so much the frequency with which you Displace, but rather what happens when you do. Did Andrew ever tell you about his trip to Port Royal after you went there?'

'No.' Sam frowned. 'Why did he do that?'

'He wanted to check on the situation, make sure that you had prevented Quentin from doing whatever it was he was there for.'

'Andrew told me that you had detected a disturbance in the time-line before I went?'

'Yes, and then when you got back it disappeared, but we didn't realise what had happened until you told Andrew about your Displacement. Anyway, he went back to take a look around, try to find out what you had done and how you had done it and he found something unusual. Something we thought was impossible.'

'What?'

'They remembered you. They weren't fully formed memories, just vague recollections of having met you and fought with you, but they knew who you were when they really shouldn't have.'

Sam blinked. 'What does that mean?'

'We think it means that you are able to affect the time-line directly, or at least manipulate it and have it accept the changes, but the energy required to do that has to be so great that it might be what is affecting you physically and causing the hair and such.'

'So… I'll be alright to Displace just as long as I don't try to change anything. Great…'

James laughed. 'Yes, just use it to go on holidays and leave Quentin to us. After all we're doing *so* well…' He turned serious again. 'I wish that were an option, I really do, but unfortunately we need you to keep doing what you can to stop him, and it looks like that's going to start to take its toll on you.' He sighed. 'All I can tell you is that we are working on finding a way to protect you and in the meantime you should keep the Displacing down to a minimum.'

'Maybe that vase I got in Egypt will have something in it that will help.'

'Hopefully… Maybe…' James slapped his hands gently on the arms of his chair and changed track completely. 'Anyway, come on, it's time for bed; it's late and we've got an early start tomorrow. I've told your parents that I'm going to show you some of my old haunting grounds and they're going to let me have you for the next few days. If you want, that is. We'll go to Headquarters and you can have a look around, then we'll meet up with Andrew and the lovely Rachel. Your parents said something about taking Violeta to some of the museums that they've already taken you to; Science, Natural History and so on, so they don't mind too much.' He grinned. 'So, do you want to come with me and play with your friends, or would you rather go with them?'

'I think I'll go with you, please, Grandad,' said Sam with a grin.

'I thought you might, somehow.' He laughed and winked then took another sip of his tea. 'Well, you need to get some rest; there's a lot for you to do over the next few days, not least of which is that you'll be Displacing, and I'm sure you'll want to have your wits about you for that. Besides, you need your beauty sleep for when you see Rachel.' He chuckled and shooed Sam away. 'Go on, away with you!'

Sam stood up and moved to the door. 'Goodnight, Grandad.'

'Sweet dreams, Sam!'

CHAPTER 7
HEADQUARTERS

James snuck into Sam's room early the next morning and shook him awake.

'Come on, up you get,' James whispered so as not to wake up Violeta, who was snoring gently in the next bed. 'The sooner we get away the more we can do. And the fewer questions we get asked.'

Sam groaned and opened his eyes. It was still dark outside and the only light in the room was an orange glow coming through a chink in the curtains from the street lamp outside the house.

He hadn't slept very well; thoughts of the coming day had kept him awake for much of the night, but even so he got out of bed quickly and grabbed some clothes and the bag he had packed the night before. He followed James out of the room and downstairs.

'Get dressed in the dining room and I'll fix us some breakfast. You still like your porridge with sugar?'

'Please!'

Sam went into the dining room at the back of the house and changed out of his pyjamas and into his street clothes, shivering in the cold. James walked in just as he was finishing, carrying a bowl of steaming porridge and a mug of tea, both of which Sam accepted gratefully. He sat at the table and when James came back with his own food they ate together in comfortable silence, gazing out of the window into the garden, watching the sky lighten as the day began.

As soon as they had finished breakfast they left, wrapped up warm against the frosty morning. They walked around the corner to the main road and the bus stop where they boarded a number 2 bus and headed towards the centre of London.

James took the time on the bus to ask about family matters, mostly catching up on how Violeta was doing and how Sam was getting along in school. He was glad to hear that Sam's bullying problems were now resolved and he was impressed at how he was trying to change Rafa. 'In my day I would have just laid the fellow out… In fact I did, several times. Remind me to tell you about the time I was an officer in the Navy. For a day.' James chuckled to himself, then looked up. 'Press the bell, will you, we're here.'

They got off the bus and walked along the road. On the other side of the street was a brick wall topped with vicious looking barbed wire, but it looked like it just had trees behind it, which puzzled Sam; it was far too much security for a park. James saw Sam's look. 'That's the back of Buck House, but don't get your hopes up; we're not going in there.'

They were, in fact, going to a building facing the wall about fifty metres from the bus stop. It was huge, with something like four floors and part of a row of more or less identical buildings. The front door was up a short flight of covered steps between two columns, the left one of which had a shiny brass plate fixed to it at head height and Sam paused to inspect it. The plate had obviously been polished so many times that the inscription on it had been worn down until it was almost smooth, but Sam could still just about make out the same coat of arms that Andrew had as the background on his computer and the letters "H.S.D." stencilled beneath it in incredibly flowery writing that was barely legible.

James called impatiently to Sam from up the steps by the doorway. 'Come on, lad, don't dawdle! The interesting stuff is inside and besides, it's bloomin' freezing out here!'

As Sam hurried up the steps, James unlocked the door and punched a code into a keypad on the wall. He waved the brass key at Sam; it was heavy and ornate and very old-looking 'You'll get one of these today or tomorrow and the code will be sent to you by secure email. It's changed every so often and please make sure you have the right one because if you get it wrong three times in a row a cage drops down and an alarm goes off that gives me a headache every time.' He pushed the door open and led the way inside. 'We used to just have the keys, but since Quentin and friends started actively opposing us we had to add some security; we bloody gave Quentin a key when he joined, didn't we? And of course the blighter kept it when he ran off.'

'Why don't you just change the locks?'

'We probably will at some point,' he gave Sam an amused look. 'But as you well know after your gallivanting around Paris with Rachel, locks are all too easy to bypass.'

He put the key back in his pocket then held his arms out wide and beamed at Sam. 'Welcome to the Headquarters of the "Honourable Society of Displacers" or the "Society" for short.'

Sam grimaced. 'That name...'

James raised an eyebrow. 'What's the matter? Don't you like it?'

'Well it's not exactly very catchy, is it?'

The old man laughed. 'Not really, but believe me, it's better to have a name like that so people have no idea what we actually do.' He went to a small table that was just inside the entrance and fished around in a flat box for a few seconds, eventually bringing out two large rectangular light brown wooden plaques. He handed one to Sam. 'Here.'

Sam took the plaque from him and held it in his hands, feeling the texture of the grain. It had "Samuel Vives" carved, or maybe burned into it lengthwise in dark writing that was almost as flowery as the script on the brass plate on the column outside. It was surprisingly heavy, about thirty centimetres by ten and two or three thick, and had a hole bored into the middle of one of the short ends.

'What's this?'

James held up a plaque of his own. 'This is to let everybody know we're here.' He hung it from a peg on the wall next to the door. 'Looks like we're the first ones to arrive.'

There were several long rows of pegs, all empty.

Sam hung his nameplate on the peg next to James' and looked at the plaques that were haphazardly piled in the box - there were a few names that he was familiar with, but a lot more that he wasn't. He saw Rachel's plaque and reached out to touch it.

'Don't worry, she'll be here soon. God, you're like a lost puppy...' James laughed. 'Come on, let's take the tour. Heel, boy!' He laughed again and went through the door that was opposite the plaques.

Sam smiled and shook his head, then followed him.

Almost the entirety of the ground floor was taken up by two huge rooms. The one at the front of the building was a large lounge with a roaring fire already lit in a large fireplace, full of leather Chesterfield sofas and wing-backed armchairs. The walls were covered in the portraits of the members, every one with a small gold plaque underneath giving the name and the dates of the person portrayed. There were mostly paintings, although there were also a few relatively crude drawings and sketches dotted around which stuck out because they weren't nearly as professionally done as the rest, but which were nevertheless still framed and displayed as proudly as the others.

Sam went over to a pencil sketch of a woman with long hair and strong cheek bones and read the plaque beneath it. 'Winifred Belvedere, 1856 to 1883 NE.' Sam gave James a puzzled look. 'NE?'

'Never existed.' James put a hand on Sam's shoulder and guided him over to a wall at the back of the room while he spoke. 'Every Displacer since the inception of our little Society is represented here with a single portrait. If they die in the past then their portrait or photo ceases to exist with them, so the people who remember them do what they can.'

The old man pulled Sam to a stop in front of a portrait of a beautiful woman with long brown hair. It was a wonderful oil painting in a very old style, but somehow it seemed a lot newer than most of the other paintings in the room.

Sam read the plaque. 'Susan Berry, nee Hudson…' He looked up at James. 'This is Andrew's wife! I saw her at Wembley. She's your…'

'My granddaughter, your aunt.'

It was easy to forget that James was actually Sam's great-grandfather. It was even easier to forget that Sam's mother had once had a sister, who had been married to Andrew and had been killed whilst Displacing. It was easy to forget her because, like all those who died while on a mission, to everyone apart from the Displacers who had known her personally, she had never even lived. Sam had actually met her when he was young but, because his powers hadn't manifested until he turned fifteen, he had no memory of her and hadn't even known about her existence until Rachel had taken him to the 1966 World Cup Final a few months before. The woman in the portrait was a few years older than the one he had seen at the football match and had a few more wrinkles, but it was definitely her.

Over the summer, shortly after Sam's visit to Egypt, Andrew had finally worked up the courage to tell him some of what had happened to Susan. He still hadn't gone into the exact details of how she had died; he hadn't been able to, but he had told Sam that it was Quentin who had been responsible. Andrew had only told him that much because he was worried that Sam would keep running into Quentin and wanted to make sure that he knew how dangerous the man actually was. Now that Sam was at Headquarters he could always try to look at

Andrew's official report on the mission where she had died, but he didn't know if he really wanted to; he wanted to hear the story from his uncle and not go behind his back.

Sam gazed at the painting. The portrait was incredibly well done, unlike most of the others that had the annotation "NE" below them. 'Who painted this?'

'Andrew did.'

'I didn't know he was an artist.'

'He keeps it a secret and doesn't ever use his skills. He learnt to paint for her, just so he could paint her portrait after she died.' There was a slight hitch in James' voice as he continued. 'Headquarters is the only place where we can safely commemorate the Displacers that have died doing what we do and have disappeared from existence. We do it with portraits created by the only people who knew them, people who have love in their hearts but not always sufficient skill to properly do them justice. Having these here, in the place where we come to relax and socialise, serve to remind us of the seriousness of our calling and the terrible price that many of us have had to pay.'

James squeezed his shoulder gently, then turned away sadly and Sam took one last look at his aunt's portrait before he followed his grandfather.

A set of double doors at the back led through to the dedicated dining room which took up the rest of the ground floor. A long wooden table, with about forty chairs comfortably arranged around it, dominated the space and the walls were hung with dozens of paintings, mostly large landscapes. The room was brightly lit by three chandeliers hanging from the high ceiling although there was plenty of light coming through the glass windows that made up most of the wall on the far side of the room. Disappointingly, there was another building only a few metres away, so the only view was of a tiny cement patio covered with potted plants and not of the huge garden that Sam had been expecting.

There wasn't much else to see, so James took them out again, through another door leading back to the entrance hallway, explaining that Sam would have enough time to stare at the artwork while sitting through the "interminably long and boring" dinners that the Displacers and the Elders in particular liked to have.

They went up the stairs that were directly opposite the front door, just past the plaques.

They didn't stop on the first and second floors, but only lingered on the landings long enough for Sam to peer through the open doors and see that every room was filled from floor to ceiling with crowded bookcases and that each had a reading table in its centre, lit by small brass lamps with green shades like in an old-fashioned library.

The third floor was mostly taken up by one large room that hummed with computers. There were a few bookcases around the walls, but the rest of the space was occupied by large heavy wooden desks, like those that could be found in the offices of high level executives in the movies, which each held blotting boards, keyboards and large flat-screen monitors, as well as the same green-shaded lamps as the libraries on the previous floors.

'This is where we do a lot of research and most of our hunting these days.'

'Hunting?'

'That's what we call our constant search for new members. It used to be quite hard to find the people who have our talent; all we could do was watch our own families and keep an ear to the ground for anything unusual - it was all very hit and miss, actually, until we got that.' He pointed to the end of the room where six computer screens were mounted on the wall in a semi-circle, linked to a whole bank of hardware that was blinking and whirring merrily. 'John put together that monstrosity and wrote a special programme that searches through traditional media, like newspapers, as well as that awful rot they call "social media" looking for certain keywords which might indicate that someone has travelled in time. We get a lot more hits this way and, yes, most of them turn out to be false alarms, but that's better than missing someone and having them get locked up for being crazy or die in the past when they go somewhere they shouldn't.'

'Definitely!' Sam nodded enthusiastically; he himself had almost died in Port Royal and probably would have thought himself crazy if Andrew hadn't been there afterwards to explain what had happened to him.

'Unfortunately, Quentin and his group still seem to get to possible members before us and we've lost at least five that we know about to his group in the last few years alone.' James started to walk out again. 'Anyway, if you want to know more about all this, then don't ask me because I don't really understand it, ask John. He's here most days, tweaking his programme and playing games.' He led the way back to the stairs. 'Right! Onwards and upwards!'

On the next floor, the fourth, there were half a dozen bedrooms and a couple of bathrooms. 'This is a home away home for the members. They can stay here if they are working late or lose track of time having a discussion after dinner. The same woman who keeps the kitchen stocked up does the cleaning up here and there are sheets and towels in every room and toiletries in the bathroom down the hall. She's very nice, Maeve is her name, and she was quite a looker in her day, I can tell you! She turns a blind eye to what we do around here; she thinks this is some kind of club for academic weirdos, like Mensa, and of course she has no idea about what Displacing actually is.'

He took Sam in to look around one of the bedrooms. It had a huge antique four-poster bed, a couple of wooden free-standing wardrobes, a large desk against the wall underneath a window with a view over Buckingham Palace gardens and a sink in the corner. It was much larger than his room back home but still managed to be very cosy with velvet curtains on the window and the bed and thick carpet on the floor. All in all, the whole building was cosy and it seemed much smaller on the inside than it had on the outside, mostly because of how full it was, mostly of books. It was very comfortably appointed and, like James said, it was more like a home than the office building which Sam had always pictured it as being, and indeed, James mostly referred to it as a "house" rather than "Headquarters", as if it were more a home to the Society than a base of operations.

Finally, James took Sam to a solid-looking door with a number pad lock that blocked the stairs up to the final floor. 'Upstairs is the attic where we keep anything that has to stay secret, as well as the things that we bring back that are too valuable to display. I'm can't take you up there today, though, because I haven't made a request to do so and everyone, no matter who, has to explain why they want to go in before they actually do and have their request approved by the Council. Each entry is electronically logged and you'll get the code for this in the same secure email as you get the one for the front door.'

'But if everyone has the code how do you know who goes in?'

'Turn around and say cheese! That camera behind you is recording us.' He pointed at the wall opposite the door; there was a small camera covering the door and the whole of the hallway. 'It feeds into the computers on the third floor and there's also a backup somewhere, in a cloud or something equally silly sounding.' He clapped his hands together and smiled broadly. 'Well! Here concludes our grand tour! If you've enjoyed yourself please tip your guide... Fancy a cup of tea?'

James led Sam all the way back to the ground floor, where they paused briefly to check the pegs and see if anyone else had arrived - nobody had and the old man shrugged. 'We don't have set hours, so members come and go as they want. It's still early and London traffic is a pain in the arse at this time, but I'm sure people will start turning up soon.'

The basement proved to be a low-ceilinged room with small windows that were on a level with the street outside, but were covered by translucent white curtains which prevented the people outside from seeing in. A wooden table sat in the middle of the tiled room, but a lot of the space was taken up by a huge kitchen with the biggest ovens Sam had ever seen, dozens of burners to cook on, several large refrigerators and a long row of cupboards. There was also a utility room with washing and drying machines through a door on one side and a walk-in pantry on the other, but Sam barely saw them because his eyes had been drawn directly to the trays of pastries covered with cling film sitting on the work surface of the kitchen. His stomach rumbled, protesting at having only had a bowl of porridge that morning and more than an hour ago.

'This is where we eat most of the time; we only use the dining room upstairs for the big celebrations or if there are a lot of us - this table *only* seats twenty.' James winked, then waved towards the kitchen area. 'There's cereal, bread, pastries, toast, whatever you want. Grab me some croissants and something for yourself while I make the tea, would you?'

Sam searched through the cupboards and, at something like his tenth attempt, found some plates. They were heavy china, gold-trimmed and had *H.S.D.* monogrammed, also in gold, in a script that was identical to that on the brass plate outside the front door. The plates looked far too expensive to use and he shot a questioning look at James, but the old man just nodded and waved for him to take them, so he shrugged, pulled out two and started filling them with fresh croissants.

A quarter an hour later they were just finishing off their tea when Andrew came down the stairs.

'Kettle boiled not long ago,' said James; for an Englishman that was a much better greeting than a simple hello.

'Thanks, Jim.' Andrew went straight to the kitchen and made himself tea while stuffing a croissant into his mouth. He came back and opposite Sam, bringing the pastries with him, which he placed in the middle of the table within easy reach of everyone.

'Is Rachel not with you?'

Andrew shared a grin and a knowing look with James before answering Sam's question. 'No, she's staying with her mother at the moment. She'll come in by tube when she can.'

'Oh.'

Andrew looked at James and smirked. 'Perhaps we should get to business before we lose Sam to his raging hormones?'

'Sounds good to me; I'm old and I'll need to take a nap soon.'

'You're not fooling anyone, James.'

'Dammit! How's a guy supposed to get any sympathy round here? There's got to be some perks to being an Elder.'

'Free croissants.'

'Sold! To the man in the cheap suit at the back!'

Andrew and James grinned at each other.

Sam watched them, loving every minute; his grandfather had always been special to him and he had never seen him look this alive before. It was almost as if he needed this house and the people in it to really open up.

Andrew looked directly at Sam. 'Right then, I take it you ignored my advice and tried to Displace? What did you do? Think about Quentin?'

Sam looked at him with his mouth open. 'How did you…?'

Andrew tutted theatrically and shook his head. He glanced sideways at James. 'These kids think they invented sneakiness.'

James smiled wryly, 'you thought you were pretty sharp yourself, once upon a time, *kid*.'

'I still am!'

'You never were…'

They laughed and Andrew turned back to Sam. 'Obviously nothing happened otherwise you would have told us. But what *exactly* did happen?'

Sam frowned as he thought back. 'I Prepared and then thought of Quentin. When nothing happened it wasn't like Calming, it was more like when I thought of my family and home on the beach that time.'

Andrew nodded. 'Good, that means he's still in the present at least. I want you to keep trying every couple of hours or so; we need to catch him and stop him.'

'OK.'

'But I want you to be with another Displacer when you do it; I don't want you going anywhere without backup, preferably myself, but John will be here tomorrow and Rachel will do of course - I've asked them both not to Displace on their own, so they're available to go with you.'

'I would prefer to go with Rachel.'

James chuckled. 'Of course you would.'

Andrew held out his hands to Sam. 'Try with me now, please.'

Sam hesitated slightly; he'd never Displaced with anyone else except Rachel before and somehow it had become something more, something intimate, even though he knew that it wasn't; it was just a part of the job. He looked at his grandfather, who gave him a reassuring nod, then reached out to take Andrew's hands.

Andrew shut his eyes and began Preparing.

Sam could feel the energy starting to build up. It was a familiar sensation, almost identical to how it was with Rachel, but it took longer and was somehow subtly different, with its own texture and sensation. When he felt that Andrew was ready he closed his own eyes and concentrated on Quentin…

He was almost relieved when it didn't work. He opened his eyes again and quickly released Andrew's hands before looking at his grandfather.

There was compassion in the old man's eyes but also urgency. 'This is very important, Sam, more important than you know. We have to stop him.'

Sam sat up straight in his chair. He hadn't been expecting the chance to press his uncle and grandfather for answers to come so soon, but he wasn't going to let it slip away. 'Why is this so important? What aren't you telling me? I know you've been hiding something from me, so please, just be straight with me.'

The smiles completely dropped from James and Andrew's faces and for the first time they became deadly serious.

The two men shared a glance, then Andrew sighed. 'Remember I told you that the Society isn't doing very well? That we've been having a bit of a bad time lately?'

Sam answered hesitantly. 'Yes…'

'Well, it's actually a lot worse than I let on - we're fighting a full out war and we're losing. Badly. It's gotten to the point where if we don't do something soon then the time-line as we know it will be destroyed forever.'

'By Quentin?'

'Mostly, yes.'

'What does that mean?'

'It means that Quentin isn't the only one working against us - we believe that he has an entire organisation behind him, not just Diana Birch and the other four youths who we've been able to identify. In fact we first detected that someone was attempting to twist the time-line to their own advantage almost twenty years ago. However, whoever it was only managed to make fairly minor changes which we were able to counteract fairly easily and the damage never got anywhere near the point where it was irreversible.'

James chimed in. 'Until Quentin.'

Andrew let out a deep breath. 'Yes, until Quentin; he has proved to be somewhat of an expert at manipulating the time-line.'

James took over from him. 'Quentin obviously joined them as soon as he left us because things immediately began to spiral out of control and in just the last three years they have made six or seven substantial changes which have had us reeling. The balance of power has tipped heavily in their favour and no matter how much cleanup we try to do, it just keeps getting worse, especially seeing as they make major changes every few months. They have managed to get people they control into positions of power in several countries including Italy, Russia, Belarus and even Spain.'

'Spain?'

'I'm afraid so.'

Sam collapsed back in his chair, stunned.

Andrew and James looked at each other, they were reluctant to continue, but knew that they had to. In the end it was Andrew who spoke, talking softly and carefully. 'This is why everybody was so excited when we found out what you could do. I know it's a very *Star Wars* thing to say, but the prophecy we've told you about speaks of someone who will bring order, make real changes and restore the time-line to how it was supposed to be.'

'And you still think that's me?' Sam waved his hand at his head. 'Even after the hair and the dizziness?'

James nodded. 'Even so.'

There was silence as the two men watched Sam assimilate the information. They exchanged a glance then James stood up and put his hand on Sam's shoulder comfortingly. 'Come on, let's go upstairs, lad. There are some books I want you to have - some homework for you to do.'

Sam groaned dramatically, then winked at Andrew before stealing another croissant and following his grandfather from the room.

James left Sam sitting in one of the deep armchairs in the lounge while he went to fetch the books from one of the libraries and when he came back he presented him with two brown leather-bound books, about the size of paperbacks.

'I know you've been having trouble getting your head around all the rules and restrictions that we have to deal with so I dug these out for you. Take very good care of them; they're almost a century and a half old.'

Sam took the books and opened the first one gingerly. It was heavy and in remarkably good condition, the paper thick and creamy and not at all brittle. Obviously it had been made with first-rate materials, which had helped preserve it. The first page was inscribed in neat handwriting: *The Honourable Society of Displacers. 1867. Being the account of a series of Experiments and Observations by E. Lloyd to divine the limits of temporal manipulation.*

Sam looked up at his grandfather questioningly.

'The two books tell the story of some experiments in Displacing run over a period of quite a few years by a member, Everett Lloyd. He was the first to test the limits of our powers, well, the first one to document his experiments anyway. It makes for very interesting reading and I think you'll find it extremely helpful in understanding more about your powers - you can read examples of what is and isn't possible, rather than us just telling you what you can and can't do. It also might give you a bit of an insight into why we think you're special.'

'Thank you.'

'Take them home and read them later, but please, as I said, take good care of them. Normally we wouldn't let books like these out of the building, but you're a bit of a special case and you know the people in charge, which is always helpful.' James winked. He looked up as the door to the street opened and they heard the noise of the busy road outside.

Sam turned in his seat to see who it was and came face to face with Rachel. He smiled, but was disappointed when she just walked past him to James.

She kissed James on the cheek and they smiled at each other. 'Do you mind if I steal your grandson for a while? He looks like he needs a break and I desperately need to blow off some steam after wading through London traffic.'

'I guess I can let you have him for a while. He's had the tour and Andrew's already spoken to him. We didn't really have anything else planned until lunch.'

'I'll have him back in time, don't worry.' She grinned and pulled Sam out of his armchair. 'Come on you, let's go for a run. I hope you didn't eat too many croissants; I don't want you showing me up and vomiting in front of the tourists. '

Sam allowed himself to be led away. He laughed happily and waved at James over his shoulder.

Five minutes later Sam was running a few metres behind Rachel as they jogged along the pavement past Wellington Arch. They crossed the road and headed into Hyde Park, going past the Achilles statue and turning to the right along one of the smaller paths towards the 7/7 memorial.

She had barely said anything to him back at the house, just shoved him in a bathroom to get changed, then pushed him out of the door when he was ready and he was beginning to wonder if he had done something wrong. He was also beginning to regret the extra croissant just a little bit.

In the park there was finally space to run side by side without fear of knocking over pedestrians and Sam lengthened his stride in an attempt to catch her up, determined to ask her what was wrong, but she saw what he was doing and increased her pace, staying just ahead of him. He frowned and ran faster, but she easily matched him and he thought it was confirmation of her being annoyed with him until he saw the grin on her face. He chuckled and redoubled his efforts.

In a matter of seconds the gentle trot had turned into a full sprint and they were both laughing as they ran headlong, startling an occasional tourist or jogger. Sam eventually began to catch up with her and was just drawing level with her when she grabbed him and veered off the path with him, into the trees out of sight. She pulled him to a halt and he stumbled, just managing to catch himself before he fell head over heels, but then he was knocked off balance again when Rachel threw herself on him, wrapping her arms around him and smothering him with kisses.

'I'm sorry I didn't say hello to you properly before,' said Rachel when they finally came up for air. 'I want to keep our relationship at least a little bit professional when we're around the others.'

'You do know you're not fooling anyone, right? They all know.'

Rachel reddened slightly, but after a couple of seconds she just shrugged. 'Even so, let's keep the lovey-dovey stuff to a minimum, at least at HQ, OK?'

He nodded. 'OK, that's fine with me, I'm not particularly into exhibitionism anyway, especially not in front of James and Andrew.'

They looked up as a group of schoolchildren walked past on the nearby path and pulled back slightly from each other, not wanting to put on a show in case someone glanced their way.

Rachel started to drag him back to the path, but he held her back. He grabbed hold of her hands and pulled her round to face him. 'Hang on, I want to try something. Prepare for me would you?'

'What?'

'It's alright; Andrew said I have to focus on Quentin and try to Displace every couple of hours. Go on.'

'OK…' Rachel was a bit doubtful, but even so she closed her eyes and did what he asked.

Sam could feel the energy building up inside her, emanating from her, a tingling sensation against his skin, so similar to what he had felt earlier with Andrew, but *so* very different. When she was ready he closed his eyes and did the same, then thought of Quentin.

The sensation washed away and they opened their eyes.

She raised an eyebrow at him. 'Well, I didn't go anywhere and I'm fairly sure you didn't, so I guess it didn't work.'

'Nope, not this time, but Andrew said I have to keep trying. We need to stop Quentin, apparently.'

Rachel grimaced. 'Yes, so I've heard. Things don't look very good apparently.'

'Let's save the doom and gloom for Headquarters, please. Right now, we've got a workout to do.' He grinned at her cheekily. 'Race you to the Diana memorial!' He released her hands and sprinted off at top speed before she had fully assimilated what he had said.

'Oi!' She raced after him.

They ran around the park a few times and then did some sparring, making up for months of not being together by going all out and not holding anything back. Afterwards they jogged gently, letting their muscles relax, whilst talking, catching up on their news and generally just enjoying the other one being there. They stayed out the rest of the morning, then wandered back to the house on Grosvenor Place early enough so that they would have time to shower and change before lunch.

When they got back to the Society there were a lot more plaques on the pegs and a crowd of people in the lounge. Rachel held Sam back and peeked around the corner. 'Come on, let's sneak past; you don't want to smell this bad when you meet them all in the flesh for the first time.'

Then waited until nobody was looking, then sprinted past the doorway, using the skills they had learnt in Okinawa to do so silently, crossing it in milliseconds.

And ran straight into John who was coming out of the toilet.

'Sam! Great to meet you finally in person! Come on, I'll introduce you to everyone.' He took Sam by the shoulder and pulled him back towards the lounge.

'Actually, John, I was going to…'

'Hey everybody! Look who I found!'

Sam was suddenly faced by a room full of people who he had never met except on Skype, whose names he barely remembered, but who nonetheless knew everything about him. He turned to Rachel for help, but she was no longer by his side; she was at the end of the corridor at the bottom of the stairs - she had left him to face the music alone. He just had time to see her blow him a kiss and grin before he was swamped by more than a dozen members of the Honourable Society of Displacers.

CHAPTER 8
LUNCH AND SUSPICIONS

Sam had his hand shaken more times than he could count, had his back slapped enough to make it sore and was sized up from top to toe by everyone. The only person there who didn't seem completely over the moon to see him was Ralph Price. Ralph had a long time rivalry with Andrew and the fact that Sam was Andrew's protégé and nephew didn't do much to ingratiate Sam to him and he was the only one who had remained seated and not leapt to his feet when John had brought Sam in.

The members fired questions at him, every single one of them clamouring to talk to him and Sam did his best to answer them as best he could, but there was such a confusion of faces and voices, all speaking in English, which he was still not completely fluent in, that he was quickly becoming overwhelmed.

Thankfully, though, Andrew saw his difficulty and stepped in. 'Come on, people, you'll have your chance at him when we sit down to lunch. Let him go and get changed, please!'

The members complained like small children told it was time to go to bed, but nonetheless backed away from Sam and returned to their own conversations.

Sam shot his uncle a grateful look, then beat a hasty retreat through the door past John, who was grinning like a Cheshire cat.

He ran up to the fourth floor where he encountered Rachel coming out of a bathroom, a cloud of steam following her. She grinned at him.

'I see you managed to escape the clutches of the walking dead.' She mimed zombies reaching out to grasp him.

He snarled, feigning anger. 'No thanks to you, traitor.'

'Hey, I did my best to get you past there, it wasn't my fault that you got caught and my going down with the ship too wouldn't have done you any good. Besides, I *had* to use up all the hot water.'

She laughed, dancing away from him as he tried to grab her and disappeared into one of the bedrooms, slamming the door in his face.

Grumbling, Sam grabbed a couple of towels from the airing cupboard where they were stored and shut himself in the bathroom.

Sam showered and changed as quickly as he could, but he was still one of the last to enter the dining room and he stood in the doorway trying to spot Rachel in the crowded room among all the people who were milling around. He eventually saw her standing in the corner with her back to him, somehow she had found time to do her hair and put on makeup and was wearing a form-hugging dark blue knee-length dress that was making his mouth water more than the delicious smells coming from the table. She was talking with a man who he recognised from Skype as Philip, the Elder who worked at the British Museum and who was investigating the vase he had brought back from Egypt.

He began to make his way across the room, wanting to sit next to her, but was immediately grabbed by Andrew and James who sat him down in the middle of the table so that he was in reach of all of the members. Thankfully, though, instead of just throwing him to the lions like Rachel had done earlier, they took the chairs on either side of him so that they could act as a buffer between him and the other members, who were eagerly waiting to bombard him with questions.

Despite the fact that Sam had been told that lunch was going to be fairly informal, the setting was anything but, with around twenty people gathered around the table in the dining room. The chandeliers were lit, wine bottles were passed around and there was enough food to feed a small army. Sam, of course, stuck to soft drinks, of which there were plenty, but he noticed that Rachel, sitting near the end of the table between John and Julia and far too far away for his liking, had filled a glass with dark red wine.

Apparently one of the Elders, Richard, was a chef with his own restaurant in Westminster, near the Houses of Parliament, and he did the cooking for the Society on special occasions. He had studied with chefs from various nations during his Displacements; it had been his hobby, like collecting martial arts was Rachel's hobby. Understandably then, the food was superb and it struck Sam as incredibly convenient to have access to so many people who had spent lifetimes learning useful crafts and he wondered which of the members was going to be next to surprise and delight him.

However, despite it being a celebration to welcome Sam, the mood during the meal was quite sombre; the shadow of their failures to hold back the advances of Quentin's group and the current feeling of impending change was hanging over them all.

There had been a brief silence as everybody had tucked in, but conversation had very quickly started up again around the room and the questions had started to come.

Sam did his best to answer whatever he could, but much of what they were asking him was stuff that he just didn't know how to answer, like technical things about the differences between his Displacements and everyone else's - a large gap in his Displacer education was being exposed, but that was only to be expected; he hadn't been time travelling for nearly as long as everybody else and didn't have access to the resources of Headquarters or to regular conversations with the Elders, who were the source of most Displacer knowledge. Thankfully, Andrew stepped in to answer those kinds of questions for him and stop him from looking like an idiot for not knowing.

Sam took advantage of the brief times when his attention wasn't being demanded by someone or other to look around the room. He tried to familiarise himself more fully with the members, putting personalities to the names and faces, but each time, inevitably, his gaze was drawn to Rachel. It looked like John was trying to hit on Julia and Rachel was doing her best to shield a reluctant and, by the looks of it, a not a bit disgusted, Julia.

The Society looked like they were a very close group and even Ralph had put aside his frown and was smiling as he conversed, although he was the only one who hadn't said a single word to Sam, not even in greeting.

After lunch there was coffee, tea and brandy in the lounge. People wandered around, mixing more than they had in the dining room and Sam finally had the chance to sidle up to Rachel. She saw him coming and smiled at him innocently. 'Did you have enough hot water for your shower?'

'More or less... Just as well we got used to standing under that waterfall in Okinawa in the winter.'

Rachel laughed gently and Sam instantly forgave her. 'You look incredible.'

'I thought I'd make an effort just this once for your inaugural lunch.'

Sam shook his head and rubbed his stomach. 'I'm stuffed!'

'Richard keeps us well fed.'

'Just as well we went for that run before we had lunch; I can barely move now.'

'Yeah, Master Hamato always said you lack discipline.' Her right hand flicked out faster than the eye could follow and backhanded him in the stomach.

'Oof!'

She leaned forward slightly and whispered in his ear as he grunted. 'And I told you that not having a six-pack was a deal-breaker!'

Sam wheezed slightly but grinned. 'OK, I'll do some extra sit-ups tonight, just for you.'

She patted him on the head. 'Good boy!'

Sam shook his head and muttered to himself. 'Why is everyone treating me like a favourite dog recently?'

Rachel smiled and was about to answer when Andrew came up and interrupted. 'Sam, I just had a word with Philip. He's ready to open up your vase, so you, me and James are going to go to the British Museum tomorrow to be there when he does.'

'Can I come?' Rachel asked.

'Of course, if Sam doesn't mind.'

'Well...' Sam feigned reluctance, but flinched and covered his stomach when Rachel twitched her right arm slightly. He answered quickly before she slapped his aching belly again. 'Yes! Of course you can come.'

Rachel smiled sweetly. 'Thank you, Sam. Remind me to give you a Scooby Snack later.'

'Grrr...' Sam growled, making her laugh.

Andrew frowned, puzzled at the exchange, but just shook his head and didn't comment. 'OK... Well, we'll meet outside the museum at seven tomorrow morning and Philip will get us all past security.'

'Fine with me,' said Rachel. 'I was planning to sleep here tonight anyway, so I won't have to get up as early as Sam here.'

Sam groaned. 'I wouldn't mind getting up so early if it wasn't so cold in this country.'

They chuckled but stopped quickly as John came over and interrupted them. 'Hey, Sam! Do you like computers?'

'Uh, yeah, I suppose so...'

'Come on then, I'll show you the cool setup I've got on the third floor!'

'James showed me it already...'

'Ah, but you haven't seen it in action! Come on!'

John put his arm around Sam's shoulder and started to drag him away without waiting for an answer.

Sam glanced back, raising an eyebrow questioningly at Rachel and Andrew, but they just shrugged, so he allowed John to pull him out of the room.

John was huffing quite a lot when they got to the third floor and he leaned on the banisters to catch his breath before taking Sam across the computer room to stand in front of the wall of hardware with the bank of monitors. He put his hands on his hips and grinned as he admired his creation. 'This is my pride and joy - they told me to build a computer that could help them search for new prospects and I came up with this.' He stepped forward and reached out to put his hand gently on the glass front of the cabinet holding the computer. 'I won't bore you with the details but there's enough processing power in this beauty to sift through all the stuff that is posted online every day, which is a *shedload* by the way, with enough left over to easily run the day to day business as well. Of course it wouldn't be able to do that without an industrial size fibre optic link, so it's just as well this Society of ours has plenty of money because that's not cheap! None of this was in fact, but it's worth it, believe me. But do you know what the best thing is?'

Sam shook his head.

The man grinned. 'The *best* thing is that you can play a really good game of *League of Legends* with almost no ping!'

Sam blinked at him, not sure if he was joking or not.

John didn't notice Sam's confusion, he was just staring at the computer with a wide smile on his face. 'Do you play computer games?'

'Um... Sometimes...'

'Of course you do! You should come around to my place sometime, we can have a few beers, play some *Halo* and watch some old movies.'

'I'm still a little bit too young to drink.'

'Nonsense! I've read your reports, you have to be, what, more than twenty one by now! You could even drink in the States!'

Sam shrugged. 'I guess. Something like that, yeah, but my body is still sixteen.'

John leaned in close to Sam and winked. 'I won't tell anyone if you don't!'

Sam really didn't know how to respond, but it didn't seem to matter because John didn't wait for a reply. He sat down at the desk in front of the monitors and moved the mouse to bring them to life.

They were blank apart from a few icons and he waved his hand at them. 'If we were living in some crappy fictional world like *CSI* there would be newspaper pages flicking across these screens slow enough that you could see the headlines, but too fast to read them properly. In reality this baby is checking so many pages per second and the refresh rate on the screens is so low in comparison that they wouldn't actually be able to display them and you'd go mad trying to make out any details!' He pointed to an icon that looked like a rectangle made up of colourful blocks. 'I've written a specific programme that I call *Ziggy*, which has specific search parameters: simply put it looks for keywords in anything that gets posted online. Ziggy then sorts them into folders depending on how many keywords each post contains. It's not an exact science and we're still refining the keywords we search for, but we get about a thousand hits a day with four or more keywords, a hundred thousand with three keywords and about a billion with one or two keywords.'

Despite himself, Sam was impressed. 'Wow, that really isn't an exact science!'

'Nope, not even close! But if we limit ourselves to just looking through those thousand hits with four or more keywords then we still have a better chance of finding an emerging Displacer than we did before.'

'And how do you do that?'

John grinned. 'Some poor fool has to read them!'

'Not you, I take it.'

'No way! The Elders actually *like* to do that kind of thing for some reason, makes them feel useful or something.'

'How often do the hits actually turn out to be new Displacers?'

'Well, it used to be that we only found one person with the gift every twenty years or so, not counting the ones from traditional Displacer families of course, and we don't think we missed too many. Lately, for some reason, there have been more and more turning up, like mushrooms after rain. There's been at least one every couple of years for the last ten years or so, that we know of anyway, and curiously only a few of those have been from established families, like yourself and Rachel. The majority of the people we've found recently have no relation whatsoever to any Displacers that we've been able to find. Like Julia, for example.'

'So, you're saying that Displacing usually runs in families?'

'Mostly, yes - a prime example of that are the Craigs; we've had so many Hamish Craigs in the Society that we've had to assign them numbers! Oh, and it tends to be an Anglo-Saxon trait as well.'

Sam frowned. 'But Lisa is Indian, isn't she?'

'Yes, but her great, great, um, maybe there's another great in there somewhere, grandmother was a maid in a house in colonial India and let's just say the master of the house was very fond of her and brought her to England with him when he came back.'

'Ah, OK.'

'Of course, now that there are cheap flights to everywhere, we expect the talent to start spreading worldwide as interbreeding occurs.'

'That's a lovely way of putting it.' Sam chuckled, shaking his head. 'But, going back to what you were saying, if new Displacers have been turning up that often the last few years, why aren't there more teenagers like me in the Society?'

'Well, some of them refuse to use their powers and don't want to join when we contact them, others think they're going mad and block their powers behind walls of their own making - they think they're freaks or something, even with the superhero culture we have right now. And then there are the ones we lose because Quentin's lot get to them first.'

'Do you think they have their own computer looking for them?'

John shrugged. 'Maybe. Who knows?' He changed tack. 'While we're on the subject of Quentin; how is the search for him going? Have you been able to sense him in the force or anything?'

'Er… not yet'

'But you've been trying, right? Andrew said he's told you to try every couple of hours.'

'Yes.'

John held out his hands. 'Would you mind trying now? I assume you haven't tried since before lunch and I would just *love* the chance to Displace with you; that would be *such* a rush!'

'Oh, er, OK.'

Sam sat in the chair next to John and very reluctantly took his clammy hands - of all the people that Andrew had suggested to take with him to face Quentin, John was by far the one that he least wanted to go with.

John smiled. 'Great! Just make sure you think of Quentin and not something else... like Japan. Yeah, Japan! That would be cool wouldn't it? All the swords and stuff - I know you like swords, but don't think

about that, OK? No Samurai! Got that? OK? Good! Right! Let's do it!'
He closed his eyes to start Preparing.

Sam groaned inwardly; he could hardly stand to be in the same room as the man for five minutes and he couldn't imagine anything worse than spending years stuck with him in the past. However, his uncle had put the man on his list for a reason and unfortunately he was right, he should have checked on Quentin a while ago, so he went along with it. He concentrated on Quentin and tried very hard not to think of feudal Japan, during the Shogunate, which of course was right at the top of his list of places he would love to go.

He was extremely relieved when nothing happened.

John opened his eyes and shrugged. 'Oh well, better luck next time!'

Sam smiled back at him, weakly.

'Do you want to play something while we're up here? I've got a copy of the new *Star Wars* game on this machine - we can be Storm Troopers!'

'Thanks, but maybe later. I should go back downstairs; I haven't had a chance to speak to most of the Elders yet.'

'Oh, alright then, rain check!'

'Yeah, sure.' Sam smiled weakly at him as he backed away. He waited until John swivelled round to face the computer and started loading up a game, then hurried down the stairs.

When Sam returned to the ground floor, the members were too engrossed in their own conversations to pester him nearly as much as before and they started leaving not long after to go back to their daily routines, mostly to work, but in Julia's case to go back to university where she was studying a post-grad degree in psychology. Andrew had also had to leave, needing to take care of one of the several businesses he owned.

A group lunch was unusual for the Society, especially during the week; usually they laid on dinners in the evenings or at weekends, which were far more convenient for those members who worked or had family, but they had wanted to make a special occasion of the fact that Sam was visiting for the first time, something that he had to admit made him feel not just a little special. He had thought he wouldn't have anything to talk about with any of the members, except for Displacing, but in the end he was approached by one of the Elders and they sat down in front of the fire and had a long and interesting conversation about the old man's Displacement to Barcelona in the late nineteenth century where he had studied with Antoni Gaudí just as he was starting construction on the *Sagrada Família*. The time had just flown by and Sam was genuinely upset when the man, who was a well-known architect, but whose name Sam couldn't quite remember, apologised because he had to leave.

By five o'clock there were only a few people left in the sitting room and Sam finally found some time to be with Rachel and talk without someone else listening.

Sam was still feeling a bit strange after his conversation with John for some reason and Rachel could see his unease. 'What's wrong?'

He chose his words carefully. 'Does John always act, I don't know… weird?'

She laughed. 'It's not an unusual occurrence. Why? What happened?'

'He was fairly normal to start with, he told me about the computer and the programme he's written, but then he asked me to try to Displace with him. I know he's one of the people Andrew told me to try Displacing with, but he was really weird about it and pretty creepy. Then afterwards he asked me to go back to his place to play games and drink beer.'

'You should have said yes! I'd go with you; I've been before and we had great fun! I even went with Quentin a couple of times before he, well, you know.'

'Really?'

'Yes, believe it or not Quentin and I used to be friends.' She grinned at him. 'Why? Jealous?'

'No… I don't think so… It's just hard to imagine him as part of the Displacers. I've only known him as someone who was trying to kill me or acting like a psycho.'

'He was a pretty decent person once upon a time.'

'I suppose. But anyway, it wasn't just John's acting strange that got me thinking, it was the computer as well - if we've got this fantastic computer that is supposed to be finding potential Displacers better than ever before, then why are the bad guys still getting to them before us?'

'Maybe they have their own.'

'I thought of that too, but a computer won't do anything without software and John had to write his programme specially for us.'

'Ziggy.'

Sam nodded. 'Yes. What's with that name by the way? Is it some kind of reference to David Bowie?'

Rachel laughed. 'No, it's from *Quantum Leap*. Every time we let John name something, it's always some kind of reference to a TV show or a movie.'

'OK...' Sam briefly wondered why the Society would ever let John name anything, but quickly put the question out of his mind and returned to his train of thought. 'Anyway, we only have Ziggy because we have a computer genius, so either they would need to have their own genius to write their own programme, or...'

'Or steal it from us.'

'Which means...'

'We might have a spy in our midst.'

They stopped talking, aghast at the possibility. Rachel shook her head. 'No. I don't, no, I *can't* believe it.'

'Quentin went bad and then left. What's to say that somebody else hasn't gone bad without your knowing about it, but has stayed?'

'But who? Who would do that to us?'

Sam inclined his head slightly, indicating a group of three people over the other side of the room. James was in conversation with Richard, who had turned out to be a jolly red-faced and rotund little man, and Ralph.

'Ralph?' hissed Rachel. 'There's no way!'

'It would make sense; he has access, he hates Andrew, and he would be helping his own son.'

Rachel was silent for a while as she thought about the possibilities. Eventually, though, she shook her head and took a deep breath. 'You've been here one day and already you've got me second-guessing people.'

'Sorry.'

'No, it's a good thing. You've got a fresh perspective; you barely know these people and you can look at them and think more clearly than I can, without letting emotional attachments get in the way.' She glanced over at Ralph, who was laughing at something that James had said. 'You may be right about there being a traitor, or at least a spy in our midst, but that doesn't mean it's Ralph. I'll speak to Andrew next time I see him and find out what he thinks.'

'OK, but *just* Andrew though.'

'OK.'

'And I don't want to Displace with John if I can help it; I don't know, I just got a bad feeling.'

'Yeah, his hands are pretty slimy, aren't they?'

Sam shuddered dramatically, then laughed. 'That's probably it!'

James finished his conversation with Richard and Ralph and came over to them.

'You ready to go home, Sam?'

Sam glanced sideways at Rachel. 'Do you think I could stay here tonight?'

James chuckled as he looked back and forth between the two youths. 'Much as I would like you to have a Displacer around twenty-four hours a day so that you can keep trying to follow Quentin, I really don't think your parents would appreciate that too much. Don't worry, you'll see her again tomorrow, bright and early!'

Sam reluctantly agreed and said his goodbyes to Rachel, receiving a quick and discreet kiss on the lips that James pretended he didn't see, then followed his grandfather out the door and down the road to the nearest bus stop.

CHAPTER 9
EXPERIMENTS

'Don't forget, we've been to see where I grew up.' James said as they rounded the corner into McKay Road. 'You've even been on a tour of Millwall Football Club, which you found pretty boring, right?'

'I didn't want to say anything, but yes, very.'

James laughed and led the way up the front garden path to the front door.

Inside they found Sam's parents and Violeta having sandwiches and despite his huge lunch Sam decided to join them.

Violeta insisted on telling Sam all about the dinosaurs in the Natural History Museum and showing him the photos she had taken with his mother's phone that were mostly out of focus or of the floor. However, while Sam was more than happy to listen to her talking enthusiastically about what she had done, he was keen to get some time to himself so that he could start reading the books that he had brought back with him and he found his mind constantly drifting to them.

She finally tired herself out and was taken to bed. Sam's mother and father went with her; they'd had a long day chasing around after her, and Sam was left alone in the sitting room with his grandfather.

James sat in his armchair doing the crossword, discreetly giving Sam space as he lay down on the sofa and pulled the first of the books out of his rucksack. He flicked through it quickly before he began; it wasn't very long, he guessed it was less than a hundred pages, and the script was large and widely-spaced, beautiful calligraphy that was easy to read. All in all it wasn't at all like his school text books and he found that he was actually quite looking forwards to doing something related to his powers that wasn't just daydreaming.

He turned back to the first page where there was a foreword by the author and lost himself in the writings of Everett Lloyd.

Salutations, fellow Displacer and welcome!

Unlike some of our fellows, who seem to delight in showing their brilliance by the amount of words they use in their writings and expect to see it in the writings of others, I am here merely to lay down my own observations of our unique talents. So with no more preamble than that I will begin.

Many of the limits of our extraordinary abilities are already well known to us, but I will list them here for clarity before going on to document my own feeble attempts to extend the boundaries of our knowledge.

First and most important there is one rule that is absolute: nobody can Displace in their own lifetime.

This naturally brings us to the second rule: once you have lived through a specific time-line you cannot then return to it.

The book went on to list some more of the rules that Andrew had already explained to Sam, for example that you always return to your body the instant you left it. It also explained some of the terminology, like *Calming, Preparing* and the *Transition.* He skipped through all of that fairly quickly, only skimming it, wanting to get to things that he didn't know and started reading again when he got to the experiments.

They started fairly simply.

Our interactions with the normal populace whilst in the past are well documented, however we don't often get the chance to interact with others who have our particular talents. I have long been curious as to whether the same rules would apply.

Lord Price, one of our most distinguished Elders, has agreed to provide assistance in my first endeavour, although for the sake of the experiment I will not explain to him beforehand of what it consists.

In his youth, Lord Price kept a series of diaries, as many of us do, that are now to be found in the library at the Society. I propose to go back to the year before my birth, to when he was yet a young man, and seek him out. I will persuade him of my status as a Displacer and prevail upon him to enter his encounter with me in said diaries. I will further leave a small token, a visiting card with my own name engraved upon it, which I will personally place in the diary.

I believe that this simple experiment will serve to determine the results of various separate interactions.

On returning to the present, the relevant diary was consulted and, while the visiting card was indeed present, there was however no corresponding entry. I further consulted with Lord Price, who racked his brain in vain for any recollection of my visit, neither could he explain how the card came to be within his diary.

In its partial failure the experiment has nonetheless revealed that we are not exceptions to our own rules.

The language that Everett Lloyd used was a little archaic and long-winded, but Sam understood the implications of the experiment easily enough, though, and read on, fascinated.

Having determined in the previous undertaking that interactions with objects are far more complex than interactions with persons, I have devised a new experiment to further plumb the depths of these new possibilities.

I have enlisted the aid of young Master Abraham Hudson, our newest member, in this latest quest.

There are many fine portraits in our lounge, some of which are small and very portable. For this experiment I will send Master Hudson to retrieve one of them and then, when he has returned, after a suitable amount of time to allow the time-line to "settle" as it were, I will go myself to an earlier date to retrieve the same portrait. We will see which of us takes home the prize.

The results were both surprising and unsurprising. Master Hudson brought home the portrait and we waited until the next day before I went to retrieve it myself. (As a side note I would like to exclaim at the willingness of our predecessors to participate in these experiments and the readiness with which they believe us when we turn up in their time-line!)

I had the portrait in my hands when I came home but, to my surprise, as soon as I arrived I found that I no longer held it; it was once again in Master Hudson's possession. It seems that his claim had preference over mine.

I can only conclude that in these matters it is the current time-line that takes precedence over the historical one.

(Afternote: I did not ask Master Hudson to take the portrait back to whence it came because I believe that this would have cancelled out the experiment and destroyed all evidence of it having happened. The absence of the portrait from the lounge has never been noted or remarked upon, however, and this fact in itself brings up some interesting philosophical questions which are perhaps better left for more suitable minds than mine to debate.)

Sam glanced over at James quizzically, 'Abraham Hudson?'

'My own great-grandfather and the first Hudson to become a Displacer. One thing you'll soon discover is that most of our Society come from well-to-do families; most of them not quite aristocracy, but certainly moneyed. Abraham was one of the first members to be accepted from what was, at the time, considered to be a lower-class family; times were very different then. That isn't to say he was the first of the family with the ability, just the first to have it recognised by our illustrious Society.' James smiled wryly and went back to his crossword.

Sam took the hint and turned his attention back to the book. He reviewed what he had just read and thought about what it meant for him - basically, if he or Quentin or anyone else brought something back that the other side wanted, they couldn't just go to an earlier time when it was still there and get it for themselves.

He went on reading, eager to find out more.

There are many occasions when we deem it necessary or advisable to Displace with a partner, for example when there occurs a particularly large disturbance in the time-line or in a dangerous time-period. Up until now we have assumed that physical contact between the travelling partners is necessary. My next venture is designed to prove or disprove this theory.

I have once again enlisted the help of young Master Hudson to aid me in my exploits. (He is more than happy to assist because I am afraid to say that, so far, his has not been an altogether happy association with our Society; his training has been sorely neglected and he has yet to be assigned a part in any mission of note. Unfortunately, our esteemed Elders continue to cling to their belief that the Society and its work is not suitable for the lower classes, an attitude that I believe will see us extinct before too much longer if it does not change.)

The experiment is simple: Master Hudson and I will test the limits of possibility, both in the separation of distance and the separation of time, by attempting to Displace to the same time-line without physical contact. We will each take with us a piece of paper, which will be signed by both parties whilst in the past. The experiment will be deemed successful if both papers remain signed by both parties when brought back. An unsuccessful experiment on the other hand will result in one or both of the papers returning with only a single signature, signifying a Displacement to the same time-period but without the power of interaction given by being in the same time-line.

The first experiment by necessity is the one that will dictate the success or failure of all subsequent activities. Master Hudson and I will Displace together to the same destination but while I will be in the lounge of the house he will be in a bedroom on the fourth floor. We will synchronise our watches and, monitored by two colleagues, we will attempt to Displace at the same exact time as best we can.

The result of this first attempt is positive, we have both brought back papers with a pair of signatures.

(Personal Note: I am relieved; if this first experiment had failed then it would have forestalled any further experiments along the same line and dictated that we would be forever limited to physical contact when wishing to Displace with a fellow Society member.)

Having determined that a small physical separation is no obstacle to success, the next logical step is to determine if there is a maximum distance at which two Displacers can be separated. Due to logistical difficulties I will not be testing too great a distance for now, but I hope that an occasion will arise whereby a Displacement can be coordinated with a member on sojourn in a far away country. I have therefore sent Master Hudson on a train journey to Edinburgh - unfortunately, our colleagues are reluctant to take the time necessary for the journey to aid us in this, so Abraham has had to go unaccompanied and unsupervised. I am assured by him, however, that his rough upbringing has more than prepared him to survive a few days on his own and that I should trust him to fend for himself. Our watches have been synchronised as before and a time and destination agreed upon.

Success! We cannot have been said to have been physically linked in any quantifiable way while we journeyed into the past and yet we have the proof of four signatures on two separate pieces of paper to prove my hypothesis.

I would like to add a thought of my own at this juncture, that, while it is possible to Displace together while separated by some distance, it is vastly preferable to do so with physical contact. Not only is the strain on the body lessened when one is directed by the other, it is also far more accurate: arriving in the same time and space is almost guaranteed. There have been documented instances where this has not occurred, but any errors in temporal geography are invariably small in nature and most often due to social circumstances. In our case, however, something, perhaps the difficulty in accurate coordination, caused Master Hudson to arrive days earlier than I did and necessitated his lingering until my arrival.

Finally Sam was beginning to see how he could have interacted with Quentin in the past and it seemed that it was entirely possible that he wasn't special, just extremely lucky.

The next experiment is in reality various experiments all designed with the same purpose in mind.

Now that we have determined that physical separation is no obstacle, I have devised a series of tests to determine whether the same can be said of a temporal separation.

The usual result of meeting a Displacer on an earlier journey into the past is the same as that of interacting with anyone else, which we now know includes those

Displacers whose natural time-line it is; the interaction is not recalled by the other Displacer upon his return to his own time. Usually this second journey is being undertaken months if not years after the one by the first Displacer, but there may be an amount of time before the time-line becomes "fixed" where it is still flexible enough for a second Displacer to arrive in the same time-line as the first.

(I apologise if my explanations are becoming rather vague and wordy; we are starting to get to areas that are more philosophical in nature than I am accustomed to and I find that I am somewhat lacking in the vocabulary and eloquence necessary for the task. The results, however, will speak for themselves.)

For the first in this series of experiments I had Master Hudson Displace normally with a piece of paper (there is only the necessity for him to take the paper in these experiments) wait a few days, then come back, at which point I immediately Displaced, met up with him in the past, gave him my signature, and then returned.

The experiment failed. Abraham did not remember my interaction with him and his piece of paper languished with only the one signature on it.

This would have been the end of this particular branch of experiments if something had not occurred to me - my morning walks around the park often provide me with moments of inspiration, just as the proverbial bath did to Archimedes, and I wondered if an, albeit brief, interaction between myself and Master Hudson in the present had nonetheless served to solidify the time-line in the past, or in other words cause it to immediately become history for us both. I hypothesised that if we were not to meet in the present then I would not "know" that his Displacement had happened and in this way the time-line might remain flexible enough for me to insert myself into it.

Eureka! In the next experiment I remained separate from Master Hudson and while he Displaced from his own home on the Isle of Dogs I remained in the Society here in Belgravia. We agreed on a time for his Displacement and precisely five minutes later I joined him in the past, signing his paper and then coming home. Master Hudson then joined me, brandishing his paper with two names and excitedly stating that his memories of me in the past were intact.

It appears that my supposition was correct and that personal interaction with the target of the Displacement does indeed fix the past in place.

Now it only remained to determine how long the past stayed fluid and subsequent experiments over the next four months, which I will not bore you with, dear reader, placed it at approximately three hours.

It seemed frivolous to spend too many further Displacements to fix this figure more exactly since the attentions of myself and, not before time, Master Hudson were wanted in service of the Society - I was also informed, in no uncertain terms, by the Council of Elders that our powers are not just tools to use to satisfy my own curiosity, that they are needed for a much higher purpose, so I have declared the experiment concluded, at least for now.

So, Sam now knew that he had a window of about three hours to join Quentin after he went into the past before his acts became set in stone and it followed that Andrew must have known that when he had told him to keep trying every couple of hours.

Sam rubbed his eyes and yawned; it was getting late. His grandfather was now snoozing, leaning to one side against the high wingback of his armchair and the newspaper with his finished crossword was on the point of falling from his lap.

Sam put the book down and stood up. He crossed the room and gently shook James' shoulder. 'Come on, Grandad, time for bed.'

'Wha…?' James' eyes opened and he looked up, quickly focusing on Sam, his mind instantly sharp. 'Oh, have you finished?'

'Not quite, but I'm done for the night. Let's get you up to bed; we have an early morning tomorrow.'

'Fine, give me a hand will you?'

Sam gently helped his grandfather to his feet and took him upstairs, getting him settled in the small third bedroom - his one was always given over to Sam's parents while they were visiting because it was the largest. That done he went back downstairs. He got himself some water from the kitchen, then went back to get the book from the lounge; it wouldn't do for his parents to find it if they came down in the middle of the night for some reason.

He did the rounds of the ground floor quickly, making sure that the doors were locked and the lights were all off, before climbing the stairs and sneaking into the bedroom. He changed into his pyjamas quickly, making sure not to wake Violeta, and fell asleep listening to the soothing sounds of her gentle snoring.

CHAPTER 10
THE GRAND OPENING

It was extremely cold standing around outside the British Museum at seven o'clock in the morning and Sam was hopping up and down trying to keep warm.

James stood beside him, bundled up and perfectly happy, watching him bounce up and down with a slightly bemused look on his face.

Rather than waiting at the main door where the tourists entered the museum, they were round the side by the door to the new extension where all the laboratories were, something that disappointed Sam somewhat; he had been hoping for a little look around while there were no people, wanting to see if he could still read any of the hieroglyphics on the Egyptian relics.

They hadn't been waiting for long before they were joined by Andrew and Rachel. Rachel stood in front of Sam and exaggeratedly watched him bouncing up and down for a few seconds before tilting her head to one side and asking him innocently, 'are you cold, Sam?'

'Just a little bit.'

She pulled him close, interrupting his hopping and ruffled his hair. 'Aw… poor puppy!'

'Gerroff!' Sam played at trying to get away, but not too hard; he was rather enjoying Rachel's close proximity.

'Now, now, you two, we're outside the British Museum. They're not going to let in two ruffians who might wreck the place.'

'Sorry, Andrew.' Rachel grinned and roughly pushed Sam away to arm's length. She reached out and grabbed his hand, though and they stood close together as they waited for Philip.

They all looked up as a cheerful voice called out to them. 'Mornin', everybody! Cold, innit?' It was John, dressed in a big red puffy jacket that made him look like the Michelin Man dipped in paint.

'John? What are you doing here?' Andrew was as surprised to see him as everyone else, apparently.

'Seeing as I'm part of the "Sam gang" I thought I'd tag along. See what's inside that vase.' He grinned. 'It's a historical moment and I want to be there when Sam's godhood is confirmed!'

Sam groaned, but Rachel squeezed his hand and grinned at him. 'You'll have to change your name, Sam. Gods are called Thor, or Athena or something tough.'

He returned her grin. 'I don't know, Sam the God has a nice ring to it.'

They were interrupted when the door opened and Philip appeared. 'Good morning, everyone... John? What are you doing here?'

'Why does everyone keep asking that? Can't I have an interest in all this stuff?'

'I think the fact that you're calling it "stuff" answers your question quite nicely.' Philip was obviously a bit disdainful of John and his lifestyle, which saw him mostly sitting in front of a computer during his waking hours. 'Anyway, come on in, please, before someone starts asking awkward questions.'

He ushered them inside and saw them quickly through an electronic security gate, past an ancient-looking guard who barely looked up from his newspaper as they went by.

The new extension was very modern and light, with lots of windows and was not what Sam expected from a museum like this one - he had been expecting a dusty basement and was vaguely disappointed. However, it was big and there was a lot of space, which meant that Philip had his own personal lab and didn't have to hide anything from any co-workers.

As Philip led them upstairs and along empty corridors, Sam lagged slightly behind and tugged Rachel's arm to make her stay with him. She looked at him quizzically, but he motioned for her not to say anything. When he was sure the others were far enough ahead he whispered to her. 'Did you get a chance to speak to Andrew?'

'About there being a spy?'

'Yes.'

'He says that he has been considering it as a possibility for a while now and what you said about the software makes sense.'

'Really? And does he think it's Ralph?'

'He said he was pretty sure it *wasn't* Ralph, even with the family connection and the rivalry. He says that Ralph is as loyal to the Society as he is.'

Sam shook his head. 'I'm still not convinced.'

'Neither am I. Anyway, he knows you have doubts about Ralph and he said he'll keep an eye on him, but he also said that we should keep our own eyes open for any other possibilities.'

'I really don't know who else it could be, but alright.'

Sam wanted to say more, but their conversation had to come to an end because they had arrived at Philip's laboratory and caught up with everyone else.

Philip let them in, then closed and locked the door behind them.

Waiting for them in the lab was Lisa. Philip had hired her straight out of university years ago; like the Elder, ancient civilisations were her main area of interest - she had a degree in Classical Archaeology and Ancient History from Oxford University and that, combined with the Displacements she had made, meant that she was an invaluable assistant for his work at the museum.

After exchanging greetings with her, they followed Philip over to a glass cabinet set against one wall. It was similar to the one that Sam's school had in the chemistry lab for manipulating corrosive liquids and such, but much newer, cleaner and probably a lot more expensive and useful. It had four holes in the side with built in rubber gloves so that things inside could be manipulated without breaking containment and sitting inside was the vase that Sam had brought back from Egypt.

Sam put his face right up against the glass and peered at the vase. It appeared exactly the same as it had when he'd brought it back, as if nothing had been done to it.

'Lisa and I have done all the tests that we can, tying to take a peek inside and see if we can get an idea of what's there before we open it, but so far it has resisted our every effort. The vase itself is made of lead, which has made it impervious to many of the scans...'

'Cool, it's Superman proof!' John interrupted with a laugh.

Philip stared at John with his mouth open, his train of thought completely broken, and there was an awkward moment of silence while John grinned at the group and the rest of them just stared back at him.

Andrew quickly tried to get them back on track. 'Anyway... Philip?'

'What? Oh, right. Where was I? Oh, yes. I haven't been able to look inside, but carbon dating of the vase itself places it as originating from around six thousand years ago. That fact and the design gives me the idea that it is from Predynastic Egypt, but that is all I have been able to ascertain up until now; there are no markings or patterns to be seen that give any clue as to the vase's contents.'

'And that has taken you this long to work out?' John was incredulous and evidently had as little time for Philip's pomposity as Philip did for him.

The Elder drew himself up indignantly as he defended himself. 'The proper form has to be maintained! No risks could be taken with a find of this potential magnitude.'

'Quite right Philip.' Andrew turned and gave John a scowl. 'Please keep quiet, John, and let Philip talk.'

John made a zipping motion across his lips and rolled his eyes.

'Some of the test are very complex and time consuming, and I do have other work to do.' Philip tried to justify himself.

Andrew appeased him. 'We know, Philip, and we are very appreciative of your efforts.'

The Elder didn't look at all happy, but continued anyway, pointedly ignoring John who was still smirking slightly. 'Having exhausted all possible tests on the vase itself, the only thing that remains to be done is to open it.'

'Duh.' John said, very quietly.

Thankfully, Philip didn't hear him, or at least pretended not to. He motioned to the glass cabinet behind him. 'This is a state-of-the-art vacuum chamber, it will serve both to protect the contents from possible contaminants in the air and will also protect us from any possible harmful agents in the vase itself.'

'Like those often found in Egyptian tombs that are opened after thousands of years,' added Lisa.

'Indeed.' Philip nodded.

He turned to the chamber and put his hands into the gloves, then waited for Lisa to join him.

They worked well as a team, manipulating the vase between them with barely a word necessary. While Lisa held the vase steady Philip used tools that were already in the chamber to unravel the wire that was wrapped around the top, holding the wax stopper in place. The wire was extremely fine, gold according to Phillip, and unwrapped easily despite its age. They then delicately manipulated the stopper, moving it millimetre by millimetre, drawing it slowly out of the vase.

It took many minutes, but eventually the piece of wax came free and Philip placed it carefully to one side. He then picked up an endoscope and manipulated it so that its tip was resting just inside the neck of the vase. Lisa turned on a screen mounted behind the back of the cabinet and they watched Philip carefully feed the scope into the container.

Almost immediately they got their first view of the contents.

'It looks like a scroll,' said Lisa cautiously.

Philip manipulated the endoscope slightly before replying. 'Remarkable! It looks like some kind of animal skin. It's incredibly well-preserved if it is and it could well be the oldest example of its kind in the world!' Philip was getting more excited with every passing minute, but he was still disciplined enough to proceed with caution. He picked up some very fine pincers, then very carefully inserted them next to the endoscope and gently grasped the edge of the scroll.

He pulled it out and laid it on the table next to the stopper before inserting the endoscope into the vase again.

Despite the fact that everybody was impatient for him to open the scroll and could plainly see that there was nothing else in the vase, Philip refused to be hurried and had a good look around, inspecting the inside walls of the vase as well, just in case there were any markings.

Eventually, though, he laid the endoscope to one side, satisfied that the vase was not going to reveal any more secrets. He picked up a couple of sterile metal implements and turned his attention to the scroll. 'Right, let us see what we have here.'

Philip made an unhappy noise when he touched the scroll for the first time - it was still tightly rolled and hadn't loosened at all after it had been liberated from the vase. He turned it to find the opening, then gently prodded at it, trying to open it up, just as you would a roll of sellotape. However, just like a roll of sellotape, it was stuck fast. 'Oh.'

'What?' Andrew asked.

'I can't open this right now.'

'Why not?'

'There is a distinct possibility that if I try to do so then it might be irreversibly damaged.'

'Oh, just do it, already! We need to know what it says!' John was annoyed; he had gotten increasingly impatient and restless over the almost two hours that it had taken Philip to open the vase and extract the scroll and couldn't contain himself any longer.

Philip turned to him with a shocked expression on his face, but it was James who answered with a disapproving tone. 'Have you not learnt *any* patience over your years as a Displacer, John? Perhaps we should send you to a monastery for a few decades?'

'Am I the only one thinking that this has taken long enough?' John couldn't believe the others didn't agree with him and it showed in his voice and his wild gestures. 'There may be information in there that we can use to stop the dark side from totally messing up time once and for all! Information we need *now* if Sam is going to have a chance at stopping them this time, or any other time!'

Andrew tried to be the voice of reason. 'I agree, John, there may be vital information on that scroll, but if we have to wait a few more hours or days or weeks to get to it safely and not risk losing it forever, then we will wait.' He gave John a long hard stare before turning to Philip. 'How long until you can open it?'

'A day at the most. We have to treat it and make it more pliable before we can open it. I haven't got anything else to do today, so I should be able to open it by this time tomorrow. If it is in a language that I recognise then I should be able to tell everybody what it says tomorrow evening at the Christmas dinner.'

'Then that will be an appropriate and appreciated present for us all.'

John still wasn't happy. 'Yeah, he can write out the translation and put it in the crackers…'

Andrew ignored him and turned to the group. He clapped his hands gently and smiled. 'Come on, let's leave our esteemed colleagues to their work. I don't know about you, but I need a cup of tea!'

Ten minutes later they were in the café of the British Museum, watching the tourists flood in. Lisa and Philip had stayed to do their work and John had left in a huff, so it was just a cosy group of four that sat down for tea, toast and pastries.

'Well, that was a bit of an anticlimax!' said Andrew with a wry laugh as soon as they had gotten settled and taken a few bites of their food.

Sam looked a bit downcast. 'Yeah, we already knew it was going to be a scroll with something written on it.'

'So, was I the only one that thought it was going to be a magic wand that conjured up unicorns and rainbows?' James asked the group with a surprised expression.

Sam looked at him, puzzled and opened his mouth to reply. It took him a few seconds to get the fact that his grandfather was making fun of him, but then he laughed with the others.

'Of course we all thought it was going to be something written, my boy!' James said as he ruffled his hair.

There was a comfortable silence as they ate and drank a bit more.

Sam looked at Andrew. 'Uh, Andrew? I wanted to ask you a favour…'

'Yes?'

'If possible, could I not Displace with John, please?'

Andrew took a moment to assimilate Sam's request. 'I understand your reluctance, I do and he has been acting up a bit lately, I know, but he's still a good man and a good operative and he could help you out enormously.'

'He makes me uncomfortable…'

Andrew considered for a few more seconds before he sighed and nodded reluctantly. 'Alright then, if we can avoid it we will… But speaking of which…' He held out his hands, one to Sam and one to Rachel, then looked pointedly at Sam.

Sam knew what was expected of him and he took a deep breath as both Rachel and Andrew closed their eyes.

James watched them and out of the corner of his eye he saw an old woman at a nearby table watching them as well. He turned and winked at her. 'Prayer group. We're praying for the souls of the poor people who believe all this science nonsense.'

The old woman quickly looked away.

James winked at Sam and Sam returned his grin before he closed his eyes and concentrated…

Nothing.

They all opened their eyes and Andrew shrugged. 'Oh well. Keep trying, OK, Sam?'

'OK.'

'The Elders still say that the past is disturbed, but not fixed, so we've still got time to stop him.'

James tutted. 'Come on, Andrew, let's just enjoy the rest of our tea and stop worrying about that for a while. So, Rachel… Is Sam a good kisser?' The old man looked at Rachel with a mock serious expression and she laughed. Sam of course went a bright red.

While they finished the rest of their brunch they spoke about inconsequential matters, purposely ignoring the looming shadow and spending time together as a family. At one point Sam's hand found Rachel's under the table and they didn't let go of each other until they left.

They went as a group to Headquarters, but then James told them that he needed to talk to Andrew and they hurried off together to one of the reading rooms leaving the two youths feeling slightly rejected.

Rachel turned to Sam. 'Fancy a run?'

'Oh yes!' Sam leapt at the idea.

They went for a long run around the park and came back in time for lunch, which was just the four of them so they ate in the basement.

Sam and Rachel went back out in the afternoon, but just for a walk, going past Buckingham Palace, where they stopped to watch the changing of the guard, then along the Mall to Admiralty Arch and Trafalgar Square. They went into the National Gallery for a while, but when they started getting funny looks from some of the security guards they realised they had unconsciously been casing the joint with an eye to robbing it and hurriedly left, laughing.

There were a few more members at Headquarters for dinner in the evening, but most of them didn't stay long after learning that there wasn't going to be any news about the scroll that day. James didn't see much point in hanging around either and all too soon he was hustling Sam out of the door without a chance to properly say goodbye to Rachel.

As soon as they got home, Sam was roped into a game of Monopoly with his family that lasted for nearly two hours and was exhaustingly hilarious and a whole lot of fun, but it didn't leave him any time to read more of Everett Lloyd's experiments. However, after such an early morning, he was too tired to have really concentrated on it anyway, so he just went to bed and almost immediately fell into a deep sleep, despite his excitement about the next day's possible revelations.

CHAPTER 11
EXPECTANCY

Sam awoke refreshed and anxious to get going with the day, which was a shame because James had decided to have a bit of a lie in and seeing as he was Sam's excuse for not being with his family, that meant that he couldn't make his way up to the Society without him.

He had his breakfast and decided to go to the sitting room and read for a while until his grandfather was ready. He flicked through the first book until he reached where he'd gotten to and saw that he was actually near the end of the first diary; the handwritten text was so big that it took up a lot more space than in a normal book.

Now that it has been determined that a tandem Displacement remains possible with both physical and temporal separation, I wish to ascertain whether the method of fixing a destination is also the absolute it is assumed to be. Until now we have had to have very clear in our minds a time and a place and we are all very familiar with the feeling we have when we do. What, however, happens if we fix on a person, *rather than a* place? *Can we Displace to them? This would be particularly useful if we wish to Displace to a* time *and a* person *without knowing their exact location. It could also be an alternate way to accompany someone on a Displacement, someone with whom we have no physical contact. (Although personally I can think of no situation in which one would not know the destination of a colleague with whom you have arranged a tandem Displacement.)*

My partner in crime, Master Abraham Hudson, once again joined me for this experiment which was as follows: we arranged for him to journey into the past from his own home to a destination that was unknown to me but had been previously arranged with the Elders, a suitably stable destination that neither of us would be called upon to go to during the normal course of our duties. I would then wait an hour before attempting to join him and would only have him *to concentrate on as a focal point for my own journey. Once again, proof of success would be provided by signatures on a piece of paper that Master Hudson carried with him.*

The experiment was successful in that we achieved our aim. However, I would not qualify it as a complete success. While I did indeed Displace to the correct time period to encounter Master Hudson I did not however arrive at the same exact time as him nor in the same place and it took considerable effort and once again much patience on his part for us to meet.

In the two subsequent months we tried again and in each instance the experiment was ultimately successful, but the results were equally inconsistent.

It is possible, *therefore, to use a person as a locus, but it is inaccurate, to say the least, and it remains infinitely preferable to tandem Displace using the more normal method.*

That was the end of the first diary, but with the final experiment that Everett Lloyd had documented, if he read it right, Sam had confirmation of what he had already concluded; that his method of concentrating on Quentin was the possible source of his meeting him in Egypt. However, it still left the question of how he had ended up in the same time-line as him in Port Royal open - the only explanation remained sheer coincidence. Unfortunately, the diary also made it clear that, even though he would arrive in the same time-line as Quentin, it was entirely possible that he could arrive several months before or after Quentin's arrival and possibly in a completely different country. That made the probability of stopping him a lot worse, unless he was very lucky, and Quentin could well have time to do whatever it was he wanted to do and leave before Sam even got to the time-line. Then, the only thing that Sam could do was try to clean up the mess as best as possible, if he could even find out what changes the man had affected, of course, because he might do something so small as to not be noticeable until many years later.

Sam had never quite managed to fully understand most of the complex paradoxes and rules that were involved with being a Displacer, but he had to admit the diary was helping to make things a little bit clearer. However, he could feel himself getting a headache, as he often did when he tried to think about time travel, so he closed the book and went looking for his grandfather.

He found the old man just finishing his breakfast and managed to get him to hurry along a bit and a quarter of an hour later they headed out.

James was unusually quiet on the bus ride into London and there was a constant frown on his face as he stared into nothing; whatever he and Andrew had shut themselves into one of the rooms to speak about the previous day seemed to still be on his mind and he obviously wasn't very happy about it.

Sam took the opportunity to gaze out of the steamed up windows at the city that he still didn't really know. The bus went through mostly residential areas, but as they crossed the Thames they passed the MI6 building that featured in the *James Bond* films, then stopped briefly at Victoria train station, giving Sam a good view of some of the theatres that were grouped around it.

Soon they were going past the wall that kept the public out of the Buckingham Palace gardens and their destination was close, but James made no move to stand.

'Grandad?' Sam shook James gently by the arm. 'We're almost there.'

'What? Oh, right you are, Sam.' James shook himself from his thoughts and they stood. Sam pressed the button to stop the bus and they got off.

'Is everything all right, Grandad?'

He sighed. 'Not really, Sam. To tell the truth we were hoping for something more than just a scroll, even if it is a fragment of prophecy.' James paused to gather his thoughts. 'Something is different about this time; the feeling the Elders getting right now is so much bigger, so much worse than what we usually get when Quentin and company try to change things - it's like a constant throbbing in our heads. I know we've already told you that we're up against the ropes, but now it seems like it might be even worse than we thought. If they manage to pull off whatever it is they're planning, then it might be the end of the line for us; we won't be able to stop them from doing whatever they want whenever they want.'

The old man lapsed into silence again and said nothing more for the few minutes it took them to get to the Society's Headquarters.

Sam didn't need to look at the pegs to know that Rachel and Andrew were already there, because he could hear their voices as soon as they walked through the door and they found them in the lounge having tea with Anne, an elegant middle-aged woman wearing a grey business skirt and jacket, who had flown in that morning from New York and whose suitcases were almost entirely blocking the wide hallway.

Sam had seen Anne on Skype but had never really spoken to her; she tended not to say very much during the conference calls. He didn't know much about her but was keen to find out more because, according to Rachel, she was in some kind of long distance relationship with Andrew.

The American woman stood up when she saw them arrive and came over. She greeted James like an old friend, then stood in front of Sam, studying him.

'You're taller than I thought you would be.'

Sam raised an eyebrow. 'Um... Thank you?'

'Sorry, it's just that Andrew used to tell me that you had a bully problem, Rafa was it? And he always said that it was because you were small for your age.'

Sam coloured, embarrassed at the thought of so many others knowing about his past misery and weakness. 'Ah, well, I have grown a bit over the last year or so.'

She smiled warmly and nodded. 'That must be it. I bet you don't have any problems now!' She reached out and pulled him into a very close embrace and planted a kiss on his cheek. 'I'm so pleased to meet you Sam. Welcome.'

Sam would have blushed, if he hadn't already been.

She stepped back and gave him a cheeky smile. 'I can see why Rachel is so keen on you.'

Beyond all expectations, Sam's face managed to go an even deeper shade of red.

Thankfully, he was saved from further embarrassment by Rachel, who came bouncing over to them and folded him into a hug. 'Morning! What took you so long to get here?'

Sam glanced at his grandfather. He looked tired and, for the first time ever, old. 'I'll tell you later.'

She pulled back and looked at him searchingly, worried at his sad tone of voice. 'OK.'

'Do you want to go for a run? I need to clear my head.'

'Yeah, sure.' She turned to the rest of the group. 'We'll leave you grown-ups to talk. See you for lunch!'

She pulled Sam out of the room and they went upstairs to the bedrooms to get changed.

Sam had taken to leaving workout clothes in the house so as not to keep carrying them back and forth. Thankfully, the housekeeper, Maeve, had been kind enough to wash them for him.

They changed in the same room, way beyond being shy around each other, so that they could continue to talk.

'My grandfather is really worried. I don't think he slept very well last night.'

'About the whole Quentin thing?'

'Yeah, and by the way, we need a name for them, we can't keep calling them Quentin and company or things like that.'

Rachel laughed. 'I wonder what they call themselves. Probably something geeky, knowing Quentin.'

'I keep forgetting you knew him before.' Sam suddenly had a thought - maybe Rachel could come up with some idea as to who the spy was, if there was one. 'Was there anyone he was particularly close to in the Society?'

'Apart from his father?'

'Of course.'

Rachel paused, her legging half way up her legs. 'Well, he spent a bit of time in the kitchen with Philip, but I thought that was because he liked to eat.'

'Probably…'

'And of course he and John were always playing games on the computers.'

Sam stopped tying his shoelaces and looked up at her, raising his eyebrow.

She shook her head. 'No! Don't even think it! It's not him; John is one of the good guys, besides, Andrew has known him almost all his life, he would know if it was John. He introduced him to Susan and was the best man at their wedding, among other things.'

'Alright, but that leaves us back at square one, unless we want to investigate our resident chef?'

'If it is him I don't care; we're not kicking Philip out, his food is too good!' She grinned. 'You ready?' Sam nodded. 'Let's go, then.'

They went back downstairs and called out their goodbyes from the hallway, but barely got a reaction from the others so they just left them to it.

They walked up the road hand in hand, still talking.

'Neither Andrew nor I can see any of the Elders being the spy,' said Rachel.

'Why not?'

'Well, we were talking about this last night. Firstly, most of the Elders are so old they barely know how to use the Internet or the smartphones we've been issued, let alone how to pirate a copy of John's software.'

'OK. A bit ageist, but OK.'

'And also you have to realise just how many years they all worked towards the stability of the time-line. For one of them to just suddenly turn around and go against us is incomprehensible.'

Sam frowned. 'But Andrew said that someone has been working against us for about twenty years - some of them weren't Elders that long ago.'

'I don't know, he just didn't think it was very likely.'

'Well, I don't know about you, but I'm not going to rule out anyone just yet.'

'Not even me?' She batted her eyelashes at him.

'*Especially* not you.'

'Gee, thanks.' She slapped him on the back of the head and started jogging. 'Now shut up and run before I stop liking you so much.' She put on a spurt and raced ahead into the park.

Sam grinned and followed her. He caught up with her quickly and they ran side by side in silence for a while.

It was another cold London day, grey and overcast with a bit of mist on the ground, one of those days that looked like it was going to rain but never quite did, the clouds hanging low overhead and pressing down on the city. The ground was still wet from overnight rain and the people they passed were all bundled up tight against the weather. None of that mattered to Sam, though; he was happy, running with Rachel.

Until he stopped dead in his tracks.

It felt like someone had thrown a bucket of cold water over him and he shivered, suddenly cold.

Rachel noticed he had stopped and jogged back to him. 'Sam? You OK?'

Sam looked up at her. 'Give me your hands.'

'What? I…'

'It's time. We've got to go.'

'How do you…?'

'Please, Rachel. Just Prepare yourself.'

'OK…' He could see she wasn't sure, but she nonetheless did as he asked.

He watched her close her eyes and concentrate. He felt the energy building inside her and when she was ready he closed his eyes, finding his own energy already there, waiting eagerly for him to give the order.

He reached out for Quentin…

CHAPTER 12
DISORIENTATION

London, 1888.

Something was different…

Sam opened his eyes and looked down in surprise; instead of Rachel's hands he was holding a cup of tea and a small plate piled high with cucumber sandwiches.

He was in a deep, extremely comfortable leather armchair in a large, dimly lit room, with a fireplace to one side and thick velvet curtains pulled back from windows on the other, revealing the dark of night outside. Expensive looking artwork was hanging on the walls and there were a fair many people sitting around the room in other, identical dark red armchairs, drinking tea or liquors, reading newspapers or chatting. A couple of men in dark suits, white shirts and bow ties, butlers apparently, were walking around the room serving drinks or clearing up.

It looked very much like the lounge at Headquarters and seemed to be some kind of gentleman's club, but a real one, not like the Society.

He leaned forward to put the plate and cup down on a small table, then looked around, twisting in his seat, panicking slightly at Rachel's absence, and for a second didn't realise that someone was talking to him.

'I asked if you agreed, Sir Sam?'

Sam's eyes slowly focussed on the man sitting across the table from him. 'I'm sorry? Oh, yes, of course.' Sam had no idea what he was agreeing to, but he tried desperately to smile and nod and look like he did.

The man who had spoken had a round face with an expectant but jovial expression and a thick moustache under dark, slicked down hair with a severe parting. 'What about you?'

He addressed his question to the man sitting on his left, the third and final member of their small group, who had longish brown wavy hair and spoke in a faintly Irish accent. 'I am terribly sorry, Arthur, but I don't get much chance to cover such matters in my magazine; the only thing that *The Woman's World* murders is my own sense of humour.'

'Pshaw, Oscar,' said the first man. 'Your wit cuts finer than any scalpel that our friend Jack could wield.'

'Speaking of which, what *are* the police doing about the situation?'

Both men turned to look expectantly at Sam.

'Excuse me?' Sam still had no idea what they were talking about and he played for time so that he could find the memories that he should have gotten by Displacing.

The first man laughed 'Come now, Vives, don't be coy! We all know that Scotland Yard has brought in an illustrious detective to aid in their efforts. It's even in the press!'

The man that had been called "Oscar" laughed. 'Yes, a brilliant Sherlock Holmes to aid in their pedantic Lestrade-like efforts.'

Sam finally caught on that it was him they were talking about, but he had nothing to tell them; they weren't giving him the time to access the information in his brain, so instead he played one of the cards that Andrew had taught him, 'I'm afraid I'm not at liberty to discuss any details of the case right now.'

The first man sighed. 'Ah, that's a shame, but I suppose it is to be expected. Nonetheless, I do hope you don't mind if we continue to discuss the latest gossip from the dark and dank corridors of Whitechapel?'

Sam smiled at them. 'No, of course not, although if you don't mind I will not listen too closely for fear of contamination.'

'By all means!' The two men turned to face each other, not exactly ignoring Sam but no longer trying to actively include him in their conversation. 'Have you heard the rumours that the police are deliberately bungling their investigation because they are covering for someone in the Royal Family?'

Oscar laughed, 'I have had heard that one, yes, and I think it just as likely to be the Queen herself as one of her weak-chinned relatives;

they would be incapable of finding their way around the boulevards of Kensington, let alone the alleys of Whitechapel.'

Sam listened idly as they continued to chat about what the word on the street was about the Jack the Ripper case, but in the meantime he let his mind work on acclimatising himself to his new circumstances.

'There have been five victims so far and the authorities still don't have any clue as to the culprit, the word on the street though…'

Sam inspected his companions, searching his mind for their identities and couldn't quite believe it when he found out. The first man, the one with the parting and the thick moustache, was Arthur Conan Doyle, author of, among other things, the Sherlock Holmes books. That on its own would have been enough to strike Sam dumb with awe, but it was the identity of the second man, Oscar, the one with the longer hair and the languid way of speaking, that had Sam fighting hard not to allow his jaw to drop, who was the reason why Sam wouldn't have been able to speak even if he had something to say and whose presence at the table was making him want to just sit back and listen for as long as he could, for the whole Displacement if possible. His name was Oscar Wilde.

'What about you, Oscar? Do you have any theories?' asked Conan Doyle.

'I make it a point never to venture any theories until after I am proven right.'

While he enjoyed their easy and witty banter, Sam gazed around the room as discreetly as possible, searching for any sign of Rachel, but there wasn't any. He was positive that he had brought her with him, had felt her coming along for the ride as usual, but something must have gone very wrong - perhaps something to do with him concentrating on a person rather than a place and time.

Anyway, whatever had happened, it looked like he would have to stop Quentin on his own. Again.

'Well, I should be going. I have to edit the latest edition for next week.' Wilde sighed and stood up. 'It is a shame to leave behind such stimulation for favour of numbing my mind with drivel, but such is my life right now. Although if I am lucky I will have another exclusive interview with Miss Sarah Bernhardt in the near future. She may even talk about something other than her dress this time.'

Conan Doyle got to his feet with him. 'I might as well accompany you to the door; I shouldn't make too late a night of it, my pregnant wife needs me!'

Sam hurriedly got to his feet as well and shook hands with both of them.

'Give my regards to your lovely wife, Sir Sam.' Wilde said as he turned to go.

Sam frowned. 'I'm sorry? Who?'

Wilde turned back and smiled. 'Are you so in your cups that you have forgotten what state of wedlock you currently find yourself? If so, I should try the same! Your wife, Sir Sam, your wife! Please give my regards... and my sympathies, to Lady Rachel, your wonderful assistant.'

Rachel! She was here! 'I will, and thank you. You must both come to dinner some time, I'm sure she would be delighted to have the chance to entertain you.'

'We shall, you may count upon it!' Wilde nodded and together he and Conan Doyle left the room.

Sam sat back down, almost dropping into the chair in relief. So, Rachel was here after all!

Suddenly, something else occurred to him and he went white; he'd been so happy hearing that Rachel was there that he'd completely blanked out the rest of what Wilde had said - Lady Rachel, your *wife* - they were married!

He wasn't quite sure how he felt about that, even if it was a temporary state of affairs for the duration of this Displacement. Worse, he really didn't know what Rachel's reaction was going to be when she found out - it could be anywhere between blind fury and outright hilarity; she was rather unpredictable like that.

He looked around the room again but, no matter how much he wished for it to happen, Rachel didn't appear, in fact there wasn't a single woman present and he decided that it would be a good idea to leave and go looking for her.

He stood up and crossed the room, following in the footsteps of his new and famous acquaintances. A few of the men called out to him as he passed and he smiled and exchanged peasantries with them, but didn't stop; he was too eager to find Rachel.

He left the room, and found himself in a short entrance hallway with a door to his right and a doorman standing by, watching him. He went that way and just before he got to the door the man opened it for him, touching his finger to his hat in salute.

Sam nodded to him. 'Thank you.'

'Goodnight, sir.'

He went out onto the steps of the club, past a gold plaque that told him that the place was the Greek Cynic Club which Sam thought was a very strange name for a club, and stood shivering on the doorstep.

'Sir Sam?' The voice came from behind him and he turned to find the doorman had followed him out.

'Yes?'

He was carrying a hat, a cane and an overcoat and he held them out to Sam. 'You left your belongings behind, sir.'

'Oh, silly me, thank you.'

'You're very welcome, sir.'

The doorman helped Sam on with his coat, then handed him the hat and cane. Sam fumbled in his pocket for some change and came out with a couple of large coins which he handed to the man. The man's eyes widened as he accepted them and he touched his finger to his hat again. 'Much obliged, sir! Much obliged!'

'Well, goodnight again!'

'Goodnight, sir.'

Sam went down to the pavement, then stood there looking up and down the street, searching for some clue as to where he should go or even where he was.

The nighttime street was only dimly lit by gas lamps and there was a sparse fog that made everything hazy and prevented him from seeing very far - after the brightly lit streets of Barcelona and modern day London, the atmosphere was almost sinister, more like a film than real life. There were no pedestrians anywhere to be seen, and the only signs of life were a few horse-drawn carriages that went slowly by, but even they were no more than indistinct shapes in the fog accompanied by the muffled sounds of hooves against the rough stones of the road.

Sam decided to just start walking, figuring that he would soon work out where he was supposed to go - either he'd remember or his feet would just carry him along.

He got about twenty metres down the road before he realised that he was being followed - there was a carriage, a small open buggy with two horses, shadowing him, a man in a dark cloak with a tall hat pulled down low over his eyes sitting on the front of it, watching him closely.

Sam turned and took a step towards the carriage, intending to confront his stalker head-on, thinking that perhaps this would be his first encounter with Quentin or part of whatever team he had brought with him. He relaxed his body and mentally prepared himself for any eventuality. He ran several scenarios through his mind, thinking ahead, like in a chess match, instantly taking in his surroundings as he did so, noting the brick wall nearby where he could take refuge from gunshots and the low bollards along the pavement that he could use to leap from to get to the level of the driver.

The carriage advanced until it pulled up beside him and the man's head turned slowly to look at him.

Sam could barely see his eyes, but he could feel them burning into him and he tensed, waiting for the attack to come, eyeing the whip in the man's hand and watching his body language for the first twitch towards any concealed weapon.

'Where to, Sir Sam?' The man asked in a rich voice with a Welsh accent.

It took Sam a couple of seconds to realise that there was going to be no attack, but when he did he almost flopped in relief; obviously all the talk of Jack the Ripper, the missing Rachel and the stress of being in the past to try to stop Quentin was making him paranoid. Of course *Sir Sam* would have a driver or something and the man's accent just added to his feeling of security; it was hard to imagine someone with a lilting Welsh accent doing harm to anyone.

'Take me home, please.'

'Right you are, sir.'

Sam hopped up into the back of the buggy and had barely settled into the back seat before it lurched forwards, jolting him.

They made their way through London, bouncing bone-shatteringly over the cobbled streets. Sam couldn't make out much because of the fog and he had no idea where they were going, but it didn't matter; the driver obviously did and it was only a short ride before the carriage pulled up outside a small townhouse.

Sam leapt out and gazed up at the house. It was narrow, one of a row of identical houses, and it was dark, thick curtains on the windows blocking off any light that might have been coming from it.

'Will you be needing me again tonight, sir?'

'Er, no thank you.'

'Then I'll be back at nine tomorrow morning to take you to the Yard, sir.'

'Thank you...' Sam racked his brain to come up with the man's name. He was relieved when it floated into his recall. 'Constable Williams. Or shall I call you Geoffrey?'

'Call me Geoff, sir, everyone knows me by that at the Yard.'

'Very well. Goodnight then, Geoff.'

'Goodnight, sir.'

Geoff clicked his tongue and he disappeared into the fog as the horses pulled him away.

Sam walked up the short path towards the door of the house, patting his pockets as he went, looking for keys. He didn't find any, but he decided to try the door anyway and found that it was unlocked.

The house was cosily lit by several gas lamps on the walls, which revealed a staircase in front of him and a short corridor.

'Hello?'

There was a noise from behind a door to his left and he opened it to find a small lounge with a few sofas and armchairs gathered around a low coffee table. There was a fire roaring in a fireplace and the room was very inviting after the cold damp air in the street.

None of that registered to him, though, because he at last found himself face to face with Rachel.

He sighed in relief and started towards her. 'Rachel! I'm so glad…'

She cut him off before he could finish and furiously thrust a finger in his face, stopping him dead in his tracks. 'I'm a bloody housemaid! I got here and I had a bloody apron on and I was in the bloody kitchen, baking.'

Sam grinned. 'Oh, great! I'm starving!'

'I didn't bloody finish the bloody baking! I'm not going to spend all my time here cooking for you, what do you think I am?'

'My bloody wife?'

'And another thing! I don't appreciate being…' She blinked and paused. 'I'm sorry, your what?!?' She stared at him.

'Apparently, we're married… Mrs Vives.'

Rachel was struck speechless for a few seconds, but then she recovered and her scowl returned, along with the scolding tone that she had most likely been rehearsing since the moment she'd arrived in the past. 'So where the bloody hell have you been?'

Sam laughed. 'Wow, it sure sounds like we're married…'

She punched him on the arm.

'Ow!

'Answer the damn question! Where have you been?' She looked angry but there was a hint of mischief in her eyes.

'Oh, nowhere in particular, darling. I was just having tea in the club with Oscar Wilde and Arthur Conan Doyle.'

She opened her mouth to shout at him again, but nothing came out.

He grinned at her.

She went red with anger. 'You…'

'Lucky, lucky, bastard?'

She said nothing else, just punched him again in the exact same place, much harder.

'Ow! Oh, and I invited them for dinner sometime, I hope that's OK with you...'

She went to hit him again but stopped and, for the first time since he'd met her only six months but more than half a decade ago, he thought that he detected a little bit of fear in her eyes.

She spoke in a quiet voice. 'You invited Oscar Wilde...' The fear disappeared in an instant and she screwed up her eyes and draw back her hand, her playful anger coming back in full.

He dodged away from her and ran off, laughing.

Later, after Rachel had caught Sam, held him down and forced him to tell her every detail of his meeting with the two renowned personalities, they sat in two very comfortable armchairs and gazed into the fire, discussing their situation while eating sandwiches with freshly made bread - Rachel had done some baking after all; she said she had gotten bored waiting for him.

'So, what am I doing helping the police with the Jack the Ripper case? I'm not a detective. And how is it relevant to Quentin? Do you think he's Jack the Ripper?'

Rachel shook her head. 'He can't be. You can't murder anyone in the past, remember; anyone he killed would just come back to life when he left...' she hesitated before continuing. 'Except for other Displacers.'

Sam blanched. 'Like Susan.'

She nodded.

'But if he isn't Jack the Ripper, why would I be helping Scotland Yard?'

'I don't know. Maybe the case has nothing to do with Quentin; this hasn't exactly been a precise Displacement from the start - we arrived separately after all.'

'It must do, though; Wilde said you were my assistant, so you'll be helping me with my investigations - surely we wouldn't *both* be involved in the case if it didn't have something to do with Quentin?'

Rachel shrugged. 'I guess we'll just have to wait and see. How does it usually work when you go up against Quentin?'

'Normally I just kind of fall into contact with him in the natural course of events.'

'I should have guessed it wouldn't be something *you* did...' Rachel chuckled, shaking her head. 'Then we'll just have to be patient. Maybe we could go and visit the Society Headquarters; they might have some ideas.'

'That sounds good. Do you know anything about the current Displacers?' asked Sam.

'Not really, beyond that there should be family members of ours - a Price, a Hudson, a Berry…'

'We'll just have to introduce ourselves, it shouldn't be too hard to gain entrance, I suppose. Let's go tomorrow after we've been to Scotland Yard.'

'Sounds good to me.' Rachel yawned and stood up. 'We've got an early morning tomorrow, so let's get to bed.'

Sam grinned. 'Sounds good to me, Mrs Vives.'

Rachel laughed. 'Don't get your hopes up; it was very common in this era for married couples to sleep in separate rooms and I've already checked out the sleeping arrangements - there are two bedrooms made up.'

Sam was crestfallen. 'Oh… how convenient.'

She laughed again and leaned over him. She pulled his chin up and kissed him. 'Come on, you've got a serial killer to catch tomorrow.'

She pulled him out of his chair and, hand in hand, they went upstairs.

CHAPTER 13
THE CASE

Sam slept deeply, his body and mind recovering from the strain of the Displacement. Each time he travelled through time was slightly easier than the last, though, and he didn't have much trouble waking up the next morning.

The wardrobe in his room held a row of white shirts and three-piece suits in various shades of grey and black, almost identical to the one that he had been wearing the night before. They were a far cry from his usual jeans and t-shirt, but he didn't mind dressing up for Displacements; it added to the fun, and at the end of the day Displacing was still fun for him, in spite of the pressure that had so recently been heaped upon his head. He put on one of the suits, marvelling at how he knew exactly how to tie his cravat without ever having learnt, then went downstairs for breakfast.

He found a young maid laying the table in the dining room at the back of the house and she curtseyed when she saw him. 'Mornin', sir.'

He found her name in his memory as he answered. 'Good morning, Mary, have you seen my wife?' He grinned; it still cracked him up to call Rachel that.

'Not yet, sir.'

'Thank you.' He nodded his thanks to her, then went over to the table and sat down. There was toast and jam and a plate of butter as well as eggs and bacon. Sam found he was ravenously hungry, as per usual after a Displacement, but he waited patiently for Rachel to appear before digging in.

She came down the stairs only a couple of minutes later and stood in the doorway, smiling.

'Wow, you look… wow!' Sam was used to finding Rachel attractive but somehow she had outdone herself - the night before she had been wearing a loose, shapeless black house dress, but that morning she had put on a blood red velvet dress that had a tight waist that flared into a skirt that flowed languidly around her legs. It wasn't her skirts that most caught his eye, though; the dress incorporated some kind of ribbing around her ribs that managed to accentuate her breasts *quite* impressively and he just couldn't stop staring.

Rachel saw the direction of his gaze and raised an eyebrow as she grinned her lopsided grin. 'I'm guessing you approve.'

Sam blinked and started. He saw her smirking at him and coloured. 'Sorry. It's just you look amazing!'

She finally walked over to him and sat down. 'There are a lot of dresses in my wardrobe upstairs and they're all incredibly beautiful, but most of them are designed to be worn with a corset or stick out a mile backwards - I can't be bothered with any of that; I want to be able to move in case we have to defend ourselves. This is one of the few that I can wear and still breathe in, so you'll just have to get used to the view.'

Sam laughed. 'I'll try!' He put some food on Rachel's plate before filling his own and then started to tuck in without waiting for her.

Rachel looked at the food wistfully. 'I'm starving but I don't know if I'm going to be able to eat very much without bursting this dress.'

In the end she ate more than Sam.

They finished breakfast in silence, mostly because they were too busy eating to talk, and then went to sit in the lounge with tea while they waited for their ride to Scotland Yard.

Sam looked at her over the rim of his ornately decorated and absurdly delicate teacup, trying very hard to keep his eyes on her face. 'You do know that nobody ever found out who Jack the Ripper was, right? And I'm pretty sure we're here after he's already committed his last murder.'

'I don't think that will matter too much. I was thinking about this last night before I slept - I think the investigation itself probably won't be very important; I reckon it's more a means to an end, to get us where we're supposed to be. We're certainly not supposed to solve the murders, because, as you say, they weren't solved.'

'So you're saying that we should just keep an eye out for any clues to Quentin's whereabouts and activities while we investigate.'

Rachel nodded. 'Exactly.'

They both looked up as the maid came into the room. 'Excuse me, sir, but your carriage is here.'

'Thank you, Mary.'

They put on their overcoats and hats and went out into the clear and bitterly cold morning.

'Good morning, Sir Sam, Lady Rachel.' Geoff was standing in the front of the carriage wearing a police uniform and, now that there was light, Sam could see that he was tall, just over six foot, and well-built, with reddish hair and freckles, in his mid-twenties. He tipped his hat to them as they walked up to him, then opened the door for them.

'Thank you, Geoff, or should I call you "constable" now you're on duty?' Rachel asked.

'It's always Geoff for you, ma'am.' He said with a smile.

'Rachel, stop flirting with the man; you're married, remember?' said Sam with a smile.

Rachel laughed and allowed Geoff to hand her into the coach.

'I'm a married man, too, sir. Don't you worry.' Geoff said with a grin and a wink.

Sam laughed and got into the carriage.

The carriage briefly tipped drunkenly to one side as Geoff climbed up in front, then almost immediately jerked forward as the man flicked the reins and clicked his tongue at the horses.

The low winter sun gave the city a stark aspect, but it was very much the London they were used to, with the same familiar landmarks. Sam hadn't known where he was the night before, but he remembered now that the house was in the Pimlico area of London, less than a mile from Headquarters, and he started to recognise where they were only a short while later when they reached the Thames and he caught sight of the Houses of Parliament in the distance.

There were more people in the streets, away from the strictly residential areas, and he frowned as he watched them.

Rachel was also concerned. 'Have you noticed…?'

Sam nodded. 'Yes. Everybody seems so, I don't know, upset.'

Nobody seemed at all happy; they were downcast, withdrawn, dragging their feet as they made their way to work, or standing around in groups talking in hushed tones. Nowhere were there the sounds of lively conversation, or of children playing - the sounds that you normally heard even in the poorest of countries or shanty towns the world over.

They continued to study the people in silence and Sam wondered if it was just a local effect, that the people around the Houses of Parliament were there to protest about something, but things didn't get any better as they left the Palace of Westminster behind and headed down Whitehall towards Trafalgar Square.

They didn't have much time to contemplate the phenomenon any further, though, because they soon stopped and Geoff helped Rachel out, then led them inside police headquarters through the front entrance.

Inside, the main reception area was a riot of noise that contrasted sharply with the hushed atmosphere of the streets - there was a mob of people all clamouring for the attention of three harassed-looking constables behind a large desk and the pervading feeling was one of anger and frustration.

Geoff pushed his way through the crowd, shouting for people to make way and Sam and Rachel kept as close to him as possible, but often had to do some shoving of their own, receiving hostile looks and curses from many of the men and women in the mob in return.

Eventually they got to the other side of the room and Geoff held the door to the interior of the station open for them. 'Sorry, sir, I should have taken you in through the back.'

'That's quite alright, Geoff.' Sam turned to frown at the crowd. 'What's got everybody so riled up? It was the same on the streets - everyone looks very unhappy.'

Geoff closed the door before answering, cutting off most of the noise so that he could speak at a normal volume. 'There are a lot of hungry people living in awful conditions out there, sir, and they're all a bit fed up, especially with the government; they're not doing too well in nobody's mind right now.' He looked around to make sure that nobody could overhear him before continuing. 'But I think it's also got something to do with this business of Jack the Ripper; they're angry because they don't think they're safe on the streets anymore.'

Rachel smiled wryly. 'I don't think I would feel very safe if someone was murdering people on my doorstep and nobody had a clue who was doing it.' She looked at Geoff shrewdly. 'There's something else, though, isn't there.'

Geoff looked very reluctant to continue, but did. 'Well, ma'am, there's a lot of folk, coppers included, who don't think that we're doing everything we can to catch him. There are dozens of rumours flying around, some of them are a bit far-fetched of course, but others are just about believable enough for my liking. One such is that we already know who Jack is and don't want to bring him in because he's one of us or because he's one of the royal household or something. Another story is that Jack the Ripper is a Mason and that the Prime Minister himself is ordering us to cover it up because he's a Mason too...'

Sam leaned in and spoke quietly to him. 'Do you think that there might be any truth to any of that, Geoff?'

The big man thought very carefully before he answered. 'No, I don't think that any of the rumours are true, sir. But what I do know is that right now there are a lot of streets in this city where you don't want to be after dark and too many people who don't have a choice as to whether they are out in them. At the last count that anyone did we have more than a thousand prostitutes on the streets of London, because there just isn't any other work, and they are the ones that are getting attacked or killed. Every one of those women is someone's mother or sister or daughter and that makes for a lot of angry people that can turn into a mob very quickly.'

Sam nodded. Unfortunately a lot of what Geoff was saying made sense; he knew how people in a crisis could very easily blame whoever they felt were better off than they - his history books were full of examples. The people were resentful and the natural target for their anger was the government and in particular the men in it who lived in safety and luxury while they suffered. The situation on the streets was bad, therefore, and only being made worse by the rumour mill.

Geoff took Sam's nod as a signal that the conversation had finished and turned to go.

Sam allowed him to get a few steps ahead so that he could speak to Rachel without him hearing. 'I think I'm starting to get some kind of picture of what Quentin might be doing here; he could be trying to stir up some kind of social revolution using the discontent caused by the Jack the Ripper case. I just don't know why yet.'

Rachel nodded thoughtfully. 'You could be right. That would certainly explain why there are so many different rumours flying around; he's telling the people whatever gets them angry, tailoring the story to the audience.'

Geoff stopped at a door with a nameplate that read "Inspector Abberline" and waited for them to catch up before knocking.

'Come in!'

Geoff entered and stood to attention just inside. 'Sir Sam and Lady Vives, sir.'

'Very good, thank you constable. Dismissed.'

Geoff spun on his heels and gave them a nod and a smile before leaving the room.

Inspector Frederick George Abberline turned out to be a fairly short man with thinning hair and a bushy moustache. He was sitting behind a desk in a room that rivalled Andrew's flat in Barcelona for sheer untidiness with piles of paper on every surface and pinned to every wall.

Abberline hadn't looked up at them as they came in, but now he did, laying aside a tiny screwdriver that he had been using to tinker with a dismantled clock, which was laid out in front of him in pieces on a white cloth. He scrutinised them, spending more time examining Sam than he did Rachel, before he stood up and came around the desk.

He offered his hand for them to shake, then turned and sat back down behind his desk.

Sam and Rachel exchanged a glance; so far the man had not said a word to them and they were starting to wonder what was going on.

'First of all, please allow me to say that I did not request your help on this case; you were forced upon me by Commissioner Monro.' He looked at them sternly for a second before his face softened. 'Having said that I am very glad to accept any help on this case that I can get. I assume you saw the ruckus at the front desk?' They nodded. 'That is a scene that is repeated daily in every constabulary in this city. We need results and we need them quickly.'

Sam shared a look with Rachel. They both couldn't help but think about the fact that Jack the Ripper was never caught.

Thankfully, Abberline didn't see the look; he was once again engrossed in his clock and was putting it back together as he spoke. 'The constabulary faces a multitude of problems on a daily basis, but most of them can be handled easily by the men that we have - drunken brawls or thefts are well within our capabilities to resolve. This situation on the other hand is something entirely different.' He paused as he used a pair of incredibly thin tweezers to transfer cogs into the clock's mechanism, leaning over it with a lens in his eye to see it properly. Once the cogs were in place he lifted his head to peer at the two people in front of him. 'What we are seeing right now is civil unrest on a scale that has been previously unheard of. If it worsens any further then it will escalate beyond a matter for the police and will fall into the hands of the army and that is something that we are all desperate to avoid; it will mean a descent into chaos the likes of which have not been seen since the French had their little revolution. Heads will roll, literally as well as figuratively.'

He paused again and lifted the mechanism gently into the back of the clock. He closed it up and wound it. A gentle ticking noise started up. He held it close to his ear and closed his eyes, listening carefully. Nodding in satisfaction he placed it to one side on his desk, folded the cloth, then stood up. He motioned for them to join him at the wall to one side of the desk.

'Mine is a mind that is based on logic,' he gestured at the recently repaired clock. 'Cogs fit together to form a whole that ticks rhythmically. If a wedge falls into it then I remove it and make sure it works again. But this,' he tapped the wall. 'This defies every effort I have made to find a pattern and pull it apart. Perhaps you can make something of it.'

The wall was covered with pieces of paper, most of them hand-written notes, but among them was a map of London with red dots denoting the sites of the murders and about a dozen grainy but gruesome photos of the crime scenes.

'I have box after box of witness statements and relevant material next door but none of it is very useful. The so-called witnesses never actually saw anything, they just report hearing screams and every so often one of them describes a dark figure in a top hat and opera cloak carrying a small leather bag; nothing even remotely reliable.' He tapped an artist's representation - nothing more than the shape of a man, which could have been anyone.

Sam looked at the mess on the wall. It was going to take a lot of effort to sift through it all and get an idea of the case.

'Anyway, unless you have some objection, I thought we would take a tour of the crime scenes today - I always maintain that detective work is best done in person; you can never rely on the veracity of second-hand information.' Abberline went and got his hat and overcoat from the coat stand behind his desk. 'Oh, yes! Before I forget - Sir Charles Warren, the previous Commissioner, asked me to give you these.' He handed a small envelope to Sam. 'Tickets to the theatre tonight, seats in a private box. He said he would see you there. He resigned last month but still takes a personal interest in the case; he assigned me to it himself in fact. He wants to have a good look at you, apparently, see if Monro was right to bring you in.'

Sam opened the envelope and looked at the tickets, they were for an opera by Gilbert and Sullivan *The Yeomen of the Guard* at the Savoy Theatre.

Abberline went past them and opened the door to reveal Geoff patiently waiting outside.

'Constable Williams, bring the carriage round to the back door, please; we're going to the East End.'

'Right you are, sir.' Geoff saluted and immediately hurried away.

They followed in Geoff's wake at a rather more sedate pace, with Abberline leading them through a maze of corridors and staircases until they came to the back entrance, which was guarded by two large policemen. There were no crowds of clamouring people here and they were able to walk straight out and get into the carriage that Geoff already had waiting at the side of the road.

They spent the rest of the day touring the East End, going from crime scene to crime scene. The East End was an awful place, crowded and filthy, with straw strewn everywhere in an effort to absorb the horse droppings and sewage that was dumped into the streets. The smell was incredible and they found it hard to get enough air to breathe in the narrow gaps between ramshackle buildings.

There wasn't much to see at any of the scenes; each murder had taken place weeks or months before and all evidence had long since gone, but Abberline described each of them, showing them the position of the bodies and telling them of the wounds and any other details he could think of. Sam was particularly interested in the famous graffiti, cleaned away long ago, that had read "the Juwes are the men that will not be blamed for nothin", spelling mistakes and all; it seemed such an obvious attempt at diverting attention and blame, but was nonetheless diabolically clever in its near illiteracy and double negatives, which gave it so many different readings and left its true meaning completely unclear.

At first Rachel attempted to speak to the people they encountered in the surrounding neighbourhoods, wanting to get a feel for what life was like for them, but most of them took one look at her rich clothing and refused to talk to her. The few people she did manage to exchange a few words with clammed up completely as soon as they found out she was with the police and stared at her resentfully before slamming their door in her face or just walking away. Word seemed to spread that there were police around asking questions and she was soon getting some very hostile looks from everyone, so she gave up, not wanting to provoke anything.

The feelings of frustration and ire that Sam and Rachel had encountered on their ride to Scotland Yard and in the reception of Scotland Yard were far worse in the East End. The mood was almost tangible and the sense they got was almost the same as that of someone about to attack. There was never any actual violence, though, but it always seemed a very real possibility, like an explosive just waiting for a spark.

Abberline took them to lunch in a public house near Whitehall, one that was frequented by government ministers. It gave them a brief break from the overwhelming poverty and stench of the crime scenes but all too soon they had finished eating and were heading back into the East End to continue their tour.

The afternoon was much the same as the morning had been and when the day was done they were exhausted, but didn't want to go home; they were determined to take full advantage of their time in the past. They decided to go out for dinner before the theatre and asked Abberline to recommend somewhere. He did and the ended up in a wonderful French restaurant near the theatre, discussing their situation while they ate.

Seeing as it had been impossible to know where they had been Displacing to beforehand, they hadn't been able to prepare with pertinent knowledge before coming and consequently they couldn't be sure exactly how things were supposed to be at this time in London. However, they were pretty sure that there hadn't been any social revolutions in the city at this time and the one that was brewing had to be the work of an outside agency, probably Quentin. So, despite the fact that they knew the case itself was unsolvable, they both realised that staying on it was probably going to be the best way to find their enemy and helping Abberline might well prove to be the best way to stop him.

Once they had made up their minds to continue as they were, they decided to forget about the case and enjoy the rest of their meal and the night. They found it almost impossible to forget about the extreme poverty and misery that they had witnessed that day, though, and it had certainly cast a shadow over their dinner, but they were hoping that their visit to the theatre would serve to lift their spirits; it was Gilbert and Sullivan after all, which promised to be fun.

Sir Charles Warren, the previous Commissioner of the Metropolitan Police, was a perfect host to them for the evening in the theatre. He welcomed them with champagne and caviar, introduced them to his wife, Fanny, and settled them down for the evening in the best seats in his box. He was a jovial young man with an impressive moustache, although he looked rather haggard; his failure to catch Jack the Ripper had forced him to resign and obviously still caused him considerable worry.

The opera was wonderful, but it wasn't quite what they were expecting. *The Yeomen of the Guard*, they found out, was one of the more serious works of Gilbert and Sullivan with none of the topsy-turvy high jinks that were in most of their other operas and, on top of everything, it didn't end on a very happy note. The audience loved it but it left Rachel and Sam with a somewhat bitter aftertaste that suited the atmosphere in the city outside the theatre.

After the opera, Sir Charles took them to a nearby club where he had booked a small private room and they sat down over brandy to discuss the case. Sam accepted a drink and sipped at it carefully before wrinkling his nose and setting it aside, then stared at Rachel when she had the man fill her glass almost to the top and gulped down almost a quarter of it before relaxing back in her armchair.

Fanny took her leave of them and Sir Charles got down to business, pacing up and down the small room. 'Right! I'm off to Singapore soon; I'm going back to the army, but I wanted to make sure that Monro was getting things done. Your reputation precedes you, Sir Sam, as does yours, Lady Rachel, and I am confident that with both of you and Inspector Abberline on the case things will start to improve.' He became very serious and leaned forward in his seat. 'I told Abberline that I wanted to inspect you myself but that wasn't exactly true; I wanted to make sure that you were aware of the political ramifications of this case. Abberline is a fine detective but a very straightforward one with a defined methodology, it comes of his being a clockmaker before joining the police; everything has to fit together neatly for him. He is therefore quite innocent of the twisted workings of politics and how it will affect his job, and unfortunately this case has long since ceased to be purely about the murders and has become a symbol for much more - it is being used as a rallying cry for change, for revolution even and has spread from the East End like a cancer and has quickly become something with national significance.'

He stopped pacing to sit down armchair opposite them and spoke earnestly, leaning forwards in his seat. 'This case is causing civil unrest and a feeling of resentment among the people. It is turning them against the current Conservative government and in return the people themselves are suffering as the government turns away from them. Something *has* to be done and fast, before everything spirals out of control and unrest turns into open violence.' He paused and looked at them expectantly. 'Do you think you can help us, Sir Sam?'

Sam racked his brain for something to tell him, wanting to reassure him; it was obvious Sir Charles only had the interests of the people and the nation at heart. 'As you know we have only just come onto the case, but I believe we may have a… a *unique perspective* on things that will allow us to contribute in a meaningful manner to its resolution, or at least return it to its status as purely a murder case.' Which was perfectly true, if it was Quentin behind the increasing unrest.

Rachel patted Sam on the hand as if to say "well done" and Sir Charles nodded, satisfied with his answer. 'I cannot ask for anything more.' He raised his glass in salute. 'I think more brandy is in order and I'll call for cigars, would you join me, Sir Sam?'

Sam paled at the idea of smoking, but fortunately Rachel came to his rescue. 'Darling, you're not supposed to smoke, remember? Doctor's orders.'

'Oh, right, of course! I'd forgotten. I'm sorry, Sir Charles, but as my ever-loving wife points out I have been forbidden the pleasure of tobacco.'

'Pity! Oh well, just another brandy then!' Sir Charles rang a tiny bell that was on a table next to him and a butler promptly appeared and refilled their glasses. Once they were alone again Sir Charles stood and raised his glass. 'The Queen!'

Thankfully, the protocol for various situations, such as this one, was something that Andrew had drummed into him over the summer in the interminable gaps between Displacements and he stood to echo Sir Charles' words. 'The Queen!' before sipping at his drink.

Rachel, of course, remained sitting for the toast and once again took a large mouthful of brandy.

The rest of the evening passed very pleasantly. There were more toasts and quite a lot of laughter as they discussed the opera and other Gilbert and Sullivan works, which Sam and Rachel found recollections of in their memories.

When it was time to go Sir Charles got the club to arrange a Hansom cab for them - Geoff was off duty by then of course and they hadn't allowed him to wait around for them when he'd offered. They had planned to go to Displacer Headquarters after work, but it was far too late and they were both very tired, so they decided to leave it for the next day and Sam asked the driver to take them home.

They got into the back of the cab and Rachel stumbled and all but fell on top of Sam, more than a little tipsy. He wrapped his arms around her and looked down at her fondly as she giggled gently and unsuccessfully tried to right herself.

They had often spoken about their childhoods while on their long runs in the hills above Barcelona and he knew that Rachel had come from a much rougher background than him. Her mother always had a drink in her hand and naturally Rachel had followed her example - she and her school friends had regularly sneaked bottles of whatever they could pilfer out of their parents' houses and had gotten drunk in the local park on the weekends. When she had joined the Displacers she had put most of her wild behaviour behind her, but she still drank with the members at Society dinners and confessed to having an occasional beer at home. Sam on the other hand had only ever had the occasional small glass of *cava* with his family to toast with during meals until he started Displacing - he had had a few cups of sake with Master Hamato in Okinawa and some cognac and wine with Jacques in France - but even then he had never gotten properly drunk.

Her upbringing had been so different to his, so much rougher, that he was sometimes amazed that they got on so well and it had occurred to him that she should by all rights be helping Rafa bully him.

Rachel's head cleared quickly in the night air and soon she was sitting up by herself, which disappointed Sam a little because he had been enjoying her leaning against him.

She took a few deep breaths and her eyes focussed on him. 'It was good, what you said to Sir Charles.'

'And it was true; if we stop Quentin, things should start to improve immediately, even if we don't solve the Jack the Ripper case. The only thing that worries me is *whether* we can stop him; we can't even find him.'

'Finding him is the hard part, after that it should be fairly easy. We have a distinct advantage over Quentin; he can only affect his changes indirectly, whereas we can be as direct as we want in dealing with him.'

Sam frowned. 'You mean kill him? I don't think I could...'

She had a very hard look in her eyes and was almost angry as she continued. 'Have you forgotten what he did to Susan?'

'No, of course not...'

She cut him off abruptly, colder than she had ever been with him before. 'She was family, Sam, to both of us - your aunt and the wife of my uncle - and he killed her with his own hands! But she's not the only one who is dead; his organisation has been responsible for other deaths over the years. And I'm not just talking about Displacers; the changes they've made in the time-line have destroyed the lives of so many people. If we don't stop him he will destroy the time-line as we know

it, so we *cannot* baulk at killing him if the opportunity presents itself...
He certainly won't if he gets his hands on us!'

Sam couldn't quite believe what she was saying. 'Could you really
do it? Could you kill him?'

Some of the anger went out of her face as she looked away, refusing
to meet his eyes and when she spoke again it was with a very quiet
voice. 'If it was him or me... Or you... Then yes, I could. I would.
Definitely.'

Sam fell silent. He wasn't sure what to think; he really couldn't see
Rachel as a killer, couldn't see himself as a killer either, but Quentin
had made it very clear on various occasions that he didn't have the
same qualms about it as they did.

He was prevented from saying anything more by the cab coming to
a halt and he looked up to find that they were already outside their
house. He got out and offered Rachel his hand. She took it and he
helped her step down to the pavement, not nearly as unsteady as she
had been before.

He paid the driver and watched the cab drive off into the growing
fog before turning to the house.

He took only a single step before he froze in horror.

A man was standing behind Rachel, holding her against him with
one arm around her neck. His other hand held a long knife to her side.

'Sorry about this, guv, but I'm going to need your money.' There
was a scarf wrapped around the man's head just below his eyes, hiding
his face, and it muffled his voice, but they clearly hear the unhealthy
rasp that it had.

For a second Sam had thought that Quentin had found them and
that they had already lost, but when the man spoke he realised that they
were just unfortunate enough to be the target of a mugging. He sighed,
relieved, which was a very strange thing to feel when the woman he
loved was being threatened at knifepoint.

Sam ignored the man and spoke to Rachel. 'Are you alright?'

'I'm fine, Sam.' There was clear confidence in her voice; they both
knew that she could easily take the knife away from the man, he just
wondered why she hadn't.

He took a closer look at the man - it was a very cold night but the
man didn't have an overcoat. He was wearing trousers and a jacket that
looked very thin and hung on his frame as if he were just a skeleton.
Newspaper stuck out of the toes of his shoes where the sole had come
away from the leather and he was filthy. He was coughing every few
seconds and the hand that held the knife was shaking slightly.

'Sam, get out your wallet.'

Sam emptied the contents of his wallet into his hand and held it out to her. There were only a few coins - he had found a large sheath of banknotes in his bedroom that morning, but he had only taken a few pounds with him and they had spent most of it on lunch and dinner.

Rachel took the money from him and looked at it. 'There's not much here, it will only feed you for a few days.' She held the coins up to him and he released her neck to snatch them.

Sam's heart leapt, his adrenaline surging and he shifted his weight forwards to the balls of his feet, ready to help her, but she again didn't take the clear opportunity to overpower and disarm the man.

The man started to back away. 'I really am sorry, guv, but me family are starving.'

He turned, about to run, but Rachel called out to him. 'We have more money inside! And food! Perhaps you could take some with you for your family?'

Sam frowned. 'Rachel…'

She held up her hand to stop him from saying anything more.

The knife wavered in the man's hand and he coughed. 'What are you two? Some kind of religious nuts?'

Rachel laughed. 'Far from it! Let's just say that we don't like what we're seeing in London these days and want to do something about it if we can.'

The hand with the knife dropped a couple of inches as the man hesitated, then it went down and stayed down. 'You're not going to call the police on me?'

It was Sam's turn to laugh. 'We *work* for the police!' He saw the alarm in the man's eyes, the knife twitching upwards again, and instantly tried to put him at ease. 'But you have my word that you may leave unharmed at any time. Please, come inside, we have more food than we know what to do with.'

The man finally agreed to go with them, but refused to enter, insisting that he was too dirty for such a "lovely domicile" as he put it. He remained in the hallway, standing on the doormat, shifting from foot to foot nervously and trying not to touch anything.

Mary was still awake so Rachel sent her to package up some food from the kitchen while Sam went upstairs to get some more money for the man.

As soon as Sam had gone and they were alone, Rachel smiled at the man, trying to put him at ease, then gently began to ask him questions.

It seemed like the man felt that he owed her at least a few answers for attacking her and after only a little prodding he opened up - it turned out that his name was Bert and he was trying to survive in the Stepney area with a wife and a baby. 'We're not well, none of us. If we're lucky it's coffin houses for fourpence if we got it, two penny hangover if we don't, which is most nights. I wouldn't normally do nuffin like this, ma'am, but I was desperate like, the baby's got cholic...'

Rachel hushed him. 'There's no need to explain; we've seen what the situation is like in the East End. Scotland Yard just brought us onto the Jack the Ripper case and we're going to be doing what we can to help.'

The man looked doubtful but nodded anyway.

Sam came back and handed Bert a spare coat and a couple of old blankets that he had found in a cupboard, which made the man's face light up in joy. He then gave him the ten pounds he had peeled off the pile of notes in his room, which made Bert hang his head in shame.

'I'm so sorry, sir, I...'

'Never mind, what's done is done. If you still feel bad about it when you get home you can use some of the money to feed a few of your friends. Tell them that Sir Sam and Lady Rachel, as well as Scotland Yard, see their plight and are doing what they can.'

'I will, sir, I swear.'

Rachel spoke up. 'Now, Bert, you can do something for us.'

His face lit up at the chance to redeem himself at least a little and he looked up at her. 'Anything, ma'am!'

'We're looking for someone, his name is Quentin Price, he's a...'

'Oh, I know him well, ma'am.'

Rachel shared a surprised look with Sam; they couldn't believe it was true, or their luck if it was.

'Really?' asked Sam.

'Oh, yes, sir, ma'am, he's a regular round the East End, always making speeches, and stirring up trouble.'

Sam nodded, that sounded like him, but he needed to be certain. 'Are you sure his name is Quentin Price?'

'Quite sure, sir. Shifty young man he is, got a strange way of talking about him. Keeps using words that nobody understands but sound impressive, if you know what I mean. Eyes never resting in one place, but always lookin' around like he's worried someone's after him. Doesn't like it if anyone talks back, gets very angry if they do.' Something occurred to him suddenly. 'Oh, and he's always got a woman with him, right looker with red hair, if you'll pardon me, ma'am.' He touched his fingers to his forehead and nodded to Rachel in apology. 'Goes by the name of Breech or Bark or some such. Always stands behind him when he speaks out but never says a word. Got a lovely smile but a vicious temper - might be Irish, but I've never heard her speak. I have seen her break a man's finger who got too close to her, though. Word of that got around, I can tell you, and nobody even looks at her no more.'

'Diana Birch.'

Bert's face lit up in recognition. 'That'll be her, sir! Birch! Yes! She's always with him and there's two big buggers, oh, sorry, excuse me ma'am, big blighters, a man and a woman, who I think are hired protection. Look like they're brother and sister maybe.'

Rachel shared a look with Sam; Quentin had them outnumbered. 'The Twins.'

Sam nodded and Rachel turned back to continue questioning Bert. 'Where exactly have you seen these people?'

'It was in a pub near the docks,' he looked ashamed again. 'I had a couple of extra pennies after getting some work and stopped in for a drink with me mate to celebrate. They were there, preaching to the crowd, like, telling them that it was the government's fault that they are in such a bad shape and that the police are covering up Jack the Ripper's real identity. That's the only time I've seen them and by all accounts they go from place to place, talking to different people every night.'

Rachel reached out and touched the man on the arm. 'Thank you, Bert. You've been a great help to us.

He looked down at her hand in shock, an expression that quickly changed to gratitude at her treating him like a human being, the beginnings of a tear in his eye. 'Don't mention it, ma'am.'

'Please send us a message if you know where Quentin is going to speak; we need to find him.'

'Right-o ma'am.'

Mary arrived with a large parcel of food which she gave to Rachel with a disapproving look at Bert.

Rachel ignored her and handed it over to the now burdened man. 'Thank you, Bert.'

'God bless, ma'am, sir. Goodnight and God bless.'

He backed out of the door, trying to carry his packages and bow at the same time.

Sam waved with a smile. 'Good night, Bert. Take care.' He closed the door, trying to spare the man as much embarrassment as possible.

Rachel dismissed Mary for the night, then she and Sam went into the sitting room where the maid had started a fire for them.

They stood together, hand in hand, in front of the fire, warming themselves and gazing into the flames.

'Well, he's not alone.' said Rachel.

'But this time neither am I.' He smiled at her.

CHAPTER 14
FAMILIAR GROUND

The next day Abberline kept them at Scotland Yard and they started wading through the case files. They were filled with photos, maps, medical reports, the reports from the officers who had discovered the bodies and all of the witness statements. Everything was handwritten, of course, and it was very tiring trying to decipher reports that were either illegible, incomprehensible or both. Even so, they slowly began to get a clearer picture of why Jack the Ripper was so hard to track down; beyond his victims and the methods he used to kill his victims there was no other pattern, no way to predict what he was going to do next and no possible way of identifying him from the often contradictory statements.

They were both keen to go looking for Quentin as soon as possible, now that they had found out what he was doing, but they knew that going into the East End and searching the public houses for any sign of him would be time consuming and probably pointless given the sheer amount of drinking places there were in the rough area. They couldn't enlist the help of Abberline and the police either, because they had no evidence against Quentin, no reason for them to arrest him yet - although, if they could get a few more people like Bert to come forward and tell their stories they thought that maybe they could bring him in under incitement to riot or something. That was unlikely, though, considering the reluctance of the people to talk to the police, so their best course of action was to hope that Bert would be able to help them track Quentin down before too long and continue to work on the case with Abberline and stay around Scotland Yard, just in case he slipped up.

In the meantime, they still felt that it was a good idea to go to Displacer HQ, not only because the Society might be able to help them in their search, but also they needed to warn them about the rogue Displacers in their time-line. So, as soon as they left the Yard at the end of the day, Geoff took them to the house in Belgravia in the police buggy.

They stood on the pavement looking at the house. Aside from the gas lighting it was more or less identical to the one they knew. The road hadn't changed very much either, the only difference being that the wall around the Buckingham Palace gardens opposite didn't have the barbed wire across the top that it did in the present.

They went up the steps and stood in front of the door.

Sam took a deep breath. 'So, how do we do this?'

Rachel shook her head and smiled wryly. 'You really do have to start learning the basics, Sam; we have had a protocol in place for exactly this kind of circumstance for almost two hundred years. Just watch and learn, noob.' She rang the bell, a pull chord by the door that also wasn't there in the present version of the house, and a bell jangled inside.

After a few seconds the door opened and a dark-haired young man in a butler's livery looked down his nose at them. 'Yes? May I help you?'

Rachel looked up at him. 'Sorry to disturb you, but have you got the time?'

The man's eyebrow raised a few millimetres - the only thing that betrayed his surprise. He stepped aside and held the door for them. 'Please come in.'

They stepped inside and he closed the door behind them.

'Wait here, please.' He left them in the hallway and disappeared into the lounge.

While they were waiting Sam turned to Rachel and raised an eyebrow. '"Have you got the time?" Really?'

She grinned. 'Yes.'

Sam shook his head and chucked. 'Very subtle.'

The butler didn't come back, instead a man in his early forties appeared. He was dressed in a rough suit and trousers that looked a bit out of place in the refined surroundings of the Displacer house. 'It is a quarter to six.' His accent was as unrefined as his clothing; he sounded more like he belonged in the slums with Bert than in a place which had a butler and silverware everywhere.

Rachel smiled her winning smile. 'Thank you, but that isn't our time.'

The man took a deep breath and nodded. 'That may be so, miss, but I'm afraid I still can't let you in.' He indicated for them to leave.

Rachel refused to move and her brow creased in puzzlement. 'Why not, may I ask? I thought that hospitality to other Displacers was part of the tenets of the Society.'

The man nodded and his expression hardened. 'Normally so, but we have been warned of rogue elements in our time-line so the normal rules have been temporarily suspended by the Council of Elders. Please, don't make a fuss.'

Sam and Rachel shared a look, understanding immediately that Quentin had beaten them to it.

Rachel was crestfallen and she turned to go but Sam put his hand out to stop her.

'Would you be Abraham Hudson by any chance?'

The man nodded, his eyes widening in surprise. 'Yes, that's me, do I know you, sir?'

'Unfortunately not, but I know of you, sir I have read the accounts of your experiments with Everett Lloyd.' The man couldn't help but shoot a glance upwards towards the library where such books were kept and Sam nodded. 'Yes, I have had access to those diaries, because I'm afraid you have been hoodwinked - we are the true Displacers while the people you have met, Quentin Price and Diana Birch represent the "rogue element" as you so rightly put it.'

It was amazing how the pompous vocabulary just flowed off the tongue in this time-line - perhaps the next time he had dinner with Oscar Wilde he wouldn't be struck so speechless.

Rachel looked at him, suitable impressed. Abraham, however, wasn't easily convinced. Sam saw this and continued quickly. 'Come to think of it, you don't know me, but you know my family. My great-grandfather is James Hudson.' Abraham's eyes widened slightly. 'And you, I believe are his great-grandfather.'

Rachel could see that the man was wavering and she decided to deliver the coup de grace. 'Quentin's education in Displacer matters was sorely lacking and Diana had no connection with us whatsoever, so I am assuming that neither of them was able to provide any kind of inside knowledge. In fact I'm willing to bet that Quentin just went straight to his ancestor here in order to gain admission, Lord Price isn't it? Did he even know the proper protocols? We, however, are more than willing to answer any question you care to ask,' she paused and shot a scathing glance at Sam. 'Although Mr Vives here is rather new to us and hasn't been doing his homework very conscientiously.'

'Hey!' Sam feigned annoyance, but grinned at her.

Abraham had been listening carefully but it seemed to be the *way* they were saying things rather than *what* they were saying that eventually convinced him and he grinned at their joking around before looking intently at Sam. 'So, you're my great great great… I don't know, maybe another great, grandson?'

Sam grinned and nodded. 'I am.'

'Very pleased to meet you!' He shook Sam's hand vigorously with a hand that was more calloused than Rachel's and obviously used to physical labour. 'I knew there was something off about that Price fellow right from the start, but I couldn't say anything with his high and mighty Lordship there.' He rolled his eyes then turned to Rachel. 'And are you Mrs Vives?'

'He wishes.' She chuckled, digging Sam in the ribs with her elbow. 'No, we're only married in this time-line.' She offered her hand and Abraham bent to kiss it instead of shaking it.

'Come on in. I'll have some tea brought, unless you prefer something stronger?'

Rachel smiled. 'Tea will be fine, thank you.'

Sam groaned silently; tea, it was always tea everywhere - it seemed to be a common denominator wherever and whenever there was another Displacer.

They sat down in the lounge and the butler brought the drinks. They remained silent while he poured and offered biscuits and cake, then, when he was gone, Rachel became serious.

'I'm sorry to get straight down to business, but we have to know urgently: do you know where Quentin Price is?' She turned around and looked at the door as if he was going to walk in. 'Are you expecting him?'

'No, he's out of the city with Lord Price at his country mansion, they're shooting pheasant I believe.'

Rachel laughed. 'I think the birds are going to be fairly safe then; Quentin was always a bloody awful shot!'

'Lord Price isn't very good either, by all accounts.'

'Do you know when they will be back?'

Abraham shook his head. 'Lord Price isn't in the habit of letting us know his whereabouts. He was hardly the most reliable of Displacers and as an Elder he is not much better.'

Sam looked at Rachel. 'Shall we take a trip into the country?'

Rachel shook her head. 'It would be better if we tackle him in London rather than at the estate of a Lord who will probably have guards and obviously has access to arms. Here we have the police to back us up if we need it.'

'Good thinking.'

Rachel turned back to Abraham. 'So, Quentin has had access to the Society.'

'Yes.'

Sam started suddenly as something occurred to him. 'Has he gone into the attic?'

Abraham was briefly surprised at the question. 'The attic? Oh, right, yes, of course you'd know about the attic. No, he hasn't been up there.'

Rachel turned to Sam. 'One of those rules that you should know about is that *nobody* is allowed access to the attic except members of the Society from the *current* time-line.'

Abraham nodded. 'The theory is that if somebody needs something from up there, then they can get it in their own time-line.'

Rachel took back over. 'And if it's information they want, they can always ask an Elder.'

Sam nodded. 'Right... But Quentin doesn't have access to the attic back in our time, does he?'

Rachel looked at him in shock. 'Of course...' she turned to Abraham. 'Mr Hudson, you have to make sure that Quentin does not get access to the attic or have Lord Price get anything from it for him.'

'And if you can keep him from the Society, so much the better,' said Sam.

Abraham sighed. 'It is hard to stop Lord Price from doing anything if he gets it in his mind to do it, but I will talk to the others and try to get them to agree. I'm fairly sure that we'll be able to stay firm against him this time, especially if Sir Andrew is on my side; keeping the attic sacrosanct is one of our most important rules after all.'

'Thank you.'

Sam raised an eyebrow, 'Sir Andrew?'

'Sir Andrew Berry, he's a cabinet minister and one of our more prominent active Displacers.'

Sam looked at Rachel. 'One of Andrew's ancestors do you think?'

Rachel nodded, 'I guess so. I think I remember Andrew mentioning once that he was named after a famous ancestor of his who was quite high up in government. Andrew is a family name or something.'

Abraham was watching the exchange. 'Am I missing something important?'

'I don't think so,' said Sam. 'Just that my mentor is also named Andrew Berry.'

Abraham smiled and nodded. 'Just more proof that Displacing is in the genes.' He stood up. 'I apologise, but I really have to be going, my wife is expecting another child and I should be there to look after her.'

'Congratulations!'

'Thank you.'

They stood up with him and he preceded them to the front door and opened it himself, not bothering to call the butler.

Sam shook his hand again. 'We'll call in every evening, if you don't mind; we really need to get a hold of Quentin as soon as he gets back.'

'I'm here most days; I'm busy cataloguing the library at the moment, but if I can't be here, then I'll have one of the other members wait for you - I'll fill them in on any developments beforehand.'

'Thank you.'

They said goodbye and went out. Night had fallen with the rapidity of winter while they had been inside and the mist was rising, starting to obscure the street - the wall opposite was barely visible.

Geoff was waiting patiently for them a newspaper open on his lap. He put it to one side and jumped down to open the door of the carriage for them with a smile.

Rachel smiled back at him. 'Thank you for waiting, Geoff.'

'My pleasure, ma'am. Sir.'

Sam nodded. 'Home, please, Geoff.'

'Right you are, sir.'

They settled into the carriage and drove off into the darkness.

CHAPTER 15
THINGS THAT GO BUMP IN THE NIGHT

Several nights later, after days of monotony looking through files at Scotland Yard, waiting for news of Quentin that never came, something finally happened.

Sam was dragged out of a deep sleep and a pleasant dream of Okinawan waterfalls and secluded forest lakes at the insistence of a hand shaking him by the shoulder and the voice of Mary, hissing in his ear.

'Sir! Sir!'

Sam rolled onto his back and looked up into the maid's face, visible in the gentle glow of the lantern she was carrying. The rest of the room was pitch black - dawn, it seemed was still hours away.

'Sir!'

Sam shook away the last vestiges of sleep. 'I'm awake, I'm awake.' He sat up, rubbing his eyes. 'What is it Mary?'

'There's two men at the door, sir. Your nice policeman driver and that scruffy man from the other night.' Her expression was disapproving when she mentioned Bert. 'He's probably been caught stealing something. I don't know why you brought him into the house the other night, sir, all you did was let him see the silverware. He's probably had his eye...'

'Yes, thank you, Mary. Tell them I'm coming, please. And put the kettle on.'

'Right you are, sir.' Mary left the lantern on the bedside table for him and hurried out of the room.

Something was up and the odds were that it wouldn't be what Mary thought; Sam doubted that Geoff would have brought Bert round in the middle of the night if he didn't have a good reason and a simple theft could easily have waited until morning.

He leaned over to poke Rachel - after the first night alone in separate rooms, they had realised how silly they were being and had taken to sleeping in the same bed.

'Wasshappening?' Rachel was barely awake. She rolled over and blinked up at him, having trouble focusing. 'What time is it?'

Sam got out of bed and carried the lantern across the room. He picked up his pocket watch from the dressing table and flipped it open to peer at the hands. 'It's two-thirty.'

Rachel grumbled and turned over, burying her face in the pillow again. Her voice was muffled. 'I'm going to beat you up if you wake me again.'

Sam grinned at her back and put on a dressing gown. 'Does that go for Bert and Geoff as well? They're waiting downstairs - I think there might be a lead on Quentin.'

There was a second of silence from Rachel, then a sudden growl. She flipped over angrily and threw back the covers. 'OK, I'm coming. But you can go see what they want; I'm getting dressed before I come down.'

Sam raised an eyebrow and smirked, looking her up and down. Rachel didn't wear very much in bed, neither of them did; the nightwear in the Victorian era was just too silly for them. 'I'm glad; you wouldn't want to give them a heart attack.' He chuckled at the dirty look she gave him. 'Find me some clothes as well, please; I have a feeling we're going to be going out.'

He managed to duck behind the door just in time to have it block the pillow she had thrown at him.

Geoff and Bert were waiting in the hallway, just inside the front door. They looked up at him as he came down the stairs towards them. They both had sheepish looks on their faces, but Sam also got a sense of urgency from them - it was a curious mix.

Geoff was in civilian clothes, not his uniform, and he held a flat cap in front of him as he spoke. 'Beggin' your pardon for waking you, sir, but it is quite important.'

'That's quite all right, constable.' He looked from one man to the other, curiously. Obviously Bert wasn't under arrest and by their attitudes it looked like they knew each other.

Seeing Sam's confusion, Bert chimed in. 'Geoff and I are mates, sir, we grew up together in Spitalfields and we're neighbours of a sort now. When I can find lodgings, of course. Which I can now, thanks to you, sir.' He touched his forehead and bobbed his head in gratitude for Sam's earlier generosity. His face and hair was cleaner than they had been, but he still looked thin and didn't quite fill the cheap, but clean, suit that he was wearing. His appearance had changed a lot, but he was still recognisable as the man that he and Rachel had helped after he had tried to rob them at knife point.

'You're more than welcome, as I've said before. Now, what can I do for you?'

The policeman in Geoff took over and he straightened up, almost to attention to make his report. 'Well, sir, there's been a bit of a disturbance tonight near where we live; a man has torn up the place, causing a lot of damage and terrifying the honest folk who live there.'

'Made an awful racket he did, breaking windows and chucking stuff around.' Bert put in.

Geoff nodded. 'He hit anyone that came within reach of them, knocked out a few men who tried to take him down - big lads they were, from down the docks, but he didn't even break his stride. Last we saw him he had broken into a warehouse and he was still in there when we came here. I've got a couple of off-duty coppers, who live in the area, keeping an eye on things, but I'd rather get him under arrest sooner rather than later.'

Sam was puzzled, he wasn't quite sure why they were telling him this, but before he could ask he was interrupted by Mary's arrival. She handed pewter mugs of tea to the two men but gave Sam a china cup. 'I've got some breakfast cooking, sir, if you want it?'

'Could you make us some bacon sandwiches, please, Mary.' Both of the visitors looked up and nodded in greeting to Rachel as she swept down the stairs.

'Yes, ma'am.' Mary hurried away to comply with Rachel's request.

'So, gentlemen, you seem to have a spot of bother. Why have you come to us for help? Surely there are others more qualified?'

'I was just about to ask that,' muttered Sam under his breath into his tea cup, annoyed with how bright and cheerful Rachel could be immediately on waking up. She looked fresh, wide awake, while he was barely conscious - it was a talent of hers, learnt, she said, during her time with the SAS.

'Don't talk with your mouth full, darling.' Rachel ruffled Sam's already messy hair and smiled sweetly at him, fully aware of how grumpy he was when deprived of sleep.

Sam glared back at her playfully, only slightly meaning it.

'Well, ma'am, it's like this,' Geoff said, reluctantly. 'The people at the yard won't like being disturbed for this sort of thing and most coppers won't go into the East End at this time of night. I was going to leave things be, turn a blind eye, like, but then Bert here told me of your kindness to him and said he thought that you would be amenable to help me take down this monster.'

'Monster?' asked Sam.

Geoff winced. 'Yes, sir. The man in question is over seven foot tall and built like a brick shi...' He stopped and looked at Rachel, who raised an eyebrow with a grin and waited for him to finish. 'Um... he was a very heavyset man, ma'am.'

She chuckled at his quick change of language. 'In that case I understand you not wanting to tackle him on your own. We'd better come with you.'

'Thank you, ma'am.'

Mary arrived with a tray full of food.

Geoff took a sandwich and put his empty mug on the tray, receiving a warm smile from her in return. 'I have the coach outside waiting, sir. If you don't mind I'll go see to the horses.' He went outside.

'Help yourself, Bert, take as many as you want,' said Sam as he passed a sandwich to Rachel before grabbing one for himself.

'Much obliged, sir, much obliged.' Bert completely emptied the plate of sandwiches under the scowling gaze of Mary, biting into one and putting the rest in a handkerchief, thankfully clean, for his family.

'Could you get some more tea please, Mary?' asked Rachel, taking Bert's drained mug from him and passing it to her.

'Yes, ma'am.' Mary curtseyed, giving Bert another scowl as she left.

Rachel turned to Bert and her voice dropped until it was almost a whisper. 'What's this really all about, Bert? You wouldn't come and bother us if it wasn't important.'

Sam looked at Rachel in surprise; it hadn't occurred to him that there was some other motive behind the visit.

Rachel saw the look and patted him on the arm with a smile. 'Don't worry, darling, you'll catch up eventually.' She turned back to Bert.

'Well, ma'am, this bloke who's tearing up the place, well, I thought he looked a lot like one of those two bruisers. Y'know - the ones who were always hanging around with the Price chap you was looking for.'

Sam and Rachel exchanged a look. If this really was one of the Twins then catching him and locking him up would be a big step in the right direction. At the very least he would be forced to go home, leaving Quentin with one less bodyguard.

'I'll go and get dressed.' Sam ran upstairs.

After a minute or so Rachel joined him in the bedroom. 'You have considered that this might be a trap, right?'

Sam smiled at her as he pulled up his trousers and tucked his shirt in. 'Of course, but if it is, springing it will be the quickest way for us to get closer to Quentin. And anyway, it could be a bit of fun.'

Rachel shook her head but smiled at him. 'One of these days you and I are going to have to have a serious conversation about what is fun and what is just plain dangerous.'

'Looking forward to it.' He grinned and grabbed his coat and together they ran down the stairs and out into the night.

Half an hour later they were in Spitalfields. It was one of the roughest areas of London and the warehouse was only a couple of streets away from where one of the Jack the Ripper murders had taken place.

The two off-duty policemen Geoff had left on lookout confirmed that the thug hadn't come out of the front entrance or the rear, where the goods were loaded and unloaded. They also said that they had heard shouting and crashing noises occasionally as he found something to destroy inside, the last time only minutes before.

Sam thanked them and, their job done, the men nodded and slinked away, apparently not wanting any further part in the affair.

Geoff sighed at his colleagues' cowardice and looked shamefacedly at the Displacers.

Rachel patted him on the shoulder. 'It's fine; we'll be more than enough to stop this man and prevent anybody else getting hurt.'

She took Sam's hand in hers and they turned together to examine the warehouse, a large rundown brick building. Hazy in the fog and lit up by the almost full moon it looked sinister, like something from a low-budget horror movie, and it just screamed at them not to go in. The building was normally used to store fabric, but times were hard and it was apparently more than half empty at the moment. The huge main door was lying broken and discarded on the street; it had been completely torn from its hinges when the man had forced his way in.

'Come on then, let's go get him.' Sam steeled himself and tried to sound confident, but he wasn't fooling anyone, let alone himself; the way the door had been so roughly treated spoke to the man's strength and, if he was indeed one of Quentin's bodyguards, then he could very well have the skills to go with it. Or worse, he might be armed.

They stepped over the remains of the door and into the absolute darkness of the warehouse. Bert and Geoff had lanterns with them, but the pool of the light they shed only illuminated the nearest bundles of cloth and seemed to make what was beyond seem even darker and more threatening. As their eyes adjusted slightly they saw that there were pile after pile of the bundles of cloth creating a maze. There was no way of telling which way the man had gone, so Sam motioned for Geoff and Bert to go one way while he and Rachel took Bert's lantern from him and went another.

They started walking slowly through the warehouse. It was nerve-wracking; the cloth was stacked haphazardly in uneven piles and in the dim light of the lantern each and every one seemed to take on the hunched shape of a man about to attack.

Sam found himself jumping at shadows and jerking his head from side to side continuously. Rachel, though, seemed completely calm, moving silently and confidently, seemingly prepared for anything, and he tried to take strength from her.

'So, is there anything else you can tell me about the Twins? They've been mentioned a couple of times, but I don't really know anything about them.' Sam whispered, trying to take his mind off the danger of the situation.

'Tristan and Tessa are from an extremely rough neighbourhood in Liverpool. John's software flagged them as possible Displacers, but by the time Andrew and your grandfather got to them Quentin had already turned up and recruited them - we recognised his description from their mother. We don't know much more about them beyond their names; they completely disappeared off the radar. That was a couple of years ago and the only time they've been spotted since was in Egypt a few weeks ago, when Andrew saw them at the temple you discovered.'

'So basically we know they're big, strong and Liverpudlians… That's not exactly going to help much, unless we only want to make fun of their accents.'

Rachel was going to answer, but they both stopped when there was a creak as someone moved, someone heavy. They stood stock still, listening, waiting for the sound to come again.

'Don't you think it would be a good idea if we turned off the lantern?' hissed Sam.

'Shh!'

There was a rustling sound and another creak, but they were still unable to pinpoint where they had come from because the bundles of cloth around them deadened any echoes. However, they were followed shortly by a deep grunt which clearly came from above them.

They looked up.

It was only their reflexes, honed through years of training, which saved their lives.

They threw themselves to the sides, away from each other, barely evading the huge bale of fabric that thudded to the ground where they had been standing.

There was a whooshing sound and a sudden sensation of heat in the freezing air; the lamp had smashed and flames were spreading across the floor towards the cloth.

Geoff and Bert came rushing up, attracted by the noise and the light. They skidded to a halt, staring at the flames and the two detectives, lying on the ground.

'Are you…?' Geoff started to ask, but Sam interrupted him as he leapt to his feet.

'He's above us. You two make sure this place doesn't burn down. Come on Rachel!'

In the sudden light of the flames he had spotted a large shadow hunched over on a catwalk high above them, watching them. There was a ladder leading to it leaning against one wall and, closely followed by Rachel, he raced towards it.

'You there! Stop! This is the police!' Sam called out as he ran and was mortified when he heard Rachel laugh from beside him.

'Really, Sam?'

'It's what they say in the films and I thought… oh, never mind, just run…'

They were almost at the ladder when it came crashing to the floor, again forcing them to leap to the side.

The dark figure above them laughed and shook its fist; the man had beaten them to the ladder and unhooked it from its supports. He shouted something incoherent at them and ran along the catwalk towards a window just under the roof.

'I didn't get that, was that a Liverpool accent? I'm not very good with English accents.'

'Now is not the time, Sam. You take the low road, I'll take the high road.'

Rachel ran towards the nearest pile of cloth and started climbing it.

Sam allowed himself the liberty of admiring her for a second - her dexterity was astounding and she was almost running up the bales of cloth, despite her long skirt. His skill and agility wasn't bad by any means, but he was pretty sure that he wouldn't have been able to do what she was doing, even with the training he had received from Jacques and Master Hamato - it was at times like these that the difference between his own and Rachel's experience became evident.

He tore his eyes away from the incredible spectacle and ran, dodging around piles of cloth that were only faintly illuminated in the flames from the spreading fire.

He was gaining swiftly and he thought he saw another ladder just ahead which would allow him to cut the man off, but all hopes of that were dashed when the man threw something else - a barrel this time, thankfully empty - and he was forced to dodge to one side and roll along the floor.

'What is this? Bloody *Donkey Kong*?' Sam picked himself up just in time to see the man unhook the ladder, sending it crashing to the ground with another laugh, then duck out of the window and climb out onto the roof. He swore and ran on, heading for what he hoped was the loading bay and a way out.

He burst out into the wide road running behind the warehouse, deserted so late at night, and ran to the opposite side to look back at the building, craning his neck to peer up at the roof above. The warehouse was bracketed by wide streets at its front and back, so if the man was going to escape across the rooftops it would have to be to the buildings on either side, limiting his options to only two directions, but Sam didn't want to choose the wrong way and leave Rachel chasing the man on her own.

Patience wasn't his strong point, though, and he was just about to choose a direction at random when he caught sight of Rachel leaping across a short gap between houses a short distance down the street to his right. He immediately sprinted after her, sticking to the other side of the road in order to keep her in view.

After the pitch black inside the warehouse, the moonlit world outside was almost dazzling in its brilliance and he could clearly see her determined look as she ran across the roof. He couldn't see the man, though, but that didn't worry him; all that mattered was keeping up with Rachel - she would have her prey in sight. However, what did worry him was that, knowing her, she wouldn't wait for him to catch up before trying to take on the gigantic man.

Running on the ground was a lot easier than across the roof, Sam was steadily pulling ahead of her and it wasn't long before he caught sight of the man. He was moving with a lot more agility that he would have expected from such a large person, but even so Sam was overtaking him quickly.

He scanned the street ahead, looking for an opportunity, some way to join Rachel and grinned; this was just like the new *Assassin's Creed* game and it was everything he had hoped a visit to Victorian London would be.

Spying his chance he changed direction sharply, sprinting towards the wall of the nearest house. He jumped, bouncing off a crate and onto a windowsill. From there it was a short leap outwards to latch onto a hanging pulley which he used to swing on and gain height so that he could latch on to the guttering. With a short scramble he was able to crawl onto the sharply sloping roof.

He found his feet just in time to get knocked over as the man ran past, laughing insanely.

Sam fell hard and started to slide back the way he came. He scrabbled for a hold on the slick roof, but couldn't find one. He was only inches from falling back to the street and suffering a probable broken limb when a small but strong hand caught him by the wrist and in a single sharp tug pulled him back up.

Rachel looked down at him and shook her head. She said nothing, just resumed her sprint after the man.

Sam picked himself up with a wry smile; Rachel was almost certainly going to rub this in for a long time to come, but he didn't mind at all - one of the things that kept their relationship interesting was the rivalry that they had, as each strove to outdo the other. However, it wasn't a battle for superiority, it was just part of the fun and served to push both of them to greater heights of skill and ability.

He sprinted after her, determined to make up for his mistake and not let her get all the glory, because that would *really* make her insufferable.

The chase ended before he could catch up with her, though. She skidded to a halt ahead of him and when he pulled up next to her he found that the man had nowhere left to go - the row of houses had come to an abrupt end and he was standing on the edge of the roof looking down at the street, three storeys below.

The man turned around slowly and for the first time they got a good look at him. He was dressed in the same scruffy, brownish clothes that most of the men in the East End seemed to dress in with a flat cap pulled low over his eyes and a scarf wrapped around his mouth hiding most of his face. He straightened up to his full height, towering over them.

He pulled down the scarf and threw the hat away, revealing his face.

Rachel growled. 'That's not Tristan.'

'It's not?' Sam was puzzled; it was far too much of a coincidence that a man matching the description of the male twin would go on a rampage in the East End.

Before he could say anything, though, the man grinned insanely. 'Hello, Matey! You must be Sam Vives. I was told you would be the only one with the guts and stupidity to follow me across the roofs.' He leered at Rachel. 'And who's your little friend here? She looks good enough to eat. When I've killed you I'll make sure she's taken care of, don't you worry.'

'Told? By Quentin Price, I assume.'

'Yeah, that's right. He paid me well to rough you up a bit.' The man cracked his knuckles and started advancing on them, 'but I would've done it for free if he'd just asked me to; it's a good bit of fun.'

The man's eyes lit up with mad glee as he swung his fist.

Sam had been expecting the punch, but even so it was so quick that he barely had time to sway back out of reach of it and he felt the wind of the man's strike passing only millimetres from his nose.

The man's hand was so big that it momentarily blocked his vision so he didn't see Rachel counterattack, but suddenly the man was staggering backwards, doubled over, clutching his ribs and Rachel was retracting her foot from where it had lashed out.

The man straightened up and grinned, displaying a distinct lack of teeth, but the grin disappeared almost instantly as his weight continued to go backwards and his arms windmilled as he toppled from the roof.

'Oops,' said Rachel dryly, not sounding at all like she regretted her actions.

There was a crash from below and they raced to the edge of the roof to carefully look down into the street.

The man had landed on his back on a pile of wooden crates, smashing them to smithereens. They watched as he made an effort to get up, but in the end the fall proved too much for him and he crumpled to the renewed noise of breaking wood.

They made their way down to the ground, taking a much slower and safer route than the man had and approached him cautiously. It was immediately obvious that he was still alive, his snores made that more than clear, and Sam was relieved; he hated people being killed on his Displacements, even if he knew they would come back to life when he left, even if they had been trying to kill him - the talk of killing Quentin had made him feel bad enough, he didn't need someone else's death on his conscience.

Rachel produced a pair of handcuffs and Sam raised an eyebrow at her. 'I didn't know you had those.'

She shrugged and grinned at him. 'Keep your mind out of the gutter, please.'

The cuffs barely fit around the man's wrists, but eventually she had them in place and they hurriedly stepped away from him; the man reeked of alcohol and there was almost a haze around him.

Geoff and Bert came running up, they were covered in soot and coughing occasionally from smoke inhalation but otherwise unharmed.

'Is the fire out?'

'It's under control, sir. Nobody wants nothing to do with a bit of drunken violence, but a fire is a different matter - we've got a couple of dozen people dousing it.' Geoff eyed the big man who was still barely conscious. 'Nice work, sir.'

'Thank you, Geoff.' He grinned and gave Rachel a look.

She rolled her eyes, but said nothing; she was only supposed to be Sam's sidekick in the past so naturally he had to walk away with the credit for anything she did.

'If you'll excuse me, sir, I'll wander back to the warehouse; I've got one of me mates running to get a paddy wagon and they'll need to know where we are.' With a quick salute, Geoff jogged away.

Bert squinted down at the man. 'Is he the one you was looking for, sir?'

'I'm afraid not, but it seems like he was hired by Quentin to lure us here for some reason.'

Sam was prevented from saying more as the man woke himself with a particularly loud snore.

He looked up at them with bleary eyes and smiled his toothless smile again. 'Sammy boy! I have a message from Mister Price. He says hello and that he'll see you soon.' The man laughed maniacally before his eyes crossed and he passed out again with a groan.

Sam and Rachel exchanged a puzzled glance, completely mystified as to what Quentin's motives could possibly be for arranging the man's destructive rampage.

Neither of them saw the dark carriage pull away from the other side of the street where it had been positioned to see everything.

CHAPTER 16
ANOTHER ONE

It took four policemen to lift the man into the back of the wagon to bring him to the Spitalfields police station, and four more to carry him to a cell. He didn't wake until after he was locked in, which was fortunate because he would have hurt quite a few people if he had decided to resist arrest. Sam and Rachel spent an hour interrogating him but he knew little beyond what he had already told them - that he had been paid by Quentin Price to attract Sam's attention, kill him if he could, and failing that give him the message. They gave up fairly quickly, not only because it was pointless, but also because he wouldn't take his eyes off Rachel and his lascivious look was making both of them uncomfortable.

By that time it was daylight and, despite their exhaustion, they decided to go straight to Scotland Yard to start the day - with that night's excitement proving to be a dead end as far as finding Quentin, they had nothing else to do except continue going through the Ripper files while they waited for Bert and the Society to find some sign of Quentin. They were hoping that the more familiar they were with the cases, the more likely they would be to spot inconsistencies in any future murders that might lead them to Quentin. It was boring work, but Inspector Abberline always made sure that they were more than compensated by entertaining them during their frequent breaks for lunch, dinner, elevenses, afternoon tea and so on, showing them many of the delightful things that Victorian London had to offer that they wouldn't have even known existed otherwise.

Four days after the incident in the East End, they were still sorting through the files for what seemed like the fifth time and it had gotten to the point where all they were really doing was moving paper around aimlessly. The novelty of the situation had worn off very quickly and now they were wishing that something, anything, would happen to relieve the boredom.

They say to be careful what you wish for, though, and not long after they had arrived in the morning a panicked constable banged loudly on the door, then burst in without waiting for an answer to deliver some bad news.

'Sir! Sir! There's been another one, sir! Jack's killed again!'

Rachel and Sam shared a puzzled and not a little troubled look; there shouldn't be any more Ripper victims, unless, of course, Quentin had been able to affect significant changes in the time-line.

Abberline stood up and walked quickly to the door where he stopped to look back at them, raising an eyebrow. 'Well? Are you coming?'

They leapt to their feet and rushed out of the room after him.

Less than half an hour later, after a scarily fast ride through central London in Geoff's buggy, they were standing in a wide, but dingy street in Whitechapel, another of the boroughs that formed the East End of London. There were over a dozen policemen already there, trying to control the hundreds of people that were milling around and stop them from contaminating the scene of the crime.

At first sight it had all the appearance of another Jack the Ripper murder; the scene was reminiscent of the others and both the location and the victim, another prostitute, perfectly fit the profile that they had been building up - if it had happened originally then there was no doubt that it would have been attributed to the Ripper, which meant that it *had* to be due to Quentin's influence. They just had to hope that he had been careless and left behind clues to his whereabouts.

Rachel accompanied Abberline to inspect the body, but Sam didn't want to go near it; he still had uncomfortable memories of his brief visit to the bloody battlefields of World War One, so instead he stood to one side and looked at the people crowding around, taking in their mood.

Despite it being the middle of a work day there were a lot of people just standing around gawking and Sam remembered what Bert had said about unemployment rates being high in this part of the city. From what Sam could see the general feeling of the crowd was one of anger rather than fear and he was disappointed to see that much of that anger was being directed at the policemen, who were having trouble keeping them at bay - it looked like a riot could break out at any moment.

Sam glanced at where Rachel and Abberline were still bent over the body - they didn't seem to have noticed the angry atmosphere and were too engrossed in their own discussions and their inspection of the body to pay any attention to the world around them. He tried to follow their lead and began to wander around, looking for anything unusual or out of place.

There was nothing, beyond a chalk drawing of a rabbit at the base of the wall on the other side of the road from the body which he was fairly sure had no relevance to the murder or Quentin, so he decided to see if there was something that he could do to help the policemen calm the increasingly unruly crowd.

He surveyed the people, searching for some kind of leader among them, someone with whom he could reason or remonstrate - anything to defuse the situation that was worsening with every second. He looked from face to face, studied their body language, watched the way they spoke among themselves, looking for something, anything, that would show that someone was being deferred to, but then his breath caught as the vagaries of the crowd caused a brief opening and his eyes locked with those of a beautiful woman watching from some distance away. They were a brilliant green, as mocking as they were seductive, framed by hair of a deep, luscious red and were gone in an instant as the shifting people hid her again, but it had been more than enough time for the flame of recognition to kindle in him.

He craned his neck, trying to see over the top of the crowd, desperate to confirm his suspicions, but he couldn't see her; there was too much movement and too many people in the way - he had to get closer to have a clearer view.

With a last glance at Rachel and Abberline, who were still engrossed in the body, he slipped past the police cordon and began pushing his way through the throng, leaving behind the relative protection of the crime scene. Many of the men in the crowd redirected their angry shouts and shoves at him as he passed, but he ignored them and kept going, refusing to be turned aside from his quarry.

He burst from the back of the throng, immediately searching for her and swore under his breath when he saw that she was no longer where she had been, but then there was a flash of colour in the corner of his eye which was so out of place in the drab grey of the surroundings that it was impossible not to see and he turned his head to see her walking away from him, about fifty metres to his left, down a narrow street between two rows of ramshackle houses.

The woman was wearing an emerald green dress that shone brightly as she passed through one of the few rays of winter sun that penetrated the permanent murk of the London slum - the dress and matching hat were far too expensive for the area that they were in and made her stand out a mile, but it was the unmistakable shade of the hair that cascaded down her back which told him without a doubt who she was and as she turned the corner at the end of the street he finally got a good look at her face.

He'd been right.

It was Diana Birch.

Not wanting to lose her he broke into a run, heading for where he had last seen her.

He skidded to a halt just before the corner and peered around it, fully expecting to see her just ahead of him, but she was almost as far away as she had been before and was moving quickly, purposefully, almost as if she were late for a meeting. He drew on the surveillance tricks that Jacques had taught him and started after her, moving quickly to close the distance, but only slightly; he didn't want to catch her yet, he wanted to follow her and with any luck at all, that meeting she was late for would be with Quentin.

Things went well for a while; the streets and alleys of Whitechapel were filled with shadows and doorways which he could use for concealment and he easily kept her in sight while remaining unseen himself, but then they got to an area where there was hardly any foot traffic and suddenly his task became much more difficult. It became infinitely worse when the street opened up, becoming much wider, and the shadows disappeared completely. The only thing he could do then was to follow in her footsteps and hurry from what scant hiding places there were to the next, spending as little time as possible in the open.

He never knew what provoked it, but for some reason, just as he was most exposed, she glanced back over her shoulder. Her eyes widened and her mouth opened in an expression of sheer panic as she saw him. There was an instant when they were both frozen in place and he thought he saw a hint of something in her eyes - satisfaction, or possibly, impossibly, regret - but the moment passed and she whirled, breaking into a run, her long skirts flapping behind her and her hat flying off to hang down her back by its strap.

He sprinted after her.

He chased her through damp dark streets, around carriages and horses, through low arches and across main thoroughfares.

She was fast, almost as fast as he was, even in her impractical shoes, and under normal conditions Sam would have caught her easily, but his smart, flat-soled shoes were utterly useless for running and he slipped and slid on the filth that encrusted every surface with every step, slowing him down.

He would have caught her even so, but she was crafty and used several little tricks to stall him: she whistled to call the attention of men in the street and he nearly knocked into them as they turned into her wake to leer at her; she scattered coins on the floor as she passed a group of children, forcing him to dodge frantically as they fell at his feet and scrambled to collect them; she took him into a market and dodged around the stalls, making him lose sight of her almost immediately - he thought she'd gotten away, but another flash of green had him racing after her again. Nothing worked, though.

Eventually she began to tire and, as he inexorably closed the gap on her she became more frantic in her efforts to escape, like a rabbit being chased by a wolf, turning this way and that, seemingly without any plan. She raced down a narrow alleyway and Sam charged in after her, only seconds behind, but came skidding to a halt when he found her about ten metres in, standing waiting for him, bent over with her hands on her knees, panting for air.

The alley was a dead end - she had nowhere to go.

She gazed up at him like a scared child as he advanced on her.

'Diana, where is Quentin?'

She didn't answer and just backed away from him, retreating further down the alley while she tried to get her breath back.

'Diana!'

He scowled, completely out of patience, and was about to grab her when she straightened up. All signs of her being out of breath were instantly gone and her frightened look was replaced with a smirk.

'Oh, Sam… you really are a fool.' She lifted her eyes and looked over his shoulder.

'Wha…?' He turned to find out what she had seen and barely had time to make out two hulking figures before his world went black.

So absorbed were they in their work that it took about five minutes for Abberline and Rachel to realise that Sam wasn't looking at the body with them and by that time he was nowhere to be seen. They called Geoff over and Abberline asked him if he'd seen Sam.

Geoff shook his head. 'No, I haven't, not for a while anyway, sir. I'll go and ask the boys if anyone's seen him.'

They waited as he made the rounds of the constables who were trying to keep the crowds back. It took a while because he could only talk to them one at a time; he had to lean in close to each of them and shout in their ear to make himself heard over the noise of the increasingly agitated crowd. He finally got a positive answer from one of them and waved Abberline over. 'He was seen running off down this street a few minutes ago, sir.' He motioned for the constable to tell the story.

'He went through here, sir. Lit off after a woman he did, nice looking bit of... oh, er, begging your pardon, ma'am.' The man coloured as he noticed Rachel watching him.

'Never mind, constable, just tell us - which way did he go?'

The man pointed them in the right direction, then he and his fellows cleared a path for them through the people.

'Does your husband often do this kind of thing, Lady Rachel?' asked Abberline.

'You mean, does he often chase after strange women on the street?' She laughed at Abberline's tact. 'No, Frederick, he does not. But I'm sure he had a very good reason to do so; we have developed a bit of a theory and are looking for a man and a woman in relation to the case - perhaps he saw the woman lurking around and went after her.'

'Let us hope he caught her then; we need a stroke of luck if we are going to get anywhere.'

As they went, Geoff and a couple of other constables asked the people they found in the streets for information, getting accounts of a well-dressed man chasing a beautiful woman through the streets. It wasn't hard to follow in Sam's footsteps; his passing had caused quite a stir and after only twenty minutes they made it to the alleyway, where the trail finally went cold.

Abberline turned to the constables. 'Ask around please, see if anyone saw anything unusual.'

'Frederick!' He spun at the sound of Rachel's panicked voice from the alleyway and, together with Geoff, he ran towards her.

They found her kneeling near the end of the alley; Sam's hat was lying on the ground, crumpled almost flat. She hesitantly reached out and picked it up, then gasped in shock when she turned it over and found the inside wet with blood.

One of the constables came running back and spoke urgently to Geoff who hurried over to them.

'A few people saw a man being bundled into a carriage by three people, one man and two women. They think he was dead.'

The hat fell out of Rachel's suddenly numb hands.

CHAPTER 17
HOSPITALITY

Sam came awake very slowly from an unpleasant dream where he was playing a game of *Whac-A-Mole*, but it was him popping up through the holes and his head hurt, just as if it had been real. His body ached as well, especially his shoulders for some strange reason, and he frowned, wondering why a dream should have had an actual effect on him.

Thinking to tell Rachel about his nightmare, he tried to roll towards her and his eyes shot open in shock when he couldn't.

The first thing he noticed was that he wasn't in the bedroom of the house in Pimlico, the next was that Rachel wasn't beside him and the third thing - which he realised should probably have been the very *first* thing he'd noticed - was that he was tied to the bed.

He twisted his head to look up, causing a sharp pain to shoot through his temples, and saw that his wrists were bound with rope to the metal frame of the bed he was lying on. He pulled at them, wincing as his shoulders protested, but his bonds didn't shift; they were too tight. The bed didn't look like it was going to break any time soon either, unfortunately. Not one to admit defeat without a fight he struggled for a few more seconds, which only made his head hurt worse, then gave up and instead inspected his surroundings.

A single gas lamp illuminated the room dimly, barely enough for him to make out that it was fairly large, rectangular in shape and easily five or six metres to a side. The roof over his head was low with bare wood beams that slanted upwards at an angle from his left to the right, so he figured that he was in an attic. The walls were bare, painted plain white, and there was a single wooden door at his feet. There were no windows and a wooden chair by the door was the only furniture aside from the bed.

He shivered with cold and glanced down at himself. He was dressed only in the white shirt that he had been wearing in the street and the white linen shorts that served as his underwear. He was also wearing socks but no shoes and there was something wrapped around his head which he assumed was a bandage of some kind. There were no sheets on the bed though, just a pillow on a bare mattress, which was why he was shivering in the winter air.

'Hello?' He called out, his voice croaking in his dry throat. He winced as his head throbbed again with the effort and the sudden noise, but nevertheless he tried again, a bit louder. 'Hello!'

There was sound of footsteps climbing a flight of wooden stairs, then a key rattled in the lock and the door swung open to reveal the red hair and beautiful face of Diana Birch.

'Oh good, you're awake! I was beginning to worry that Tessa had hit you too hard.'

She was wearing a black dress, very different to the green one she'd had on in the street - it was black and while the skirts were voluminous, the body was tight to her, revealing curves that Rachel didn't have. It also had a very low bodice that showed much of the swell of her breasts. The overall effect was overwhelmingly sexual.

She noticed the direction of his gaze and smirked slightly as she moved into the room, swinging her hips more than was strictly necessary. She came to stand by the side of the bed and looked down at him. 'There was an awful lot of blood and for a while I was sure you were going to die, but we managed to patch you up no problem and here you are, alive and well!' She rearranged his bandages, then stroked his hair as she looked down at him with obvious sympathy. 'I'm sorry about this.'

Sam chuckled, wryly. 'If you're so sorry then why don't you let me go?'

Diana just shook her head and continued to stroke his head as she smiled down at him. 'I wish I could, Sam. I really do.'

To Sam the smile looked like the grin of a hyena assessing its prey. 'So why didn't you just kill me?'

'Quentin gave us strict instructions not to; he wants to take care of you himself, apparently. He's not the most forgiving of people and you've shown him up twice now - it's become a bit personal for him

I'm afraid.' Her hand traced the line of his jaw then moved over his shoulder before coming to rest in the middle of his chest. 'Anyway, I'm afraid you're my guest until he gets back - Lord Price has taken him to Paris for the weekend so it shouldn't be too long, just a few days.'

'That sounds delightful, he seems to be having a wonderful time while you are left to carry out a murder for him.'

Sam was gratified to see a slight lessoning in the girl's smile, but apart from that she didn't react to his provocation and she continued as if he hadn't said anything.

'There's no point in shouting for help; we're in a big house on the outskirts of London, there are no neighbours for a hundred metres, and we have no servants to hear you - it's just me and the Twins here. They don't like noise very much, though, so if you disturb them they are likely to gag you. Oh, and Quentin also told them that if you try anything then they should feel free to break a few of your bones, so I really hope you won't annoy them too much.'

Sam was already cold, but her words chilled him further and the hand on his chest seemed to radiate heat into his body through the too-thin material of his shirt, making him uncomfortable in more than one way, but then she lifted it to point at the bindings around his hands.

'By the way, you're tied up for my protection; the Twins aren't here right now and Quentin doesn't trust me to look after myself around you - he knows all about your little trip to Okinawa and the training you do most days with your little girlfriend and he doesn't want anyone getting hurt. When the Twins get back we'll untie you and let you move around a bit.' She looked down at his body and smiled, the hand returning to caress his chest softly before dropping further down. She growled appreciatively as she found his hard stomach muscles. 'The Twins stripped you to search for weapons, but if you behave, then maybe you can put your clothes back on later when we untie you. That would disappoint me, though.'

Her frank appraisal of him was beginning to make Sam decidedly uneasy; nobody had ever looked at him the way that she was, even Rachel had never been quite so blatant about it. Her hand moved down further and he started to become alarmed, wondering how far she was going to go and whether his teenage body would betray and humiliate him.

She noticed his discomfort and lifted her hand slowly with a regretful smile. She stood up suddenly, startling him, her eyes widening as if something had occurred to her. 'Oh, I'm sorry, you're probably really hungry! I'll go and get you some food. Don't go anywhere!' She giggled flirtatiously and skipped girlishly out of the room.

Sam watched her go, then let his head drop back onto the pillow with a sigh of relief. He had gotten the distinct impression that Diana was trying to seduce him, but that was ridiculous; he was tied to a bed and shivering with cold after being hit on the head by one of her friends. Even so, the dress… the caresses… It certainly looked like that had been her intention and if so he would have to be on his guard; the people from this time-line might see him as an adult, but he was still a teenage boy and he couldn't be sure his hormones wouldn't make him do something stupid.

To take his mind off the image of Diana in her revealing dress he turned his thoughts back to what she had said. She had already as good as confirmed that Quentin was in the past only with her and the twins and he wondered what else he could get her to divulge just by having a normal conversation with her, perhaps he could even get her to tell him their entire plan.

He shifted in the bed, trying to get comfortable and groaned as the movement sent a sharp pain through his head. He closed his eyes, willing his headache to go away, using all the meditation techniques he had learnt from Master Hamato, but nothing worked - it was bad, an all-consuming ache that barely let him think and the cold wasn't helping his concentration either.

He must have dozed off because before he knew it Diana was coming back into the room with a tray of food. She turned up the lamp to shed more light on the room and Sam winced as it stung his eyes - he was starting to get the feeling that he might have a concussion or something.

She put the tray on the floor and dragged the chair over to the side of the bed, then helped him to sit up a bit, putting the pillow behind him, but it was hard for him to move much while he was tied up.

She picked the tray up again and balanced it on her lap as she sat down. Sam saw a bowl of something hot and brown, like soup, some water and a thick chunk of bread.

'I'm sorry, but I'm going to have to feed you.' Her voice was apologetic, but she didn't look particularly upset about the prospect.

'You can untie me, I promise I won't do anything.' Sam put as much honesty into his voice as he could even though it was a blatant lie.

Diana just laughed and started to spoon soup into his mouth.

The hot liquid did a good job of warming Sam up and he realised how hungry he was. He took huge bites out of the bread when it was offered and thirstily gulped the water.

All too soon the food was gone and Diana laid the tray to one side and stood up. She returned the chair to its place by the door and then came back to stand over him. She smiled down at him, gazing into his eyes and laid her hand on his chest again, then ever so slowly moved it up his body until it was cupping his cheek. Her mouth opened slightly and her tongue flicked, wetting her lips.

Sam didn't know if it was the concussion or what, but he felt himself getting lost in her incredible green eyes. She was a very beautiful woman and he would be lying if he didn't say he was at least a bit attracted to her.

Suddenly she leaned over and kissed him full on the mouth.

Sam's eyes widened in shock. Every rational thing in him screamed at him to stop her, to turn his head away, to tell her to go, but inexplicably he found himself responding.

The kiss continued, the hand on the side of his face burning into him and all thoughts of Rachel and the fact that Diana was his enemy were forced from his mind as his whole being centred in the contact of their lips.

Eventually, though, she pulled back. 'You know, all this would be easier and so much more fun if you'd just join us.'

Sam had to catch his breath before he answered. 'I'm sorry, it's not going to happen.'

She laughed gently, not unkindly. 'We'll see.'

She picked up the tray and left the room. There was a loud clunk as the key was turned in the lock and Sam was left alone with his thoughts.

Finally, the motive behind her attempted seduction of him was clear and his opinion of the girl dropped considerably.

There was nothing else for Sam to do, so he slept as best as he could, resting and trying to recover; he would need his strength if he was going to be able to escape.

With no view of the outside world, Sam had no way of knowing what time it was or whether it was night or day, but after what must have been at least four or five hours, a pressure started to build. It prevented him from sleeping and eventually he was unable to hold out anymore. He took a deep breath, steeling himself against the inevitable pain in his head and called out. 'Hey, I need to go to the toilet!' He listened for a few seconds and when there was no response he called out again. 'Hey! I'm going to make a mess if you don't help me out here!'

Very shortly there were footsteps on the stairs. They were a lot heavier than Diana's dainty steps, though, and Sam wasn't surprised when the door opened to reveal a young woman, who he assumed was one of the large forms that he had merely glimpsed before being knocked out in the alley. She stood in the doorway and glared at him, arms crossed. She had dark brown, dirty looking hair and the arms that were crossed in front of her were almost as thick as Sam's legs. If anything she reminded Sam of the big woman knight from *Game of Thrones*.

Sam smiled at her. 'I don't believe we've been properly introduced, I'm Sam Vives and you must be Tessa, right?'

'You try anything and I'll bash your head in again.' Her voice was almost a growl as she stomped across to the bed and started to undo Sam's bindings.

Sam had indeed planned to do something when he was untied, but the strength he was seeing in her arms and his continuing headache changed his mind very quickly. The fact that he would probably wet himself if he was hit in the stomach also did a fair amount to convince him to bide his time.

The big woman freed his hands, then grabbed them to roughly pull him off the bed.

Sam almost screamed as the blood rushed back into his hands and his shoulders rotated in their sockets for the first time in hours. He stood unsteadily for a second, his bare feet cold against the bare floorboards, trying to stop his head from spinning but he didn't have much time to recover because Tessa immediately shoved him towards the door. He stumbled slightly, only just managing to catch himself on the foot of the bed. With the solidness of the floor and the bed to centre him, his head cleared enough for him to straighten up and continue to the door. He was walking relatively easily, although there was a shakiness to his limbs that he didn't like, as if he'd run to the top of Mount Yunaha and back, fought ten rounds with Rachel, and *then* had to face Master Hamato.

Outside the door was a short stairway heading down. At the bottom of the steps there was an open door and he went through, finding himself in the middle of a short corridor with a couple of closed doors on either side of him. There was a floor to ceiling at the end of the corridor to the right through which he could see the tops of some trees and an expanse of clear blue sky.

He paused and looked inquisitively at the woman and she motioned for him to go left.

At the end of the corridor was a landing overlooking a large open space that looked like it might be the entrance hall. There was a wide flight of stairs going down and he thought he spotted a pile of coats underneath the stairway near the bottom.

He tried to stop and look around to get a better idea of the house, but a hand in his back kept him going and he was led to the other side of the landing where there was another short corridor that was identical to the one he had just left behind - this was obviously a very large house. There were three doors leading off this corridor, two of which were open and led to rooms that were sparsely furnished and the third, which he was pointed towards, revealed a small bathroom with a deep tub and a rather dirty white porcelain toilet.

Sam went in and was just about to pull his underwear down when he realised that the woman was standing in the doorway watching him. 'Do you mind?' When she didn't answer he pointed at the tiny window that was the only other way out of the room aside from the door and which he obviously wouldn't be able to fit through. 'I really don't think I'm going to go anywhere. Or did you want to watch?' He gave her a cheeky smile.

She snarled in reply, but took a step back and closed the door.

The smile immediately faded from Sam's face and he slumped slightly. He had to prop himself up against the wall with his hand as he did his business; his head wouldn't stop swimming and his legs were like jelly.

There was water in a bowl by the tub with a cloudy mirror and he took the opportunity to wash his face, then turned his attention to inspect the wound on his head. The bandage was stuck to his hair with dried blood and he grimaced in pain when he pulled it away. Underneath, his hair was matted with dried blood and he was unsurprised to find a large lump and a horrible-looking bruise, as well as a moderately-sized gash which had been sewn together quite neatly. The cut was healing quite well and he poked the area around it, ignoring the sudden agony, looking for any damage to his skull. Thankfully there didn't seem to be any.

He was interrupted by a thump on the door which shook the mirror on the wall and chuckled as he put the bandage back into place then quickly washed his hands again.

He opened the door to reveal the scowling face of the big woman.

'Thank you.' He smiled and gestured to the toilet behind him. 'Do you need to go while we're here? I can wait out in the hall for you, if you'd like.'

She snarled again then grabbed his arm in a huge fist. She dragged him back to his room and locked him in without a word, but didn't bother to tie him up, which he was very glad for because his shoulders really hurt.

Now that his bladder was emptied and he was free to move around he did so, running through some gentle exercises to limber up his body and clear his mind, forcing himself to do them even though his head was killing him; he had to be in perfect condition to act if a chance came along and he wanted to know how much his injuries would hold him back if he did.

The exercises tired Sam out far more than they should have and he fell asleep again immediately after doing them. He had gotten a bit more used to the cold in the room and he was no longer in shock after the head wound so he actually managed to get some decent rest instead of just being unconscious.

It must have been several hours later when the door opened again, this time to admit Diana accompanied by a large man. He was obviously the twin to the woman who had taken him to the bathroom earlier; he could see the similarity in his face. His body was even bigger than hers had been and Sam thought that, if he was going to continue to make *Game of Thrones* comparisons, he would have to say that the man looked very much like The Mountain and he hoped that the old axiom, that the bigger they are the harder they fall, really was true, otherwise he was going to be in a lot of trouble when he tried to escape.

Diana was carrying another tray of food; some meat and vegetables, water, and a cup of what looked like wine. She smiled at him as he sat up on the bed. 'Good afternoon, Sam, how are you? You look a bit better.'

'I am. Much better, thank you.'

She set the tray next to him. 'Do you want me to feed you again? I really don't mind if you do.' She winked seductively at him.

'I think I can cope.' He picked up the tray and set it on his lap.

Diana went and got the chair and set it in front of him, close enough to reach out and touch him. She sat and watched him as he ate hungrily.

The giant stood in the doorway, a silent, menacing presence.

Sam jerked his head at the man in a gap between mouthfuls. 'Don't talk much, do they?'

'Tristan and Tessa?' She shrugged. 'They're not here for their conversational skills.'

'What? Quentin needs them to provide protection from the big bad Displacers?'

Sam snorted in derision, a noise which was echoed, much louder, by the giant.

Diana laughed gently and leaned forward in the chair to put her hand on his knee. 'While I know you are *very* capable, we didn't bring them for you - they are here to deal with Jack.'

'Jack? You mean Jack the Ripper?' Sam was surprised. 'You know who he is?'

'Of course.' She leaned back in the chair. 'We knew exactly when and where the murders would take place, all we needed to do was lie in wait.'

'So you caught him?'

'Well… not exactly caught, more like recruited.'

Sam stared at her with his mouth open. Thankfully he had swallowed beforehand.

'You're going to use him?'

Diana shrugged. 'We *were* going to, but the damn man died the week after we found him - he had a bad heart, which, I assume, is why he stopped killing in the first place.'

Sam laughed. 'What a shame, all that careful planning for nothing!'

'Not quite.' Diana smiled slyly. 'We still had all the information and the plan in place, we just needed a new Jack. So we went out and got one. It was easy; there were plenty of very unhappy young men to choose from, I can tell you! We chose a likely looking one and all he needed was a little nudge, a little suggestion and a few winning smiles from me to get the ball rolling. The crime scene you "found" me at was a test for him and a trap for you.'

'You knew I was going to be there?'

'Of course we did! We knew you were coming into the past after us and we were waiting for you. As soon as the papers started speaking about how the "great detective" Sir Sam Vives was going to help the police with the Ripper case we knew you were here and it was a simple enough matter to stake out Scotland Yard to find you. We've been watching you since then, while you've been blundering around looking for us.' She grinned. 'Congratulations on your knighthood, by the way!'

Sam chuckled. 'Thank you.'

'You're welcome! You certainly took your time about turning up, though, we've been here for a couple of months!' She leaned forward and spoke quietly, confidentially. 'So, who did you bring? We know about Rachel; we saw her when you met the little henchman we arranged to draw you out, but is there anyone else? Did Andrew come with you?'

'The warehouse...' He nodded. 'I was wondering what the point of that was.'

'Good boy!' She stared him in the eyes, searching for something, then nodded when apparently she found it. 'It's just you and Rachel then.' She smiled. 'You really like her, don't you? I don't blame you for only bringing her; she's much better looking than Andrew.'

'Oh, I don't know, Andrew has a certain charm.'

'If you're into that kind of thing...' She raised her eyebrow and smirked at him. 'Are you?'

It took a second for him to realise what she was suggesting, but then he went red and panicked at the thought that she might think that of him. 'No! I'm not!' He then realised that it wasn't exactly the worst thing in the world and that he was making too much of it for some strange reason, as if it really mattered what she thought. 'Um... Not that it's a bad thing, it's just that I'm, that is, I like...'

He stopped when he realised he was babbling and that Diana was grinning at him.

She really did have a very nice smile and he found himself involuntarily smiling back at her.

She put her hand back on his leg, a bit further up from the knee this time. 'I'm only teasing; I know you do and I'm very glad!' Her voice was low and husky and she smiled her nicest smile yet.

Sam pretended to be incredibly interested in his food, trying to ignore the feel of her touch through the thin material of his decidedly unattractive, but thankfully long, shorts. He sat in silence for a while, concentrating on chewing his food. He drank the water but didn't touch the wine; he wanted a clear head and he still considered himself too young to do much drinking.

It was very obvious that Diana was doing all that she could to try to seduce him, but whether it was just for information like he'd thought, or if she really believed she could get him to join them he didn't know. It didn't matter too much either way; he wasn't going to bite.

Suddenly it occurred to him that two could play at her game; he could go on the offensive and have a bit of fun while he was doing it - the only real danger in turning the tables on the woman was what Rachel would do to him when she found out.

He placed the tray to one side and in a smooth but quick movement leaned forward and put his hand on top of the one Diana had on his leg. He was very gratified to see her eyes widen almost imperceptibly in shock and her smile falter slightly - she wasn't as confident and self-assured as she wanted him to believe.

He didn't say anything, just held his hand over hers and smiled; at the moment he only wanted to plant a seed, then later, if he could get Diana on her own, he would try to talk to her. For now, though, he just wanted her off balance, wanted her to think that she might actually have a chance of seducing him over to the dark side.

She recovered quickly and pulled her hand out from under his as she stood up. 'Well, if you've finished eating, I'll leave you alone.' She picked up the tray and walked to the door. Tristan moved to one side to let her pass.

'Come back and see me again soon, please, Diana!' called Sam. He smiled to himself as he saw the slight hitch in her step, but she didn't turn.

Once again, the door locked behind them.

CHAPTER 18
FUN AND GAMES

Despite his attempts to put on a good front, Sam was very scared. He was effectively living under a death sentence, because Quentin was undoubtedly planning to kill him on his return, and it was a heavy weight on his mind.

The fear followed him into his dreams that night, manifesting as a dark, indistinct shadow of a man holding a scalpel which shone almost with an inner light. The man stalked him through the dark streets of Shadwell while people watched from the doorways as he staggered past - among them was Diana, wearing the black dress and smiling wolfishly at him, and, bizarrely, various characters from *Game of Thrones*.

No matter how fast he ran, how many twists and turns he took in the maze of alleyways and back streets, when he glanced over his shoulder the shadow was always just a few steps behind, the scalpel weaving through the air in anticipation, glinting silver in the moonlight.

He burst out into the market that he had chased Diana through. It was deserted at that time of night but the empty stalls still provided plenty of hazards that seemed to reach out for him as he passed, attempting to trip him.

He was finally starting to pull away and gain some space over his pursuer when he turned into an alley and found himself in an all too familiar dead end. He skidded to a halt as a man stepped out of the shadows in front of him - Quentin, the sneer on his face the one that Sam remembered so well and hated so much.

'Vives, the proverbial bad penny! A penny for your thoughts?' He walked slowly towards Sam, chuckling.

Sam could feel a presence at his back but couldn't turn, no matter how hard he tried; he was held in place somehow.

Quentin came to a halt a few metres in front of him. 'Before my master deals with you, perhaps you would like to spend that penny?' He laughed at his own joke and suddenly Sam was released.

He started to turn his head towards the shadow at his back, saw the glint of something sharp and wicked reaching out, probing for his neck...

'Sam! Wake up!'

A hand was gently shaking him and he came awake to find Diana sitting on the side of the bed next to him. He slowly focused on her, then glanced around the room looking for bodyguards - there weren't any, she was alone.

'Sounds like you were having a bit of a nightmare there.' She smiled down at him, the hand still on his shoulder.

He slowly uncurled from the ball in which he had fallen asleep in an attempt to conserve heat - it hadn't worked; he was still shivering and he was beginning to feel a bit unwell. 'I hope I wasn't making too much noise for the Twins' liking,'

She chuckled. 'They're sparring right now - all the grunting and groaning would drown out a herd of cows.'

'That's an appropriate analogy.' He smiled faintly, playing up the sympathy card.

'Oh, before I forget.' She bent over and picked some things off the floor - Sam's trousers and overcoat. She put them on the side of the bed next to her.

'Thank you!'

She stood back out of the way as he rolled his legs over the side of the bed. She leaned against the wall, watching him as he got dressed and he thought he caught a slight moue of disappointment as he put his trousers on, although he couldn't be sure if the look was merely a continuation of her mind games or just wishful thinking on his part. He put on the coat and hugged himself as a touch of warmth spread through his body - he could hear the patter of rain against the roof above and it had gotten progressively colder over the last few hours, cold enough that he hadn't been able to ignore it any longer.

'That's better, thank you.' With some warmth came the ability to think and Sam considered his situation - escape wasn't a viable option at that point and even if it was he might not have taken it; Diana was alone and he had a golden opportunity to talk to her without her feeling like she had to hold back for an audience - not only was there Quentin's current mission to find out about, but there was also his organisation in general, he owed it to the Displacers to gather as much information as he could and besides he could always go home whenever he wanted, if, of course, his headache would just go away.

He raised an eyebrow in what he hoped was a charming, and not creepy, manner. 'I'm still alive, so I'm guessing your boss isn't back.'

'Not yet, and he's not my boss, by the way.'

'He's not? I thought he was running the show.'

'He wishes!' She laughed. 'No, we have a boss who tells us what to do, thank god, because I don't think we'd last very long if he was in charge!'

'Yeah, he is a bit of loser.' He gave Diana his best smile. 'I don't understand why you have to take his orders and aren't giving them; he's been beaten at least twice that I know of and you don't strike me as the subordinate type.'

'I'm not, but hierarchy is very important in our organisation and there are ways of determining it - Quentin is high up not only for his connections but also for his ability.' She gave him a smile. 'If you joined us you would be very high up indeed - you'd probably be giving Quentin orders from the get go.'

'Is that's why he wants me dead so badly?'

'It's one of them, yes, but not the only reason; you've humiliated him a few times now and he is a *very* vindictive person.'

'He does have a bit of a temper, doesn't he?'

'You don't know the half of it.'

Sam chuckled. 'I bet he wasn't very happy when he found out that the mask you guys brought back from Egypt was a fake!'

'You knew it was a fake?'

Sam nodded. 'Of course.'

She laughed. 'Figures! He got a real telling off for that, but it didn't matter in the long run; the Twins went back and retrieved some of the treasure - we got what we wanted.'

'Yeah, I heard about that. So, let me get this straight - somebody had to go back into the past and clear up his mess, right? That must have gone down really well with him and your boss.'

'Yeah, the Master was not pleased.'

'The "Master"? Really? That's a bit pompous isn't it?'

Diana shrugged. 'He's not that bad, actually; he takes care of us, pays us well, and if you join us you'll be very well taken care of as well.' She smiled encouragingly at him.

Sam smiled inwardly; she was trying so hard to recruit him that she was giving him vital clues as to who was really behind Quentin's organisation - it sounded like it might be Ralph after all; he struck Sam as *exactly* the kind of person to take the name "Master" to hide his identity. He decided to press Diana harder, see what happened.

'I guess what I really want to know is why you're still with them; you don't strike me as the kind of person who is only interested in personal gain.'

'I'm not.'

'Then why are you working for them?'

She turned away from him so that he couldn't see her face as she answered. 'Because they… they found me and took me in. They gave me a chance when nobody else would.'

The fact that she wouldn't meet her eyes meant that she was most likely, finally, going to be truthful with him. Sam had no idea why she was opening up to him so easily, it might have something to do with what she was about to reveal, but also it might be that nobody had actually spoken to her like he was since she had joined Quentin's organisation. The more he thought about it, the more he suspected that was it; in Egypt Quentin had barely spoken to her and then only to give her orders.

He could see that Diana was still reluctant to share her feelings, though; he would need to tread very carefully.

He spoke gently to her, not wanting to make her angry or spook her. The best way, the only way of getting to her was to keep her talking. 'You don't owe them anything just because they found you first. We would have taken care of you as well, you know that, but we wouldn't be making you do things that you didn't want to do in return.'

'And who says that I am?'

'Come on, Diana! I can see you're not the kind of person that would willingly participate in murder, or allow someone like me to be Quentin's plaything, a focus for his vengeance to cover his own failures.'

She turned back to him, but Sam could see that he had pushed too hard, too quickly; there was anger in her eyes and he thought he detected a hint of madness as well that more than worried him. 'You don't know me! You don't know *anything* about me!' Her voice was rising in volume, becoming almost hysterical. 'My whole life I've had people trying to manipulate me! They know that, they're my friends and they wouldn't do that to me!'

There were tears forming in the corners of her eyes and Sam tried to calm her back down. 'No, of course not, I'm sure they wouldn't.' He desperately wanted to tell her that of course they were manipulating her, but now was not the time; he was getting to her, but the situation was very delicate.

He took a step towards her, intending to offer her some comfort, a hug if she would let him or a hand on the shoulder if she wouldn't, but before he could do or say anything more the door slammed open and the Twins burst into the room.

They were sweating and breathing hard from their training, which had obviously been interrupted by Diana's shouts. They were both very scantily clad, Tristan in only a pair of Lycra shorts and Tessa in a sports bra and leggings, and they were even more impressive now that Sam could see their bodies clearly, both solid slabs of muscle.

They stood shoulder to shoulder just inside the room, looking back and forth between Sam and Diana, like two people at a tennis match.

Diana stood stock still, staring at Sam through tears that were making her heavy mascara run down her cheeks in dark rivulets. She opened her mouth as if to say something, but then just turned and ran from the room, pushing her way past the Twins.

The gaze of the Twins now settled firmly on Sam and their eyes narrowed.

'Hi!' Sam smiled at them, trying to diffuse the situation.

They, of course, didn't smile back.

'We don't like you,' growled Tristan.

Tessa's voice was almost as deep as Tristan's. 'You've hurt our friend.'

Sam was lost for words; he wasn't quite sure if they were referring to Diana's tears, his previous defeats of Quentin, or both.

The Twins looked at each other and they smiled.

Sam really didn't like it when they smiled.

'The boss never said we couldn't play with him.'

'No, he didn't.'

Their heads swivelled slowly in unison to look at Sam, then they stomped forward.

The Twins dragged him to an empty room on the floor below that had obviously once been a library; there were shelves on every available space of wall, but there was not a single book to be seen. It was a corner room and there were windows along two of the walls letting in a lot of light and giving a lovely view over the surrounding countryside, but he had no time to admire it before Tessa had pulled his coat roughly off of his back and the bandage from his head and thrown them to one side. Then, while Sam was distracted watching them fly across the room, Tristan slammed his fist into Sam's stomach.

Sam collapsed onto his knees, clutching his abdomen. He hadn't been taken too much by surprise, though; he had been expecting something of the sort and had already been activating his muscles to absorb any blows that came, but the man's fist had still done a lot of damage and hurt more than he could have thought humanly possible.

While the Twins laughed cruelly, Sam remained on his knees, taking his time to recover fully. He didn't know what kind of fight this would be or whether it was going to be a fight at all - they might just be intending to hold him down and beat him - so he decided to test them a little by staying down longer than he needed to; he would learn a lot by whether they hit him while he was still on the floor or dragged him to his feet. To his relief he felt hands on his shoulders and he was lifted bodily into the air and deposited back onto his feet.

He found himself facing Tristan while Tessa, who had picked him up, backed off and leaned against the wall to watch, smiling expectantly. Tristan had an identical smile on his face, which widened to a full, mocking grin when Sam brought his hands up into a defensive position.

Sam desperately wanted to wipe the smiles off their faces, but he really didn't think he was going to be able to.

He faced off against the giant man and assessed his possibilities, looking for any weak spots in the man's guard or physique - there weren't any, which meant that he had to hope that the man's technique and speed were inferior to his.

Those hopes were dashed immediately as Tristan surged forwards on the attack. He was fast and the punch that flew out towards Sam's face wasn't the wild barroom brawler swing that he had expected but rather a crisp boxer's jab.

Sam swayed back from it, just managing to stay out of reach and the man smiled even more; the jab had just been a test and the real attack was the one that followed. The big man stepped forward again and launched another, quicker jab, which was immediately followed by a second, deeper one, then a right cross to Sam's mid-section.

Sam swayed and twisted, only just managing to stay out of range of the jabs, but he couldn't do the same with the cross and he had to block it with his elbow. A shock ran up his arm at the power of the blow and the arm drooped as it went numb.

He scuttled backwards, trying desperately to stay out of reach while his guard was wide open, but the man followed him closely, stalking him around a room that was much larger than a boxing ring, but that suddenly seemed so small.

The fight could easily turn into a shameful fiasco, with Tristan chasing him while he ran around the room like a coward, if he didn't do something drastic - it was time to change tactics.

He waited until Tristan had gotten into a rhythm of chasing him and then, just as his adversary was stepping forward, he reversed his direction and slammed an open palm into Tristan's nose, using his momentum against him, looking to end the fight in one huge strike. There was a snap and blood immediately spurted from a broken nose, but unfortunately it was a nose that was used to being broken and Tristan didn't even break his stride; he threw out a quick but heavy combination that had Sam reeling back, his lip cut and an eye swelling closed.

Usually in a bare knuckle fight, blows to the head were uncommon because they tended to do as much damage to the deliverer's hand as to the receiver's head, but Tristan didn't seem to have any qualms about it whatsoever.

Sam's head spun and he blinked, struggling to recover. He cursed himself; he had been too slow in getting back to a guarding position after his strike - he had thought the single blow would be enough to knock Tristan down or at least give him pause, he certainly hadn't expected him to just shrug off his attack as if it were nothing.

Tessa laughed cruelly from the side of the room and it was the humiliation as much as anything that made Sam get back into the fight. He pretty much had the full measure of his opponent now, he thought, and while this was going to be very tough, it wasn't by any means impossible.

Tristan had obviously dedicated a lot of time to physical training, both in the past and the present, much more than Sam had, but there was much more to fighting than just training, like instincts, willpower and cunning, and Master Hamato had always praised Sam for those very things.

Sam went on the attack, using every ounce of technique that he had honed with Rachel and Master Hamato, employing all his speed and cunning to put Tristan on the back foot. He wasn't going for a knockout blow anymore, instead he was trying to wear his opponent down gradually, frustrate him and hopefully get him to open up enough to land a few more damaging strikes.

Tristan was surprised at first; he probably hadn't ever had someone go on the attack against him, or even last long enough to fight back, except for his sister and Sam was gratified to see a worried look briefly cross the man's face.

His satisfaction didn't last more than a couple of seconds.

There was a laugh from the side of the room as Tessa showed her delight at her brother's discomfort, which in turn provoked an angry look on Tristan's face and a furious reaction. He immediately stopped retreating and launched a furious counterattack that terrified Sam - the man was no longer playing, now he was aiming to kill or seriously maim his opponent and there was a murderous light in his eyes which matched the killing power behind his fists.

Sam was again forced to back off around the room and he had to use every trick and tactic he knew to avoid or deflect the blows - blocking them completely was out of the question; the force behind them would have broken his bones or at least made his limbs unusable. Despite his best efforts, a few punches still got through, although, thankfully, he was able to negate most of their force by twisting out of the way at the last moment and they barely grazed him, but even so they were still powerful enough to hurt and would undoubtedly leave a bruise.

The effort Sam was having to put in just to dodge was extreme and he was tiring quickly, but so was Tristan and his swings getting wilder and wilder as the unnecessary power he was putting into every one took its toll; in his anger, blinded with the need to destroy his opponent outright, Tristan had lost all control.

With renewed hope Sam continued his evasive manoeuvres, knowing that his chance would come.

Soon, the brute was nearing exhaustion, his blows slowing and his steps faltering, which in turn gave Sam a chance to recover. His evasive actions got easier and easier until suddenly his chance came; a particularly wild swing opened Tristan up and he pounced - he placed his retreating foot firmly and pushed off of it, spinning in place and landing a vicious back kick on Tristan's ribs. The kick on its own would have done a lot of damage, but Tristan's own momentum again worked against him and there was a sharp crack as Sam felt something give under his foot.

Tristan cried out and dropped to his knees, gasping for breath and clutching his chest - his inability to control his anger had indeed proved to be his downfall.

Sam stepped forward quickly, intending to deal a finishing blow and knock his opponent out, but before he could, he was shoved hard from the side, knocking him off his feet. He hit the wooden floor hard and slid a good few metres, only coming to a halt when he crashed into the wall. He looked back to find Tessa standing over her brother with her hands on her hips. Strangely, she was laughing at him and his rasping efforts to breathe.

She reached down and pulled Tristan to his feet, then punched him in the stomach and all but threw him to the side of the room, just as easily as she had Sam. 'You've had your fun, little brother, now it's my turn. Go sit down, you wimp.'

Tristan staggered to the wall next to the door and leaned heavily against it. He doubled over in pain and gave Sam a hateful look.

Sam grinned at him and shrugged. He had had a few seconds to rest and he stood up.

He brushed himself down trying to act like he was still fine even though he was anything but, then looked at Tessa and gave her what he hoped was a seductive smile, but which in reality was probably twisted by the pain he was in. 'May I have this dance?'

She threw her head back and laughed, but when her eyes met his again they had a fire in them that worried Sam; the look in Tristan's eyes had been that of a wild animal, a savage, she on the other hand had the cold stare of a killer. He swallowed, nervously, and brought his guard up, already positive that the result of his next fight was going to be quite different from the last.

He was right but, while she didn't quite beat him into a pulp, she gave him enough of a pounding to teach him a lesson and exact a modicum of revenge for the damage he had done to her brother, mercilessly focusing much of her attention on his ribs, probably because that was where he had hurt Tristan. That wasn't to say she didn't hit him anywhere else and he took a fair amount of punches to the face as well, adding to the damage that Tristan had already done, but luckily she didn't break his nose or knock out any of his teeth; thanks to the rules of Displacing any damage that he sustained in the past would be taken back with him when, or if, he got back to his own time and he was quite fond of the way he looked.

There was real disappointment in her eyes when he didn't put up nearly as good a fight as she had been expecting, but he was far from his best after having faced Tristan and after ten minutes she tired of playing with him - a single punch to the side of his head that he barely saw coming dazed him enough that he could no longer stand. She caught him as he toppled and carried him to his room as if he were a child, throwing him on his bed and laughing when the ribs that she had cracked grated and made him scream.

She locked the door and left him alone with his pain, bleeding on the pillow and struggling to breathe. Before long, though, his one good eye closed and he didn't resist as darkness took him.

It wasn't sleep; it was unconsciousness, and this time the nightmares couldn't follow.

When Sam woke up, he opened his eyes to find Diana sitting in the chair by the door underneath the gas light, watching him.

She was looking the worse for wear. Her hair was untidy and her clothes looked slept in and her eyes were puffy and red from crying.

Sam tried to sit up, but groaned and collapsed back. He could barely even turn his head to look at her either; his neck hurt so much.

'I'm sorry.' Her voice was very soft. 'I was feeling so sorry for myself that I had no idea what they were doing to you.'

Sam laughed, but very briefly because it hurt. 'That's fine, I needed the exercise.'

She came over to the bed and stood looking down at him. He could see the indecision in her eyes, the doubt as to which way to turn and who to trust, and he knew that he had almost won.

'I got into this because it sounded like fun - running around time, sightseeing and making a bit of money bringing back treasure. They told me it was going to be an adventure, harmless, a bit Robin Hood actually.' Her eyes defocused as she remembered past events and when the words came they were disjointed and hesitant. 'It was Quentin who recruited me. He was a bit geeky, self-conscious, but full of himself and he knew exactly what I had been dealing with. My Displacements before I met him had been uncontrolled and disastrous - I had gone to nightmare places without understanding what was happening or what I was doing and I was on the point of asking my parents to get me help because I thought I was going crazy. Quentin was the first person who told me I wasn't insane, that what I had seen and done was real.'

She sat down on the bed next to him and put her hand lightly on his chest, caressing it absent-mindedly as she continued. 'I've turned a blind eye to what they've been doing over the last couple of years; I haven't wanted to see, but it's impossible to totally ignore what they've been doing. They've become more and more ruthless in achieving their objectives and the objectives themselves have become much less Robin Hood and more Sheriff of Nottingham. I've gotten more and more troubled with what I've been doing, with what I've had to do, but still I stuck with them, did what they told me, because they were all I had. And because I thought that they were all there was.'

She looked at him, meeting his eyes for the first time and Sam saw pain in them but also a note of determination. Her voice was also stronger. 'Talking to you, getting to know you better, has been the last straw. Up till now they've been painting you Displacers as the bad guys, the uptight self-proclaimed rulers of time, but now I can see that you're not. *We* are the bad guys and Quentin is murdering people here just to create a distraction!'

Tears were streaming down her face now and somehow Sam could tell that they were genuine. She was so close to turning from Quentin and he knew he had to be gentle with her so as not to scare her off, but he needed information and he might not have another chance to get it. 'A distraction? For what?'

His direct question brought her out of her self-pity a little and she shrugged. 'I don't know, he wants something from the attic at Displacer Headquarters, he didn't tell me what - I don't need to know apparently.' She sniffed and wiped her nose with a lace handkerchief from her sleeve.

'Is that the main objective then?'

'The murders are pretty important as well. We're supposed to cause enough trouble for the ruling party to be ousted in favour of the opposition, but Quentin is off out of the city with his ancestor, working hard on getting whatever it is from the attic, so I guess that's what's most important.' She grimaced as she remembered her own role in things, dropping her head into her hands and turning away from him in shame. 'While Quentin has been away in the country doing god knows what I've been stuck here with the Twins, keeping an eye on the man we've found to be the new Jack. Arthur. It's my job to point him in the right direction and get him to kill the right people in the right parts of London, according to the Master's plan.' She shuddered. 'The Twins like to watch him work. They make bets on how much his victims will scream and laugh at the crudeness of his technique. I can't stand it, I hate them!'

'I can imagine,' Sam reached out and put his hand on her shoulder. 'That's really not you, you shouldn't have to do that kind of thing. You deserve much better.'

Sam felt ashamed; he had been playing her, trying to turn her manipulation back onto her, but he was slowly coming to realise that she was not the cruel and heartless femme fatale that she wanted everyone to believe - underneath she was as uncertain and vulnerable as he was. She could have been like him if Andrew had gotten to her first and she needed his help to be who she should be and not what she had been made into.

Her voice fell until he could barely hear her. 'You're the first person who has ever been nice to me.'

Their eyes met and Sam could see such longing in her eyes, a desire to be treated fairly and, he hoped, to escape from the clutches of the Master and Quentin.

Sam found he was almost shaking with the adrenaline surging through him and his injuries were all but forgotten with how important the conversation was proving to be - it could be the key to the Jack the Ripper case, this Displacement, and maybe pave the way to destroying Quentin's group forever. So many things went through his mind in such a short time and he saw so many possible outcomes, a multitude of different paths unfolding before him, all stemming from Diana's defection, cleansing the time-line forever and returning the world to the peaceful existence that it should have been leading rather than the nightmarish present that the Master had fabricated.

It was a moment of sheer clarity, but in none of the visions that flashed before him did he see what actually happened next.

She leaned down and kissed him on the lips.

This was very different from any of the kisses he had shared with Rachel, it was not as tender as it was with her - there was passion and desperation in it, seemingly in equal parts, but there was also a need that made it so much different than the one that she had given him earlier, the one she had given him purely in an effort to seduce him. The one she had probably been ordered to give him.

Sam knew that it would be so easy to just go with it and kiss her back - use the confused woman's feelings against her to give him a way out of his current situation and it was certainly tempting; Diana was very attractive, beautiful in fact, more so than Rachel even, and Sam would have been happy to be with her, but he just couldn't. It wasn't just about betraying Rachel, it was about what was *right*, and it wasn't right to take advantage of her; it might well destroy whatever fragile hold her mind had on reality. It was also exactly the kind of manipulation that someone in Quentin's group would do.

No matter what it cost him he wouldn't do that to her, to anyone.

However, that meant that he had to reject her advances and her emotional state was such that he had no idea how she was going to react.

Fortunately, the state of his body gave him an easy way out - he couldn't breathe through his nose and had to turn his head away from her to gulp in air, breaking the kiss. He groaned in pain as his cracked ribs grated against each other at the sudden movement.

She pulled back and he was relieved when he saw concern and not anger. 'I'm sorry, I forgot about your injuries. It was selfish of me.'

She stood up and went towards the door as if to leave, but then she hesitated with her hand on the knob. She stood like that for a second, but then she turned around and the look on her face made Sam rejoice; it was one of determination mixed with compassion. She came back to him, her strides purposeful.

'Come on, I'm going to get you out of here.' She held out her hands to help him stand, but before he could take them, the door swung open and crashed against its stop with a thunk and she jerked back from him, startled and spun to face the newcomer.

In the doorway stood Quentin Price, Sam's enemy - his nemesis. The man who had threatened to kill him on various occasions and had tried to at least twice. The man who had killed the aunt that Sam had met but never known and who had given instructions for Sam to be held until he could come and take care of him personally. He was a sadist and Sam didn't doubt that there was going to be more pain and suffering in his immediate and probably brief future. He was dressed in a tweed suit, which was rumpled and creased, with a white shirt underneath, the collar of which was almost black from contact with greasy hair that was much longer than it had been when Sam had last seen him - it seemed that he had been so keen to see his prisoner that he hadn't taken the time to change or rest and there was an insanely cheerful grin on his face as he took in the sight of Sam lying bruised and bloody on the bed that was all too familiar.

'Well, well, well, Vives. Fancy meeting you here! Always turning up like the proverbial bad penny, aren't we?'

Sam was shaken when Quentin used almost the exact same phrase that he had in his nightmare, but he buried the fear it sparked in him and tried to put on a confident face. 'Actually, Quentin, I rather think it's you who is the expert on trick coins.'

'Touché, captain!' Quentin nodded, acknowledging the reference to Blackbeard's double-headed coin that he had used to cheat in Port Royal and deliberately using a fencing term to flaunt his knowledge of

Sam's recent activities at school. 'Anyway... I'm sorry I wasn't here to greet you in person, I'm afraid I had more pressing matters to deal with than just one little boy, but now we're going to settle this once and for all.'

'No need to rush on my account; I'm quite comfortable - plenty of exercise, good food... although I must admit the company leaves a lot to be desired.'

Quentin laughed once, very briefly, then stepped to one side and motioned to someone outside the door. 'You two, take him down to the garden, I don't want to put this off for any longer.'

The smiling faces of the Twins appeared from the shadows of the stairwell and they padded into the room like the predators they were, swiftly closing the distance to the bed, where they immediately grabbed Sam, ignoring his growls of protest as they roughly handled parts of him that were begging to be left alone.

'Diana!'

The girl hadn't taken her eyes off Sam the whole time, but when Quentin said her name they shot to him. Her concern for Sam and her fear that Quentin somehow knew what she had been about to do were written plainly on her face and Sam held his breath, wondering how the man could possibly not notice.

Quentin was completely oblivious, though; his attention was riveted on his rival - brought low and helpless before him. He snapped at her without even looking in her direction. 'Go get my duelling pistols from my room; we're going to have a bit of fun.'

While the Twins were dragging him down the stairs Sam looked back and saw Quentin whispering something to Diana as they followed behind, chuckling all the while and grinning malevolently at Sam.

Diana was frowning at his words and she glanced at Sam, concerned. He could see she was torn about something; it was quite obvious she wasn't at all happy with what Quentin was saying, but he was still her boss and she had as good as said that she would be punished if she didn't do what she was told.

He wanted to tell her that he wouldn't blame her if she did what she was told, but he lost sight of her when the Twins frogmarched him around the corner at the bottom of the stairs and he couldn't help but feel that he had also lost his only opportunity to escape.

CHAPTER 19
THE DUEL

Sam was dragged all the way to the ground floor then to the back of the house and through a large but sparsely furnished dining room which had only a few chairs grouped around a small table. They pushed him through some French doors, thankfully opening them first, then across a small paved patio and down some steps onto a lawn surrounded by overgrown hedges and an ornamental pond that was green with scum. The lawn looked like it might once have been meant for croquet; it was square and perfectly flat, but it hadn't been taken care of and the grass was above Sam's ankles and infested with weeds.

It was the first time he was seeing the outside of the house and it looked much bigger than he had imagined - three stories tall and rather wide. It was quite grand, although it had obviously stood empty for some time and was as rundown as the gardens.

The Twins stood either side of him, making sure that he didn't make a break for it. It wasn't really necessary, though; he was fairly sure he wouldn't be able to get very far even if he did try something - his body was battered and his ribs would prevent him from drawing enough air to get more than a few hundred metres before he passed out.

He turned his head up to the sky, relishing the feeling of sunlight on his face after so long inside. His breath misted in the cold air and he shivered, not for the first time wishing he still had his coat; he hadn't gotten it back after the fight.

By the height of the sun it had to be around noon. He wouldn't have been at all surprised if that were the case; arranging a duel at "high noon" sounded very much like something that Quentin would do. However, Sam realised that he had no idea what day it was noon of; the fight against the Twins could have been only hours ago, but it could just as well have been the day before, or two days - he had no way of knowing how long he'd been unconscious, just as he didn't know how long he'd been unconscious after the ambush in the alley. Bizarrely, he found himself hoping that he had slept through several days; that way Rachel and Abberline would have had more time to find him. Although, by the look of things, they were going to be a bit late...

It was a good few minutes before Quentin came out. He was wearing a clean white shirt, pressed black trousers and polished black shoes. He had also taken the time to wash his hair and it was wet and brushed back into a ponytail.

Diana was a few steps behind him. She was carrying a small wooden case in front of her on her upturned hands and was trembling slightly. She refused to meet Sam's eyes so he turned his attention to Quentin and watched as the man swaggered across the patio and down the steps onto the lawn. His usual supercilious grin was plastered on his face, but there was a sadistic hint to it that had Sam especially worried - he definitely had something up his sleeve.

Quentin stopped a few paces away and looked Sam up and down. He raised an eyebrow. 'I see you've been well taken care of.'

Sam smiled back at him. 'I had a bit of fun with the Twins here. Whatever you're paying them it's too much; they're big softies.'

Sam heard matching growls from the two thugs standing behind him, but Quentin just threw his head back and laughed his peculiarly evil laugh. 'I think they went easy on you; your face is a state and I can see you're barely able to stand, but I've seen them do much worse - be thankful you still have four limbs; they tend to act like Wookies sometimes if they lose.' He chuckled at his own joke then gestured for Diana to come forward.

Diana gave Sam a warning look that Quentin couldn't see before doing as she was told.

Quentin turned and opened the wooden case to reveal two beautiful duelling pistols.

'I thought that we would settle this little feud of ours like gentlemen.'

'That will certainly be a change for you; your usual style is more to kick someone when they are down, isn't it?'

Quentin laughed again, nastily. 'Winning is everything, the tactics you use don't mean anything.'

Unfortunately, that seemed to be true and Sam thought that it was one of the biggest reasons why so much was wrong with the world and there was absolutely nothing gentlemanly about that kind of attitude; it just encouraged cheating, especially in sports like football where winning had become everything for players and supporters alike.

He didn't share his opinions with Quentin, though, he just smiled confidently at him. 'It will be good to face you on a more or less even playing ground; I seem to recall that last time we met like this I beat you fairly easily.'

Quentin snarled. 'You caught me on a bad day and I underestimated you. I won't do so again.'

'We'll see.'

Quentin took the pistols from the box and handed one to Sam. 'Keep it tipped up, Vives; you wouldn't want the shot to fall out the end. Diana, you officiate, Tristan you'll be Vives' second, Tessa you'll be mine.'

Sam inspected the pistol. It was ornate and heavy, with a carved wooden grip, a long metal barrel and an antique flintlock mechanism that looked like it was plated in gold for some reason. They looked more ornamental than functional, but they were well balanced and Sam could tell they would be lethal in the right hands. He raised an eyebrow at Quentin. 'Pistols? Do you need this to be like a video game so you have a chance? Why not make this fair and bring out some swords?'

Quentin smiled. 'You'd like that, wouldn't you, Mr Fencing Champion?' The smile dropped from his face and he snarled. 'Not a chance!'

Sam shrugged and returned a cheeky grin. 'It was worth a try.'

Quentin led the way to the middle of the lawn. 'This should do. Shall we say ten steps each? Do you think you can hit me from twenty metres or so?'

'I'll give it a go.' Although he had very little experience with guns, Sam was fairly sure that, if he could throw a chopstick through a straw dummy at thirty metres, he could hit Quentin with a pistol from twenty, in whichever eye he chose.

'That's the spirit! OK, we'll do this properly; it's more fun that way.' Quentin turned his back to Sam and lifted his pistol onto his shoulder.

Sam was "helped" into position by Tristan and he lifted his own pistol up to his shoulder. The big man then backed away into position a few metres away, ready to "act as his second" which Sam thought was probably a euphemism for "catch him if he runs."

It hurt him to stand upright and he was still having trouble breathing. His main worry, though, was his depth perception; with one eye still swollen he was effectively going to be aiming with only one, although thankfully his right eye was fine and that was his dominant one. He spoke to Quentin over his shoulder. 'I suppose you won't change your mind and settle for a handshake and letting me go, right?'

Quentin just chuckled in reply.

'And what about the fact that duelling is probably illegal?'

'Are you really worried about doing something illegal? In the past? *Seriously?* This is our playground! You can do what you want here!'

He laughed and there was a note of something like hysteria in his voice when he continued. 'You still don't get it, do you? I've won! I've beaten you, Vives! You're still trying to be smart, but you're going to be dead in a few seconds! I'm going to kill you, not just for my own considerable pleasure, but also because if I get rid of you then the people back at your Headquarters in this time-line will forget that you ever warned them about me - I'll just walk right in and take whatever I damn well want!'

He smiled in satisfaction at Sam's surprised face and his voice dropped to a more normal level. 'Oh yes, I know about your little visit to poison them against me. My idiot ancestor was going to let me in until they took him to one side and had a quiet word. So, I'm going to kill you, then I'm going to go straight back to Grosvenor Place, wipe my feet on the welcome mat, drink their tea, laugh in their faces and take whatever I damn well want! Now, come on, let's get this done! Diana! Start counting.'

Diana sighed and then spoke. 'Ten steps, gentlemen, then turn and fire. Are you ready?'

'Just get on with it, will you?'

Quentin sighed in exasperation, but Sam gave her a warm smile and nodded, trying to let her know that he didn't blame her for what was happening, but then he put her out of his mind, along with Quentin's taunting revelations, so that he could concentrate on the duel.

Diana continued. 'Then on my count… One.'

Both men stepped forwards.

'Two.'

Sam continued to walk forward, but he was barely listening to the count; he was still puzzled by why Quentin would propose a duel.

'Three.'

Quentin had no way to win in a fair fight. Rachel had said that he wasn't a very physical person and he most likely had very little training in anything to do with fighting and shooting and Sam doubted that the light gun games he undoubtedly played would be much use in preparing him to use a real pistol.

'Four.'

Unless, of course, Quentin's confidence came from the thought that Sam was so injured he wasn't going to be able to raise and aim the heavy pistol.

Sam rolled his shoulder gently as he stepped forward.

'Five.'

His shoulder was fine, more or less, and he was going to have no trouble lifting the weapon.

'Six.'

Anyway, Sam would have to be unconscious or dead for Quentin to be as confident as he was.

'Seven.'

There had to be something else.

'Eight.'

There were of course other ways for Quentin to have cheated things in his favour.

'Nine.'

Sam glanced at Tristan, who was standing nearby, arms at his sides and weight on the balls of his feet, ready to pounce on Sam at any sign of treachery. Perhaps he was going to prevent Sam from firing? He was a bit too far away for that, so probably not.

All further thoughts of possible betrayal were put out of his mind as Diana finished the count.

'Ten!'

Sam turned slowly to find Quentin already facing him with his pistol raised and aimed, a half smile and intent look on his face.

There was a loud bang and a spurt of smoke and Sam felt a sharp tug on his already injured ribs. He would have screamed if there had been any air in his lungs, but it had been driven out of him with the impact.

He staggered on already weak legs, only just keeping himself from falling over. His vision narrowed and darkness threatened to enclose him, but he drew a ragged breath and shook himself, forcing his muscles to obey his commands. He steadied and after a few more breaths the cobwebs cleared away. He put his left hand to his side and it came away sticky and red - he was hurt, but not seriously; the bullet had grazed his ribs but not penetrated.

He lifted his head to look at Quentin.

His adversary was standing with a wide grin on his face, the discharged pistol lowered to his side. The grin faded to a look of annoyance, though, when he saw that Sam was not as wounded as he had originally thought. He laughed and threw his pistol to Diana. 'Reload me; I going to need another shot.'

Diana caught the pistol easily, snatching it from the air with a grace that impressed Sam, but she didn't even glance at it, she just held it in her hands, looking back and forth from Quentin to Sam.

Quentin's grin disappeared and he scowled at the unmoving Diana. 'I said reload it!'

Diana hesitated a moment longer, obviously reconsidering obeying him, but then she sighed and knelt down to begin loading the gun from the implements in the wooden box.

Satisfied, Quentin turned back to Sam, his mocking smirk once more in place. 'Well, come on then, fire! Kill me or we'll just keep trying!' He held his hands out to either side, presenting his full body to Sam.

Sam lifted the pistol again, but hesitated; he was still not sure that he could kill a man, any man, even Quentin, who had killed his aunt, who had attempted to kill him at least twice and had threatened to do so on various other occasions, who had done so many hateful things and was part of the group who were endangering time itself and twisting it to their own ends.

Did his reluctance to kill Quentin make him human? A good person? Or just stupid?

He pointed the pistol at Quentin's chest. His hand trembled slightly with the effort of holding it there, but he knew that he could easily put the bullet right through his enemy's heart, killing him instantly.

But still he didn't do it.

'Come on! We haven't got all day!' Quentin laughed but maintained his open, inviting stance.

Sam frowned, the man must have had some kind of death wish. Either that or he knew something that Sam didn't. Brief thoughts of Clint Eastwood and iron plates went through his mind but the shirt wouldn't hide anything like that.

Suddenly he realised that he didn't care about Quentin's motives; this could only end one way.

He shot.

Quentin dropped to the ground screaming in agony, his voice high-pitched and not particularly masculine.

At the last second Sam had decided not to kill him, he just couldn't; no matter what the man had done, Sam just didn't have it in him to do it. So he had adjusted his aim slightly and shot him in the right arm. He had aimed for the bone because, even though he didn't want to kill him, a bit of pain would be just fine and the thought of Quentin not being able to play computer games properly for a few months was actually quite amusing. Plus, as a nice bonus, he wouldn't be able to aim well enough to shoot Sam again.

Quentin writhed on the floor, clutching his arm. Tessa bent over him and tried to help him but he just screamed at her to leave him alone.

Sam chucked the pistol to one side and smiled weakly, enjoying the show despite his own pain.

Quentin struggled to his knees, but instead of turning on Sam, he screamed at Diana. 'You imbecile! I'll see you get what's coming to you for this!'

She shrank back from him a bit and shook her head. 'I'm sorry, I… With all the… I'm sorry…' She broke down into tears and ran for the house.

Tessa went to stop her, but Quentin stopped her. He turned his attention back to Sam. 'Let her go; I'll deal with her later. Kill him first.'

Sam glanced to the side where Tristan was already advancing on him. He started to back away, but knew that he wouldn't get far and fighting back was not an option - it looked like the time for games was well and truly over.

Suddenly, whistles blew, seemingly coming from all around them. Tristan stopped in his tracks and looked around in concern before looking to Quentin for instructions.

Quentin's face was waxen and white, twisted in pain, leaning heavily on Tessa. Blood was streaming down his arm and dripping onto the grass. 'Get me out of here, I need a hospital!' He looked around frantically. 'The pond - that should be deep enough! Quick!'

Tessa picked Quentin up and lumbered towards the ornamental pond.

Tristan stepped towards Sam, intending to carry out his orders, but then whistles sounded again and he hesitated, his huge hands only inches from Sam's neck, looking back and forth from his victim to his sister. He snarled in frustration, then broke into a surprisingly fast run after Tessa.

Sam tried to run after them, thinking to delay them, but after a couple of steps he collapsed to his knees, wheezing, too weak to continue and was forced to watch while they escaped.

He was amply compensated, though, by the spectacle of Tessa throwing Quentin bodily into the pool before she and Tristan all but belly flopped into it and he laughed when fat Koi carp, forgotten but somehow still alive, flew into the air, displaced along with most of the water. However, a couple of seconds later, the surface of the pond was perfectly calm again, the fish undisturbed and the filthy water back in place; they were gone from the time-line and all trace of their having been there was gone with them.

Sam knelt, staring at the pond, fascinated by it for some reason, but was brought back to the present when the whistles sounded again and he remembered that his job wasn't done; Diana was still there. He struggled to his feet and staggered towards the house.

He was stumbling up the steps to the patio when Rachel and Abberline appeared around the side of the house accompanied by Geoff. A few other Bobbies ran into the garden at the same time, appearing from all sides; apparently they had surrounded the house, hoping to cut off anyone trying to escape. Unfortunately, though, Quentin was always going to have a way out that they didn't know about and could never hope to block.

'Sam!' Rachel almost screamed his name when she saw him, saw his injuries and the blood soaking his white shirt.

At the sight of them all fight went out of Sam and he collapsed to his knees, but he had one thing left to do before he could give in to the pain. As they rushed up to them in concern he pointed to the house. 'Diana. She went inside.'

While Geoff sent the uniformed policemen into the house to search for Diana, Rachel knelt next to Sam and helped him to lie down on the patio. She put her hat under his head for a pillow, not caring if it got crushed and stained. 'Sam! I was so afraid you would be...' Her sentence went unfinished when tears sprang forth at the corners of her eyes and her throat constricted.

Sam smiled, reaching up to stroke her cheek as she leaned over him. 'How did you find me?'

'That would be my doing, sir.'

For the first time Sam noticed the man who had been standing unobtrusively in the background.

'Bert! Then it looks like I owe you my thanks and my life!'

Rachel nodded. 'When you disappeared and we found out that you had been abducted I went looking for Bert. I told him that we had found out that Quentin was with Lord Price and he suggested using some kind of servants' network to find out which of Lord Price's estates he was staying on. We knew you wouldn't be there, though, so we waited until he left and followed him here. We didn't know things were going to move this quickly, though, and it looks like we took too long organising the rescue party.'

'You did cut it a little bit fine, yes; Quentin had just given the order for the Twins to finish me off.'

Rachel's concern was instantly forgotten, replaced by anger and she swiped her sleeve across her eyes, scrubbing away the tears, before scanning the garden, looking for a target for her blossoming rage. 'Where is he?'

'Long gone, I'm afraid, but I gave him a nice little souvenir to remember me by - I'll tell you all about it later.' He chuckled, then gasped as a fresh pain shot through his ribs, sending stars shooting behind his eyes. He wrapped his arms around himself; the pressure seemed to make them hurt less.

'Let me see.' Rachel pushed his hands away then carefully pulled Sam's sodden shirt away from his body and inspected the wound. The bullet had scraped past his ribs, taking some of his flesh with it as it went - it was bleeding a lot, but it wasn't very deep or life-threatening. She grunted in satisfaction. 'You'll live.' She grinned. ''Tis but a scratch.'

Sam grinned. 'Just a flesh wound.'

Abberline didn't share their opinion of the wound's seriousness, neither did he get their *Monty Python* reference. 'I'll send for a physician.' He walked off around the house, muttering about "taking a stiff upper lip a bit far" and shaking his head in exasperation, tactfully taking Geoff and Bert with him to give them some time alone.

Rachel leaned in to kiss Sam gently and when she pulled back her eyes were bright with moisture once more. 'I thought I might never see you again; given Quentin's track record I was pretty sure you would be dead already.'

'He left orders for me to be kept alive while he was away in the country because he wanted to kill me himself. He wanted to have a duel, of all things.'

Rachel frowned. 'Why would he duel with you? Surely he knew you could kill him easily with just about any weapon he chose.'

Sam thought back. Recent events were rather hazy because of the pain and all the times he'd been hit in the head, but he recalled Quentin's confidence and what he had shouted at Diana after Sam had shot him. The pieces slowly fell into place. 'I get the feeling that Diana wasn't supposed to load my pistol; I reckon that Quentin told her to put powder in it so that it made a bang, but not any shot, so that he wouldn't be in any danger. He was *very* surprised and *extremely* unhappy when I actually hit him.'

'I wish I could have seen the look on his face.'

Sam grinned. 'I think you would have liked his high-pitched girly scream even more.'

Rachel hit him lightly on the arm. 'Don't insult girls by comparing us to Quentin! I've warned you about that before!'

'I'm sorry; you're right… Have you ever met Tessa?' He waved at his face. 'This is mostly her work. She hits like a truck.'

'She's built like one too... Yeah, I've met her. It wasn't a very pleasant experience.'

Sam shivered, feeling very cold all of a sudden. 'Should I go home, do you think?'

'You'll certainly get better medical care at home.'

Sam considered his options. His brain seemed to be working much slower than it normally did and it took much longer than it should have, but finally he shook his head. 'I should stay; this might not be over. Besides, it would be better for me to heal first; we don't want to scare the people in Hyde Park with all this blood and I don't particularly want to have to explain a bullet wound to the police or my parents if I can help it.'

Rachel smiled. 'That's my boy! Finally thinking like a Displacer!' She ruffled his hair and frowned when he didn't push her away like he usually did. 'OK, we'll stay, but you'll probably have a lovely scar and at the first sign of any infection we're going home without any arguments.'

'That sounds good.' He smiled at her and was going to ask her for another kiss, but right that moment Abberline came back around the house with a doctor in tow.

Rachel moved back as the doctor started prodding at Sam's wound, drawing gasps from his patient.

Abberline stood next to her and they watched the man work. 'I can't believe that one woman is capable of causing so much trouble…'

Rachel rolled her eyes. 'I thought you were married, Frederick.'

He gave her a puzzled look. 'I am. What has that got to do with it?'

'Never mind.'

They watched the doctor work in silence for a while. He finished his inspection then fished in his bag for a glass bottle containing a clear liquid which he poured on Sam's wound, drawing a hastily stifled scream from his patient and sympathetic winces from his audience. He then began to sew it closed.

'So, did you catch her?' asked Rachel, looking away from the blood that had begun pouring even more freely from Sam's side at the doctor's manipulations.

Abberline shook himself, pulling his attention away from his fascination at Sam's treatment. 'Oh, yes, silly me, it completely slipped my mind! We have her in the dining room.' He raised his voice so that Sam could hear. 'She's asking for you, Sir Sam; she refuses to talk to anyone else.'

'Right, you're done, Sir Sam,' the doctor interrupted. He snipped the end of the thread then started to pack his bag.

'Thank you doctor.' Sam looked up at Abberline with eyes that were having trouble focusing, feeling suddenly light-headed. 'Right, let's go see the dastardly Diana!'

He smiled, tried to get up, failed and passed out.

CHAPTER 20
HEALING

Sam was shaken gently back into consciousness by a hand on his shoulder. He was warm for the first time since he'd been abducted and the temptation to go back to sleep was almost overwhelming and he tried to shrug away the hand, but the hand shook him again and he reluctantly opened his eyes with a groan to find Rachel standing over him.

She smiled down at him apologetically and gave his shoulder a last squeeze before letting him go. 'Sorry to wake you but the doctor said that he didn't want you to sleep too much in case you had a concussion.'

'How long?' He mumbled the words through lips that were cracked and dry.

'Only an hour.'

He grumbled but he understood the necessity. He felt a bit better, he was still very weak but his head had cleared somewhat. 'It's alright, I have to talk to Diana anyway, or has Abberline taken her away already?'

He lifted his head to look around the room, half-expecting to find her sitting in the corner. She wasn't, but he was obviously in her room - the bed he was lying on had sheets and blankets, there was a fire burning in a fireplace and a rack of women's clothing occupied most of one wall. It was far more comfortable than his cell had been.

'She's here, Abberline still has her in the dining room. I wouldn't let them take her away without seeing you first.'

'Won't she just go home if you don't watch her?'

'I had a quiet word with her and she promised me that she wouldn't go anywhere. She wants to speak to you, says she's got things to tell you. I also think she feels sorry about what she's done to you for some reason. Is there something you're not telling me?'

Sam took a deep breath, now was as good a time as any to come clean about Diana and the kissing, he just hoped that Rachel didn't beat him up too much, he wasn't in any state to defend himself. 'Before we go down I have a confession to make.'

Rachel chuckled and bent down to kiss him gently on the lips. She stroked his hair as she looked into his eyes. 'There's no need, Sam; I'm assuming you and Diana spent some time alone together and you did what you had to do to survive. It looks like you had quite an effect on her, you charmer! You can tell me everything later, but for now, just believe me when I say that I trust you.'

She kissed him again, but a lot deeper, and Sam felt his head start to swim again, although this time it wasn't such an unwelcome sensation.

Too soon, though, she was pulling back. 'Now, if you're feeling up to it, let's go and see what she wants. Hey, maybe she wants to join the good guys! You never know.'

Sam smiled. 'I doubt it, not now anyway; she's pretty loyal to them. She would have been one of us if they hadn't found her first, though, I'm sure of that - I got to know her a little bit and she really doesn't belong with them; she was just about to help me escape when Quentin turned up.'

He shifted round on the bed and Rachel helped him to sit up. The pain in his ribs intensified and he clutched them, finding that they were padded with bandages beneath the shirt. 'Ow… Doesn't the doctor have any painkillers? I can barely move.'

'He does, yes, but they are pretty strong and all *very* illegal in our time - I really don't want you taking things like that, just in case we have to go home; they'd find it in your system in the hospital and that really would be hard to explain. So I just told the doc that you're a big strong boy and that you can take a bit of pain.' She smiled sweetly and batted her eyelids at him. 'I hope that's alright?'

'Yeah, thanks…' On a normal day Sam wouldn't go anywhere near drugs of any kind but with the throbbing in his head and the agony in his ribs he wasn't sure if that was the best policy.

He swung his legs of the side of the bed and began to stand up, but immediately fell back onto his bed. The room swam and he almost passed out, but he fought and clawed himself back from the brink with sheer willpower and the dizziness slowly went away. He attempted to get up again, but found that he just couldn't; his legs wouldn't support him and he couldn't straighten his body properly because of the pain in his side and ribs. He looked up at Rachel. 'Can you give me a hand, please?'

She chuckled. 'Certainly, husband of mine.'

She helped him to his feet and together they staggered out of the room.

Diana was sitting in one of the chairs gathered around the small table in the dining room just off the patio. There were five policemen spread around the room, blocking both the door and the French windows; apparently Abberline was taking no chances with such a dangerous criminal. She wasn't making any effort to get away, though, she was just sitting bolt upright, defiantly staring down at her cuffed hands on the table in front of her.

She looked up as they entered and Sam thought he saw a look of compassion and tenderness cross her face before it was gone and her expression became neutral once more.

'Hi, Sam, are you alright?'

Sam smiled weakly at her, trying to keep up his efforts at winning her over. 'I'll be fine. A few days in a warm bed will get me up and fighting soon enough.'

'It might take a bit longer than that, darling.' Rachel wrapped her arm around Sam and pulled him closer, possessively.

Sam winced as she squeezed his ribs and freed himself from her as surreptitiously as he could; her jealousy was understandable, but it was going to kill him if she held him any tighter.

'I suppose you'd like to hear everything now, right?' Diana said with a sigh. She looked at Rachel. 'Do you think that I could talk to Sam alone?'

'No way am I going to leave you on your own with Sam.' Rachel said with some aggression, staring Diana down.

Sam looked around the room at the policemen watching Diana. Despite the fact that they would forget everything they heard as soon as Diana went back to her own time, things would go a lot smoother if they didn't have an audience. 'I think it would be better to talk on the ride to Scotland Yard, that way we can be guaranteed a bit more privacy.'

They searched out Abberline, who readily agreed that it would be best to get the prisoner into a cell as quickly as possible. Thankfully he didn't insist on accompanying him; he wanted to stay and supervise a search of the house for any clues to the identity and whereabouts of Jack the Ripper.

It didn't take long to organise and about ten minutes later Rachel and Geoff helped Sam into a carriage for the journey back to centre of London. The big policeman was under strict instructions from the doctor to go slowly so as not to jolt Sam around too much and this suited them fine as it would give them more time alone with Diana.

Sam settled into the rear seat with Rachel, who put an arm around his waist to hold him close in an attempt to steady him. Diana was put into the seat facing them by two of the policemen and she looked back and forth from Sam to Rachel. Sam smiled encouragingly at her, but Rachel just glared at her coldly, her hatred evident in her eyes. She seemed to deflate under Rachel's withering gaze, her head dropping and her shoulders hunching forwards and it wasn't until after they had gotten underway that she began to talk.

It was a very small voice that issued from her and the Displacers could barely hear her over the sound of the carriage making its way over the rough country roads. She recovered a bit over the next half an hour, but there was always a defeated look in her eye that made Sam feel sorry for her.

She reiterated what she had already revealed to Sam, about how they had planned to use Jack the Ripper to cause an uprising and knock the ruling party from power and she recounted their search for a replacement when he died, giving them the name and location of the replacement. 'I don't think he's going to kill again any time soon; we didn't have time to point him towards another victim and he's unlikely to act on his own - he was a bit weak-minded, that was one of the reasons we chose him. You should have time to nudge the police in the right direction before he gets bored and decides to do things on his own.'

She also told them about Quentin's desperate attempts to gain access to the attic, but reaffirmed that she had no idea what he had been looking for. Eventually she ran out of things to confess to them about her time in the past with Quentin, but by then they had more than enough information to reverse the damage that had been done.

There was a brief silence as she looked at them hopefully, seemingly desperate for their approval. For Sam's approval in particular.

Sam decided to test the relationship he had built up with her and try to get some more information from her. He knew this was the crucial moment; it was one thing giving them the tools they needed to undo the work that Quentin had done in twisting the past to his own needs, quite another to start revealing secrets about her associates, her so-called friends, but this was an opportunity that might never come again so he had to push. 'Tell me more about your organisation, Diana. How many of you are there? What do you call yourselves? Who is the "Master" you told me about?'

Diana shifted uncomfortably in her seat and turned away, suddenly unable to meet his eyes. She swivelled in her seat and looked out of the window to watch the world go by outside the carriage.

Sam could feel Rachel stirring beside him and he knew she was about to say something to try to persuade the girl, but Sam knew that would be a mistake. He squeezed her hand and gave her a warning glance and she subsided back into the seat with a nod.

They were nearing the centre of London now and the sporadic mansions had long since given way to terraced houses, which had in turn given way to townhouses. The air outside the coach had changed too, becoming smokier and dustier as they made their way into the coal fires of the city.

It was almost two minutes before Rachel seemed to come to a decision. When she turned back to them her face was set in a determined scowl and as soon as she opened her mouth to speak Sam knew that they had won. He also knew very quickly that they were in much more trouble than any of them could have ever imagined.

'We call ourselves the *Illuminati*.'

'Oh, god, seriously? Couldn't anyone come up with a better name than ripping off something like that?' Rachel scoffed, a mocking look on her face.

Diana fixed her with a deadly serious look. 'Ripping off the name of a secret society that only appears here and there in history, almost at random? A secret society that reportedly creates enough havoc to bring down governments or cause global recessions, but then just disappears? That profits from the chaos it causes to expand across the globe, but can never be pinned down?' She raised an eyebrow and a faint smile lifted the corner of her lips as something of her character and confidence resurfaced. 'Why do you assume we're ripping anything off?'

The smirk had gradually faded from Rachel's face as Diana had spoken and she was left without words as the realisation sank in - all the legends, all the events that had been attributed to the Illuminati over thousands of years, all the rumours of a secret society or select group of immensely powerful men and women working behind the scenes to manipulate events to suit their own selfish means… Unfortunately it described Quentin's group perfectly.

'Of course, not everything the Illuminati are supposed to have done was really us; you know how the truth tends to get exaggerated over time and how people are always willing to attribute anything strange to almost supernatural forces. A lot of it was, though. Quentin, and the Master before him, both like to leave clues, rumours and such, behind them. I'm not convinced that the name "Illuminati" wasn't around before they started using it; you know how time travel becomes very paradoxical, very chicken and egg, but the Master has always claimed that he came up with it and I wouldn't be surprised if he did - the whole thing suits his arrogance and self-importance.'

Sam took note of the disdain in her voice when she was talking about the Master, filing it away for possible later use. 'So, how many of you Illuminati are there running around causing havoc through time?'

Diana grimaced and shrugged. 'I'm sorry, I don't know.'

'Oh, come on, you must do!' Rachel laughed incredulously.

'I'm sorry, but it's true.' Diana waved her hand vaguely, indicating the current situation of the city. Angry shouts could be heard in the distance as a riot or a demonstration took place. 'As well as being an absolute genius at causing this kind of thing, the Master is also incredibly paranoid. As far as I know we're always organised into teams of four, but I have no idea how many teams there are in total - I know of at least two, but there might equally be dozens. Quentin's group is obviously the one that always gets assigned to the most important jobs because we're the best, but I think that might change soon,' she smiled almost shyly at Sam. 'Thanks to you. You really have put a bit of a dampener on Quentin's ambitions - it's been incredible to watch.'

Rachel gave her a sour look. 'Yes, well, that's enough about how fantastic my boyfriend, sorry, my *husband* is.'

Sam grinned at her, quite pleased about her continued jealousy. She didn't find it funny, though, and gave him an angry stare that made him realise that he would pay when he wasn't too injured for her to kick his arse. Funnily enough, the thought of that wasn't too unpleasant.

They were now rounding Buckingham Palace and going up the Mall towards Trafalgar Square and Diana was getting restless. 'I think it's best if I disappear before we get to the Yard; it'll make things easier for all of us.'

Sam nodded reluctantly. 'Fine, just answer one more question and then you can leave. Who is the Master and who is his spy in the Displacers?'

Diana shook her head sadly. 'I don't know either of those things, sorry; that's need to know information and I don't need to know. I don't think all the group leaders know who the Master is and as for a spy in your organisation,' she shrugged, 'You definitely have one, but I'm pretty sure the Master is the only one who knows his identity; he's paranoid, remember?' She glanced out the window, increasingly nervous; they were going past Nelson's Column, preparing to turn onto Whitehall and the Yard was only metres away. She smiled at Sam. 'I have to go. Now. Not all of us have your talent; most of us need some time.'

Sam looked at Rachel and she shrugged; there didn't seem much point in keeping Diana there any longer - either she didn't have any more information or she wouldn't give it to them. 'All right then, go.' She dismissed Diana with a wave and turned to look out the window.

Sam, however, was a bit kinder and he smiled at her. 'Take care, Diana; you already know that Quentin is a very vindictive person. If you have any problems, you know where we are.'

'Thank you, Sam. I'm truly sorry for what happened to you, I hope you'll forgive me. I'll try to make it right, believe me.' She shifted in her seat and for a second it looked to Sam if she was going to lean forward to kiss him, but she hesitated and the moment was gone. She settled back in her seat and closed her eyes.

Sam watched with interest as he felt Diana's energy build up. He had never seen anyone go home from this close before; the Twins and Quentin had been quite far from him when they had gone into the pond, and usually when he went into the past with Rachel they travelled back together because he never had a reason to stay on his own.

The energy slowly built until it reached a peak and then suddenly Diana was just gone. She didn't fade or pop or look like she was going down a tunnel or twist and distort or do any of the other special effects that he'd been expecting, she just wasn't there anymore.

Sam looked around the coach with interest, expecting changes, but nothing was different which puzzled him somewhat. He turned to Rachel who was now looking at him with a stony expression. 'How come the carriage is still here and I've still got a bandage around my head? Now that they're all gone there's no reason for the police to have gone to the house and no reason for a doctor to have tended my wounds.'

Rachel tutted and shook her head in exasperation. 'What did you expect? The carriage to vanish and to be left sitting on your arse in the middle of the road? It would serve you right, but it would never happen. Everybody will still forget about Diana and Quentin, but material things in our immediate vicinity are kept the way we need them to be because the time-line is still adapting to *our* presence even if it no longer has to for someone else. If it didn't we'd be falling out of planes or having cars and horses disappear under us all the time, which would be a bit silly, don't you think? And quite hard to explain to the people around us, which would just cause more problems with the time-line.'

Instead of teasing him about his usual lack of experience and knowledge she seemed genuinely annoyed by him and Sam frowned at her with some concern, wondering if he had managed to damage their relationship by his flirtations with Diana, even though she had told him that she understood.

She saw his look and sighed, her face softening. 'I'm sorry. I'm just tired, I haven't slept very well since you... Oh, Sam... Why didn't you tell us where you were going instead of wandering off on your own?'

'Because I wasn't sure it was her at first, and then when I finally got a good look and saw it was her I didn't have time to tell anybody because she would have gotten away.' Sam shrugged and grinned sheepishly. 'I thought I was going to follow her to Quentin and save the day. I guess I was wrong.'

'I was so worried for you.'

'I wasn't; I knew you would find me. That was pretty clever, by the way, how you and Bert found Quentin.'

'You do know that we could very easily have done the same thing and found Quentin without you getting captured, right?'

'Ah, but then you wouldn't have had the extra motivation and it might have taken us weeks to come up with the idea. And who knows what damage Quentin would have done by then?' He grinned. 'So, if you think about it, I was helping by getting captured and beaten up.'

'Try putting that in your report, see what James says...' She chuckled, shaking her head. 'You know, I *really* don't want to hear the details, but you are still going to have to tell me everything that was said and done in that house.'

'Everything?'

'Yes, *everything*; you never know what might be relevant and something you heard might not mean anything to you but it might to me.'

'Oh, OK then.'

'And, Sam, don't worry; as I said before, I trust you, but that doesn't mean I'm going to stand by and let some… *tart* make googly eyes at you. You're going to tell me everything that went on between you two because I have to know and then we're going to leave it at that.' She met his eyes for a second, a hard look on her face, but then she turned away to stare out of the window.

He leaned forwards to see past her as the carriage turned off Whitehall and approached the back door of Scotland Yard and almost did a double take when he saw Abberline there, but caught himself quickly when he realised it was just more Displacer stuff he had to get used to. He glanced out of the corner of his eye to see if Rachel had noticed his surprise and coloured when he saw her shaking her head at him again.

The Inspector was giving instructions to a large group of policemen assembled in ranks on the pavement, but he stopped in mid-sentence when the carriage came to a halt next to him and his face lit up when he saw the passengers. 'Sir Sam! Thank god you're alright! I was just about to send out another search party for you.'

He turned and waved at the policemen who were standing around watching, dismissing them. They wandered back into the station, many of them saluting or waving happily at Sam before disappearing and some of them even calling out how glad they were to have him back.

Abberline handed Rachel down from the carriage and she stalked into the station without a backwards look.

Sam couldn't get out on his own so Geoff came round and with Abberline's help managed to get him down to the pavement without aggravating his wounds too much.

'My word, Sir Sam, you do look like you've been in the wars! What on earth happened to you? What have you been doing all this time? I thought you were only off chasing down leads.'

Sam had already worked out that Abberline wouldn't know anything about the house or the goings on; he never would have gone there. He wasn't sure what he should say though, what explanation he could give for Rachel and Geoff coming to get him. 'Well, I…'

He was saved from having to make up a story that might not make any sense by Bert, who had been riding on the outside of the carriage beside Geoff. 'Me an' Lady Rachel done find him knocked about in an abandoned house out Harrow way. Nobody there now, though, Mr Abberline, sir; all skidaddled long ago. Left Sir Sam here on death's door to fend for himself, like.'

Abberline gave Bert a surprised look and his mouth opened and closed as he searched for reply. 'Yes, well, er…' He turned back to Sam almost immediately. 'I hope that your efforts have borne fruit?'

Sam smiled. 'I'll fill you in on everything later when I've recovered.' He inclined his head in Bert's direction. 'I owe my life to Bert here and I think he would be a great asset to the Metropolitan Police. You could use a man like him who knows the streets and the people. If not as a constable then as a paid consultant.'

Abberline's face and his opinion of Bert immediately changed and he gave the scruffy man a shrewd look. 'I think we could take you on at 4 shillings a week on a temporary basis, see how you fit in.'

Bert, who had been shrinking into himself a bit at Abberline's previous dismissal, immediately brightened up, like any good cockney, at the prospect of making some money. 'Couldn't do it for only four, guv, better make it twelve.'

'Twelve! For twelve I could have an urchin from every street corner in my pocket!'

'And you'll get that from me, sir, don't you worry! But they'll tell me the truth and not the pack of lies they'd sell to you.'

Sam and Geoff watched as Bert and Abberline disappeared into the station, haggling and having a good time while they did it - they had forgotten all about him, almost as if he'd gone home and left the time-line.

He turned his head to look up at Geoff who grinned down at him and shrugged.

'Well, Sir Sam, looks like it's just you and me now. Come on, let's get you inside; a nice cup of tea will make everything right as rain again.'

'Tea… Wonderful…'

Geoff didn't catch the sarcasm in Sam's voice as he helped him hobble to the door and into the warm station. 'If you play your cards right, there may be a warm crumpet or two in it for you as well, sir!'

Sam just groaned in reply.

CHAPTER 21
FIXING

Guiding the police towards Jack the Ripper's replacement was complicated but made much easier by Abberline's brilliance as a detective; he had already realised that the recent murder hadn't had the same *modus operandi* as the other Ripper cases and from there he had quickly figured out that they were looking for a second killer, probably a copycat and not Jack himself.

Diana had given them the name and the address of the killer, but they couldn't just give that information to Abberline because that would be too direct an action and wouldn't last after they'd gone home. They could, however, keep an eye on him. Diana had been right when she'd said he didn't have much initiative of his own and they were relieved when he went back to his own life instead of killing anybody else; it made their job less urgent and more likely to succeed.

In the end it took them six months of steady work, carefully influencing Geoff, Bert and Abberline, to catch the man. During that time there were of course no further Ripper murders and the case was declared unsolved but closed. London started to forget and the East End of the city started to calm down, especially now that Quentin wasn't there trying to stir them up in the pubs and clubs every night.

It didn't take nearly so much time for the relationship between Sam and Rachel to heal, in fact it took only one day. Sam told her everything that had happened: the two kisses, Diana's attempt at seduction to get him to defect and his counter-seduction in an attempt to bond with her and win her over. As she'd already said, she understood the need for what he'd done and readily forgave him. Sam was a little slower to forgive himself, though; he knew in his heart that he had been attracted to Diana and he would always be unsure whether the kisses had only been due to the circumstances, which would hopefully never be repeated, so in the end he chalked it up to experience and threw himself back into his life with Rachel and their task of cleaning up the time-line.

London looked like it was going back to how it should be but Rachel insisted that they couldn't go home. Apparently, in order to be sure that nobody from the Illuminati could turn up and just carry on from where they had left off, they had to stay and "fix" the time-line in place; the work of a Displacer can't be undone by another, so if they remained and kept working on calming down the populace and returning things to normal, then Quentin couldn't do anything. They had to stay long enough for the general fear and paranoia about Jack the Ripper and the anger at the government to die down completely, then there wouldn't be anything for the Illuminati to build on.

In the end they remained in the past for nearly three years.

Rachel claimed they were staying "just in case" but Sam believed that it had more to do with the fact that Wilde and Conan Doyle became regular visitors at the house and that there were a multitude of social occasions for her to dress up for, sometimes in the presence of royalty - they were even presented to Queen Victoria at one such occasion.

It was a surprise to Sam therefore when Rachel gave him a look over breakfast and pronounced seriously, but nonchalantly, 'I want a divorce.'

Sam dropped the knife he was using to butter his toast in shock before her face cracked into a grin and he realised what she was saying - she had decided it was time to go home. 'Can I at least finish my breakfast first, please, Mrs Vives?'

Rachel laughed. 'Of course you can, husband! Actually, I was thinking we could throw one last party, not here of course, somewhere bigger, and invite all our friends.'

Sam smiled fondly at her, he hadn't imagined Rachel as being much more than a tough warrior woman, but she had developed social and intellectual skills in Victorian London to rival her martial ones. To hear her debate with Wilde was hilarious, her detective skills rivalled Abberline's and the various politicians they had met over the years always looked for her opinion before they asked for his. He was almost jealous of the ease, the almost chameleonic ability with which she had completely changed her personality to fit in with the world around her and he reflected that a talent like that was probably something a Displacer had to pick up quite quickly or fail and that it was something he should work on himself as soon as he could.

They set about planning their goodbye party, sending out invitations to all of the people they had gotten to know over the years, including a few Society members like Abraham, who they had had many long conversations with. They didn't tell anybody the reason behind it, but called it a "celebration between like-minded friends". They had been getting paid generously for their continuing work with the Metropolitan Police and it wasn't as if they were going to take the money back with them, so they spent it on the party. They rented a ballroom and hired an orchestra to play, among other things, music by Gilbert and Sullivan, which somehow epitomised the time and had wormed its way into their hearts as an unofficial symbol of this Displacement for them.

The night was a great success and some of the guests even heralded it as the social event of the year. There was dancing, special appearances from singers that regularly appeared at the Savoy and Sam had employed a photographer to take portraits for whoever wanted one.

One of the hot topics of discussion was the controversy over the recent introduction of the penalty kick in association football. The men were hotly divided in opinion as to whether it was fair or not while the women were completely indifferent... until Sam sent a man out to buy a ball and proposed a competition between the sexes. They spent a hilarious couple of hours with men and women taking penalties while dressed in evening wear and jewellery, some of them too drunk to even stand steadily, let alone kick a ball.

Too soon the night was over and the guests began to take their leave. Oscar Wilde presented Sam with a hand-written manuscript of his most recent publication *The Picture of Dorian Gray* and gave Rachel a never-before-published poem. Conan Doyle in turn gave the couple a leather bound set of his novels, signed of course.

Sam and Rachel stood hand in hand in the middle of the deserted ballroom when everyone had gone, the gifts they had received held closely between them. The place was silent and seemed to echo with the sounds of joy and laughter that had filled it just moments before. They smiled at each other and without a word began to dance. There was no music of course, but they didn't need it; they knew each other as well as they knew themselves and besides, dancing was very similar to fighting and they were both experts at that.

They swept around the floor, turning circles in the candlelight as the sun rose over the waking city and the light through the long windows slowly brightened, never taking their eyes off each other.

'Well, Mr Vives, has Victorian London been all you expected it to be?'

'Not quite, no.' Sam said after a moment's consideration. 'I've seen *Mary Poppins* a few times with Violeta and there weren't nearly enough chimney sweeps for my liking.'

Rachel laughed, tilting her head back and leaning into his arms as they supported her.

Centrifugal force tried its best to separate them as they spun round and round but neither of them was going to let go of this moment.

'Forget Paris, this visit to London has been far more romantic.'

'That's just the torture and the gunshot wound talking.' Rachel took her hand from his just long enough to poke him in the ribs where his injury had been. He barely flinched; thankfully it had healed well.

They danced in silence for a few minutes, neither of them wanting the night, the moment, to end, but eventually they both sighed, knowing that it had to. Without stopping they held each other close, still so much in step that their feet interwove beneath them, in time to a music that they held in their hearts and their bodies.

'Ready?' asked Sam.

Rachel squeezed him one last time before answering quietly. 'Yes.'

She closed her eyes and Sam felt the energy build within her, then he closed his and still dancing they…

…opened their eyes to the noise and chaos of central London. They were once more holding hands in the middle of Hyde Park and while they couldn't see the traffic, the noise of it was overwhelming for a second.

Sam grinned at Rachel. 'I think people are going to start staring if we keep dancing like this.'

Rachel gave him a puzzled look before she realised that they were still shifting from foot to foot as if they were back in the ballroom. She released his hands and reached up to brush his hair back from his forehead, looking at his temples on each side. 'No grey this time, which is a bit of a shame; I thought it looked very distinguished.'

She grinned and took advantage of her hand being raised to slap him gently on the cheek. 'Come on, you haven't run in three years - I don't want you losing that six pack! Let's finish our jog and do some sparring; I'm itching to kick some arse and yours will do!'

She tucked the package with Oscar Wilde's poem under her arm and started jogging, continuing along the route they had been taking before they had Displaced.

Sam smiled then raced to catch up, fumbling awkwardly with Wilde's manuscript and the set of Conan Doyle's books.

CHAPTER 22
CELEBRATIONS

Despite the fact that they hadn't been able to do much exercise in the past, beyond a few sparring sessions when they were alone at home, neither of them could properly concentrate on what they were doing for very long; they were far too eager to get back to Headquarters and give everyone the news, looking forward to seeing the happy faces of the people they loved and being swamped with congratulations at their victory over Quentin.

The chaotic scene that greeted them was not quite what they had been expecting.

The house phone and at least two mobiles were ringing and there was a group of about half a dozen Elders in the living room talking animatedly with James and Andrew, making a lot of noise. However, they fell silent as soon as Sam and Rachel came in.

Sam barely had time to think how creepy it had looked when all the faces had swivelled towards them in unison before Andrew led what was almost an avalanche as everybody in the room swarmed towards the two newcomers. Questions were shouted out from all quarters, made incoherent by the sheer volume and number of them.

Sam wasn't sure how to deal with a pack of wild Elders, but Rachel apparently did and to his amusement she held up her hands and shouted at them. 'Shut up, everyone! Please!'

They quietened down immediately, although a few among them grumbled at Rachel's "tone of voice" and her "disrespecting her elders". The phones also stopped ringing as they were either silenced or held up so that they could hear the conversation.

'Thank you! Now what's this all about?' Rachel looked pointedly at Andrew, asking him to speak for the whole group.

'We, I mean, the Elders, felt the disturbance in time disappear about ten minutes ago. We were wondering if...' He looked at Sam expectantly.

Sam nodded and smiled.

Rachel and Sam nearly jumped out of their skins as there was a collective whoop from the Elders, who began jumping up and down in celebration in a manner that wouldn't have commanded respect from anyone.

Andrew stepped forward and enveloped both of them in a hug. 'Well done! Very well done the both of you. I knew you could do it!' He stepped back, a huge grin on his face and a tear in his eye. 'You can tell us all about your Displacement over dinner tonight, for now, go have a shower and get some rest. Go on, hurry up, before this lot realise you've gone.'

He shooed them away and they raced up the stairs, leaving behind the cheering, which was fast beginning to resemble football chants.

They got to the bedroom where they had left their clothing and closed the door, finally shutting away the sounds of Elders definitely not showing their ages. They put their souvenirs on the bed, then Rachel jumped into Sam's arms and held him tightly.

Sam wrapped his own arms around her and they remained like that for some long seconds before Rachel pulled back. She was crying but there was a huge smile on her face. 'Thank you. You've made everybody so happy, given them so much hope. Thank you.'

She kissed him. It wasn't a passionate kiss, though; it was more tender, with real emotion behind it.

When she finally pulled back she looked at him again and wiped away her tears. 'You might not be my husband any more but I still love you. Now come on, get your clothes off and let's go take a shower.'

She stepped away from him and started pulling off her sweaty running gear.

Sam hesitated a second, then grinned as he realised that he was being invited to join her.

She saw the look on his face and smiled sweetly. 'Don't go getting all excited. I just need someone to wash my back.'

Sam grinned and started taking his own t-shirt and shorts off.

They took their time showering together then went back to the bedroom to relax and go over the Displacement in their minds before writing it down. They slept for a couple of hours then Rachel used her ninja skills to sneak down to the kitchen and bring them back some food without anybody noticing her, although, according to her, the rest of the Society members seemed so completely engrossed by their animated discussions and celebrations that a bomb could have gone off and they wouldn't have noticed. Some of them even looked like they were already drinking.

By the time Sam and Rachel came back downstairs a few hours later many more members had arrived, but they didn't want to face the entire group yet, so while Sam caught the eye of his grandfather, Rachel did the same for Andrew. They went up to one of the libraries on the second floor and sat down around one of the reading tables, Sam and Rachel on one side and James and Andrew on the other.

'We wanted to tell you a few things before we give the whole story to everyone,' Sam said quietly reaching out to take Rachel's hand.

She nodded. 'We don't know who else can be trusted.'

Andrew started to open his mouth to protest but James stopped him with a look. 'Let's just hear them out.'

Rachel nodded her thanks. 'As a quick summary, we've been in London from 1888 to 1891. Quentin was using the Jack the Ripper case to stir up social unrest.'

James nodded slowly, thoughtfully. 'That makes sense, it was a pretty unstable time in London, especially in the East End. My great grandfather wrote a lot about it in his diaries.'

'It did get a bit hairy at one point, yes,' said Rachel. 'But the bad guys were also doing something else while they were there - Quentin was in contact with his ancestor, Lord Price, in an attempt to gain entrance to the attic.'

Sam leaned forward onto the table and spoke quietly. 'What on earth is up there that they would go to so much trouble to steal?'

James shrugged. 'There's all number of valuable things up there, but nothing stands out as particularly desirable, unless they're just after funds.'

Sam looked doubtful. 'I get the feeling they are beyond the stage of just looking for money.'

Rachel nodded her agreement. 'You'll understand once you hear what they call themselves; the implications are mind-boggling.' She paused for dramatic effect, but to her disappointment Andrew and

James just stared at her, waiting. She shrugged. 'They call themselves the Illuminati.'

The initial reaction from both the men was to laugh, but they both stopped very quickly as the implications sank in and they worked through the possibilities in their minds. They turned to each other with shocked expressions on their faces.

'You don't think…'

'It's not possible…'

'Surely…'

They tailed off into silence then turned back to the young Displacers, who were watching them.

James sighed. 'This is extremely troubling, we will have to discuss this with the Council.'

Rachel gave them a final warning though. 'We thought you might, but be very careful who you talk to please; we definitely have a spy amongst us. Diana Birch confirmed it.'

After James and Andrew had left, troubled looks on their faces, they had again hidden in the bedroom, going back to sleep for a few more hours, trying to recover enough from their Displacement to be able to stay awake during dinner.

They finally decided to get up about an hour before the meal was due to start; they could both feel the rising volume of noise and traffic in the house and knew that people would start looking for them soon if they didn't make an appearance. They got dressed but before they left the room Sam pulled Rachel over to sit down on the bed next to him.

She looked at him, seeing a sad look on his face. 'What's wrong?'

'I just realised something.'

'What?'

'This trip was the last straw for me - I'm not a child anymore and I won't be able to put up with being treated like one.' He sighed. 'We've spent the last three years married and living together, I've been beaten and shot. Again. I've been kidnapped and held captive, I've had Diana try to convert me and I tried to convert her in turn. I've danced with Queen Victoria and had conversations with Oscar Wilde, Arthur Conan Doyle and two Prime Ministers.' He took a deep breath and then sighed. 'My relationship with my family has to change or I'll have to leave them.'

Rachel put her arm around him and held him to her. 'I did tell you this would happen, but please, don't do anything too drastic right away;

we've just got back and things are still fresh in your mind - you might feel a little different in a few days.'

Sam frowned but nodded. 'I just don't know if I'm a good enough actor to just try to carry on as if nothing had changed.'

'No, you suck at lying and acting is just lying professionally.' She chuckled and shook him, trying to get him to lighten up. It worked to a small extent and he smiled weakly. She leaned in and kissed him briefly before ruffling his hair. 'Awww! My big grown man!'

'Geroff!' He fought back weakly, not really trying to win, and they laughed together.

They were interrupted by a knock and Andrew's head poked around the door. 'Not interrupting anything, am I?'

'If you were it'd be a bit late now, wouldn't it?' asked Rachel, mock annoyed.

Andrew grinned. 'You're too young for hanky panky anyway. What would your parents say?'

Rachel laughed, once, sarcastically. 'You know damn well what my mother would say if I got preggers *and* how quickly she'd be out signing up for government allowances.'

Andrew sighed and nodded. 'Your mother is a piece of work, yes. I really don't know where she gets it from.'

He came into the room, closing the door behind him and sat in a chair facing them. 'Anyway, I came to tell you about what's expected of you tonight - it's going to be a bit of a special occasion, more so than we thought it would be.'

'Really? Has something happened?' Rachel grinned cheekily and Sam laughed.

'I think you can say that...' Andrew chuckled briefly, then went on. 'It's very unusual for Displacers to report to the entire Society, it only happens once every few years, but as you've probably guessed we have rules and ritual set down for it.'

He smiled when Sam groaned. 'Don't worry, you don't have to learn anything, Sam. I know how you hate that!'

He shared a laugh with Rachel while Sam's cheeks reddened. 'Anyway, here's what's going to happen - I'll introduce you one by one during the soup course and you'll get up to speak. You can read your report out or just tell your story, whatever you want. Sam, as the instigator of the Displacement, will go first and then Rachel immediately afterwards. The members aren't allowed to comment while you're making your report, but for the rest of the meal they will ask you questions in order of seniority. That's not to make you feel uncomfortable, by the way, it's so you don't have to put every single little detail into your report - they'll make sure to get anything they think is relevant out of you.'

The way he said it didn't make it sound like it was going to be much fun and Sam was feeling very nervous about standing up in front of the whole Society, far more nervous than when he had duelled against Quentin. 'What about Philip? Isn't he going to tell everyone what the scroll says tonight? Can't he take some of the heat off of us?'

'He just rang to say he's going to be a bit late; he's having trouble with some of the nuances of the translation or something like that. So the spotlight's all yours!'

Sam forced a smile. 'Yay…'

Andrew stood and went to the door. 'Dinner is in half an hour, I suggest you both go over what you're going to say; I don't want relatives of mine umming and ahing and sounding anymore like fools than everybody already knows they are.'

He ducked out of the room, laughing, as two heavy pillows hit the door where he had been standing.

EPILOGUE

Sam and Rachel went over their reports again, making sure they had them correct and fresh in their minds, before going down to dinner; even though they knew Andrew had only been joking, neither wanted to come across as a blithering idiot and Sam was glad to see that Rachel was just as nervous as he was.

There was a surprise in store for them when they made their way downstairs - not only was the place as full as they had ever seen it but some enterprising person or people had gotten Christmas decorations from somewhere and decorated the entire ground floor.

Sam had actually completely forgotten that Christmas hadn't passed yet; they had celebrated three very Victorian Christmases during their Displacement, but they had been nothing like this; there was a tree in the lounge that several quite drunk-looking Elders were trying to decorate, mostly getting in each other's way, and tinsel of every colour draped on everything - it looked like someone had set off some kind of festive bomb and it certainly wasn't what Sam had expected from people who were obsessed with order, but he supposed they had to let their hair down sometimes.

While Rachel mingled, Sam stood in the doorway and watched the activities for a while, it was good to see everybody with a reason to be happy and the serious mood from earlier in the day had completely evaporated. Soon, though, James came over and dragged Sam into the room to talk to some of his friends and he spent the next half an hour listening to some of the funniest stories he'd ever heard, told by some very sprightly old men, most of whom had gotten up to a surprising amount of mischief in their youth throughout much of time.

All too soon, though, it was time to eat and they filed into the dining room. Obviously Richard wasn't able to cook for so many people all at once so he had brought food from his restaurant. It had arrived with him in three taxis, along with five waiters who were under strict instructions to serve the food and then go back to the kitchens in between courses so as not to hear the discussion - he had jokingly told them that they were a society of Masons and if they discovered any of their secrets they would have to be "dealt with".

The soup course was dished out to everyone and when the waiters had disappeared Andrew stood up and raised his wine glass. 'First of all, a toast. Merry Christmas everyone.'

His toast was repeated around the table and for at least a couple of minutes there was the sound of clinking glasses, crackers being pulled and laughter before once again silence fell and all eyes returned to Andrew, still standing at the head of the table.

'Well, as you all no doubt know by now, we have more to celebrate aside from the date.' He indicated Sam and Rachel who had been placed on either side of him so that they could better address the whole table. 'Two of our youngest members have had a little bit of an adventure.' There was some laughter and scattered applause at this and he smiled, letting it die down naturally before continuing, allowing everyone to savour the moment. 'So without further ado, I'd like to invite Sam Vives to stand up and start the ball rolling with his account.'

Andrew sat down and there was thunderous applause as Sam slowly got to his feet.

He glanced around the table. Aside for the empty chairs that had been left for Lisa and Philip, who would join them later, the room was filled to capacity and every single face was tilted to look up at him. Rachel smiled encouragingly at him from across the table and not for the first time he wished he had her next to him so that he could hold her hand and take her strength. James was also much too far away at the other end of the table, but he could still feel the love coming from him as his grandfather beamed proudly. The only remotely sour note was the look on Ralph's face, but now wasn't the time to deal with that.

'Well, I...'

Suddenly the door thumped open behind him and Philip rushed in, followed closely by Lisa.

Philip was out of breath; he'd obviously run from his car, but he managed to speak into the hushed silence that followed the crash of the door. 'Sorry, but this can't wait!'

He had a piece of paper in his hand and he waved it at the group while he gasped for air. 'Sam isn't the chosen one!'

'This is getting to be a bit of a habit, isn't it, Mr Price?' As always the screen of the laptop was blank as the voice of the Master issued from it.

Quentin was sitting hunched over on the sofa in his flat in London. The room was completely dark aside from the glow from his laptop, open on the coffee table in front of him.

'It wasn't my fault!' He whined, childlike. 'It was Diana, she disobeyed my orders and…'

'Miss Birch will be dealt with in due course, and yes, we may have to dispose of her if I deem her usefulness at an end.' There was a brief pause as the Master let his callousness sink in and watched the reaction from his subordinate. It seemed to satisfy him that the possibility of Diana's death didn't seem to bother Quentin very much, if at all, and he grunted in satisfaction before continuing. 'Did you at least make sufficiently obvious your clumsy efforts to gain entry to the attic?'

'Yes, I made sure to be suitably annoyed at being denied access.'

'Thank god for small favours, then - that should help to cloud our true intentions for a little longer. No thanks to you.'

There was an ominous silence and a bead of sweat made its way slowly down the side of Quentin's face.

After letting his subordinate suffer for a while, the Master spoke again. 'It seems that Sam Vives is not the chosen one after all. Whoever it is, they are still out there and we must make sure we get to them first.'

Quentin brightened up a bit at the news that his enemy wasn't as all-powerful as he had previously thought, but his improved mood lasted only seconds as the Master's harsh voice again rang out, immediately putting him back in his place. 'This news only makes your inability to kill the boy even more shameful! Believe me when I tell you that if there were anybody in this organisation that I thought could accomplish my goals better than you, you would be joining Miss Birch in her punishment - you are fortunate that you are all I have. For now.'

Quentin swallowed but said nothing.

'We must regroup and make plans; your incompetence has proven costly, but this is only a minor setback and victory is still within our grasp. However, I have stood by and watched you and your associates' failures for too long, it is past time I took a more active role in the downfall of the Displacers.'

There was a laugh that made Quentin shudder, but it was the Master's next words that really chilled him to the bone.

'I will enjoy *personally* bringing about the death of Andrew Berry.'

ABOUT THE AUTHOR

Simon Brading tried his hand at many things before it occurred to him that he might have a few stories to tell. As well as the odd novel he writes screenplays and also does some acting every so often.

www.simonbrading.co.uk

For news of special offers, upcoming releases, exclusive content, competitions and events, please follow me on social media.

Instagram - @sibrading
Facebook - Simon Brading Author
Tiktok - @SimonBradingAuthor

ALSO BY SIMON BRADING

The "Displacers" series - a young adult time travel adventure series for all ages.
The Time Traveller's Nephew
The Secret of the Ancients
The Whitechapel Plot
The Price of Greed
The Time for Vengeance

The "Misfit Squadron" Series - a Steampunk series set in an alternate World War 2.
The Battle Over Britain
The Russian Resistance
A Misfit Midwinter
The Lion and the Baron
The Maltese Defence
Tales from the Second Great War
The Siege of Gibraltar
The King's Mission
The Home Front
Taking to the Skies
The Invasion of Britain

The "Twin Ambitions" series - ballet books for children ages 7 and up.
Fight to Dance
Back to Basics

The "Ni Hon - The Two Books" Series - a young adult series set in a dystopian future Japan.
The Black Book

Others
Public Enemy
Empath
The Lifeboat at the End of the Universe